"Catherine Mann had pulled out all the stops in a hard-hitting story!"

—*Romance Reviews Today*

"Fans of Suzanne Brockmann will find that this book with its powerful story lines and realistic backgrounds is bursting at the seams with one electrifying moment after another."

—*Coffee Times Romance Reviews*, 5 Cups

"Simply one of the best military/romantic suspense novels I have ever read!"

—*Joyfully Reviewed*

"Mann proves once again she's a force to be reckoned with in the military romance genre with an unexpected and compelling plot… her characters are incredible and the plot is fantastic."

—*RT Book Reviews*

"Entertaining and suspenseful. One can't help falling in love with the characters. A great read!"

—*Fresh Fiction Reviews*

"A smoking hot romance… This is an author that has made me an instant and long time fan!"

—*Romance Readers Connection*

D0357634

COVER ME

CATHERINE MANN

sourcebooks
casablanca

Published by Sourcebooks Casablanca, an imprint of Sourcebooks, Inc.
P.O. Box 4410, Naperville, Illinois 60567-4410
(630) 961-3900
FAX: (630) 961-2168
www.sourcebooks.com

Printed and bound in Canada
WC 10 9 8 7 6 5 4 3

To my husband Rob and our four miracles—Brice,
Haley, Robbie, and Maggie. I love you all!

Chapter 1

IT WAS A COLD DAY IN HELL FOR TECH SERGEANT WADE Rocha—standard ops for a mission in Alaska.

He slammed the side of the icy crevasse on Mount McKinley. A seemingly bottomless crevasse. That made it all the more pressing to anchor his ax again ASAP. Except both of his spikes clanked against his sides while the underworld waited in an alabaster swirl of nothingness as he pinwheeled on a lone cable.

Wade scratched and clawed with his gloved hands, kicked with his spiked shoes, reaching for anything. The tiniest of toeholds on the slick surface would be good right about now. Sure he was roped to his climbing partner. But they had the added load of an injured woman strapped to a stretcher beneath them. He needed to carry his own weight.

Chunks of ice and snow pelted his helmet. The unstable gorge walls vibrated under his gloved hands.

"Breathe and relax, buddy." His headset buzzed with reassurance from his climbing partner, Hugh "Slow Hand" Franco.

Right.

Hold tight.

Think.

Focus narrowed, Wade tightened his grip on his rope. He'd earned his nickname, Brick, by being the most hardheaded guy in their rescue squadron. Come hell or high water, he never gave up.

Each steady breath crackled with ice shards in his lungs, but his oxygen-starved body welcomed every atom of air. Lightning fast, he grabbed the line tying them together and worked the belay device.

Whirrr, whippp. The rope zinged through. Wade slipped closer, closer still, to Franco, ten feet below.

"Oof." He jerked to a halt.

"I got ya, Brick. I got ya," Franco chanted through the headset. Intense. Edgy. Nothing was out of bounds. Franco would die before he let him fall. "It's just physics that makes this thing work. Don't overthink it."

And it did work. Wade stabilized against the icy wall again. Relief trickled down his spine in frosty beads of sweat.

He keyed up his microphone. "All steady, Slow Hand."

"Good. Now do you wanna stop horsing around, pal?" Franco razzed, sarcastic as ever. "I'd like to get back before sundown. My toes are cold."

Wade let a laugh loosen the tension kinking up his gut. "Sorry I inconvenienced you by almost dying there. I'll try not to do it again. I'll even spring for a pedicure, if you're worried about your delicate feet chafing from frostbite."

"Appreciate that." Franco's labored breath and hoarse chuckle filled the headset.

"Hey, Franco? Thanks for saving my ass."

"Roger that, Brick. You've done the same for me."

And he had. Not that they kept score. Wade recognized the chitchat for what it really was—Franco checking to make sure he wasn't suffering from altitude sickness due to their fifteen thousand foot perch. They worked overtime to acclimate themselves, but the lurking beast could still strike even the most seasoned climber without warning. They'd already lost one of their team members last month to HACE—high altitude cerebral edema.

He shook his head to clear it. Damn it, his mind was wandering. Not good. He eyed the ledge a mere twenty feet up. Felt like a mile. He slammed an ice ax in with his left hand, pulled, hauled, strained, then slapped the right one in a few inches higher. Crampons—ice cleats—gained traction on the sleek side of the narrow ravine as he inched his way upward.

Slow. Steady. Patient. Mountain rescue couldn't be rushed. At least April gave them a few more daylight hours. Not that he could see much anyway, with eighty-mile-per-hour wind creating whiteout conditions. Below, his climbing partner was a barely discernible blur.

Hand over hand. Spike. Haul. Spike. Haul. He clipped his safety rope into a spike they had anchored in the rock on the way down. Scaled one step at a time. Forgot about the biting wind. The ball-numbing cold.

The ever-present risk of avalanche.

His arms bulged, the burden strapped to his harness growing heavier. *Remember the mission. Bring up an unconscious female climber. Strapped to a litter. Compound fracture in her leg.*

His job as a pararescueman in the United States Air Force included medic training. Land, sea, or mountain, military missions or civilian rescue. With his brothers in arms, he walked, talked, and breathed their motto, "That Others May Live."

That people like his mother might live.

Muscles burning, he focused upward into the growl

of the storm and the hovering military helicopter. A few more feet and he could hook the litter to the MH-60. Rotors *chop, chop, chopped* through the sheets of snow like a blender.

The crevasse was too narrow to risk lowering a swaying cable. Just one swipe against the narrow walls of ice could collapse the chasm into itself. On top of the injured climber and Franco.

On top of him.

So it was up to *him*—and his climbing partner—to pull the wounded woman out. Once clear, the helicopter would land if conditions permitted. And if not, they could use the cable then to raise her into the waiting chopper.

Wind slammed him again like a frozen Mack truck. He fought back the cold-induced mental fog. At least when Hermes went subterranean to rescue Persephone from the underworld, he had some flames to toast his toes.

Wade keyed his microphone again to talk to the helicopter orbiting overhead. "Fever"—he called the mission code name—"we're about five minutes from the top."

Five minutes when anything could happen.

"Copy, the wind is really howling. We will hold until you are away from the crevasse."

"Copy, Fever."

The rest of his team waited in the chopper. They'd spent most of the day getting a lock on the locale. The climber's personal locator beacon had malfunctioned off and on. Wade believed in his job, in the motto. He came from five generations of military.

But sometimes on days like this, saving some reckless thrill seeker didn't sit well when thoughts of people like his mother—wounded by a roadside bomb in Iraq, needing his help—hammered him harder than the ice-covered rocks pummeling his shoulder. How damned frustrating that there hadn't been a pararescue team near enough—he hadn't been near enough—to give her medical aid. Now because of her traumatic brain injury, she would live out the rest of her life in a rehab center, staring off into space.

He couldn't change the past, but by God, he would do everything he could to be there to help someone else's mother or father, sister or brother, in combat. That could only happen if he finished up his tour in this frozen corner of the world.

As they neared the top, a moan wafted from the litter suspended below him. Stabilizing the rescue basket was dicey. Even so, the groans still caught him by surprise.

The growling chopper overhead competed with the increasing howls of pain from their patient in the basket. God forbid their passenger should decide to give them a real workout by thrashing around.

"Franco, we better get her to the top soon before the echoes cause an avalanche."

"Picking up the pace."

Wade anchored the last… swing… of his ax… Ice crumbled away. The edge shaved away in larger and larger chunks. *Crap, move faster.* Pulse slugging, he dug deeper.

And cleared the edge.

Franco's exhale echoed in his ears. Or maybe it was his own. Resisting the urge to sprawl out and take five right here on the snow-packed ledge, he went on autopilot, working in tandem with Franco.

Climbing ropes whipped through their grip as they

hauled the litter away from the edge. Franco handled his end with the nimble guitarist fingers that had earned him the homage of the Clapton nickname, Slow Hand. The immobilized body writhed under the foil Mylar survival blanket, groaning louder. Franco leaned over to whisper something.

Wade huffed into his mic, "Fever, we are ready for pickup. One survivor in stable condition, but coming to, fast and vocal."

The wind-battered helicopter angled overhead, then righted, lowering, stirring up snow in an increasing storm as the MH-60 landed. Almost home free.

Wade hefted one end, trusting Franco would have the other in sync, and hustled toward the helicopter. His crampons gripped the icy ground with each pounding step. The door of the chopper filled with two familiar faces. From his team. Always there.

With a *whomp*, he slid the metal rescue basket into the waiting hands. He and Franco dove inside just as the MH-60 lifted off with a roar and a cyclone of snow. Rolling to his feet, he clamped hold of a metal hook bolted to the belly of the chopper.

The training exercise was over.

Their "rescue" sat upright fast on the litter, tugging at the restraints. Not in the least female, a hulking male pulled off the splint Wade had strapped on less than a half hour ago.

Wade collapsed against the helicopter wall, exhausted as hell now that he could allow his body to stop. "Major, have you ever considered an acting career? With all that groaning and thrashing about, I thought for sure I was carting around a wounded prima donna."

Major Liam McCabe, the only officer on their team and a former army ranger, swung his feet to the side of the litter and tossed away the Thinsulate blanket. "Just keeping the exercise real, adding a little color to the day."

The major tugged on a helmet and hooked into the radio while the rest of his team gaped at him—or rather, gaped at McCabe's getup. He wore civilian climbing gear—loud, electric yellow, with orange and red flames that contrasted all the more up next to their bland sage green military issue. Laughter rumbled through the helicopter. The garish snow gear had surprised the hell out of him and Franco when they'd reached the bottom of the chasm. They'd expected McCabe, but not an Olympic-worthy ski suit.

McCabe could outpunk Ashton Kutcher. For the most part they welcomed the distraction at the end of a long day. McCabe's humor was also a needed tension buster for the group when Franco went too far, pushing the envelope.

End game, today's exercise hadn't pulled out all the stops for a mountain rescue. Nobody had to parachute in.

Suddenly the major stood upright as he gestured for everyone's attention. "Helmets on so you can hear the radio."

Wade snapped into action, plugging in alongside his other five team members, some in seats, Franco kneeling. The major held an overhead handle, boots planted on the deck.

"Copilot," McCabe's voice piped through the helmet radio, "have the Rescue Coordination Center repeat that last message."

"Romeo Charlie Charlie, please repeat for Fever two zero."

"Fever two zero, this is Romeo Charlie Charlie with a real world tasking." The center radio controller's Boston accent filled the airwaves with broad vowels. "We have a request for rescue of a stranded climbing party on Mount Redoubt. Party is four souls stranded by an avalanche. Can you accept the tasking as primary?"

Mount Redoubt? In the Aleutian Islands. The part of Alaska the Russians once called "the place that God forgot."

The copilot's click echoed as he responded. "Stand by while we assess." He switched to interphone for just those onboard the helicopter. "How are you guys back there? You up for it?"

The major eyed the rest of the team, his gaze holding longest on him and Franco, since they'd just hauled his butt off a mountain. His pulse still slugged against his chest. Franco hadn't stopped panting yet.

But the question didn't even need to be asked.

Wade shot him a thumbs-up. His body was already shifting to auto again, digging for reserves. Each deep, healing breath sucked in the scent of hydraulic fluid and musty military gear, saturated from missions around the world. He drew in the smells, indulging in his own whacked-out aromatherapy, and found his center.

McCabe nodded silently before keying up his radio again. "We are a go back here, if there's enough gas on the refueler."

"Roger, that. We have an HC-130 on radar, orbiting nearby. They say they're game if we are. They have enough gas onboard to refuel us for about three hours of loiter, topping us off twice if needed." The copilot switched to open frequency. "Romeo Charlie Charlie, Fever and Crown will accept the tasking."

"Copy, Fever," answered their radio pal with a serious Boston accent. "Your new call sign is Lifeguard two zero."

"Lifeguard two zero wilco." *Will comply*. The copilot continued, "Romeo Charlie Charlie copies all."

The radio operator responded, "We are zapping the mission info to you via data link and you have priority handling, cleared on navigation direct to location."

"Roger." The helicopter copilot's voice echoed through Wade's headset, like guidance coming through that funky aromatherapy haze. "I have received the coordinates for the stranded climbers popped up on a data screen and am punching the location into the navigation system. Major, do you copy all back there?"

"Copy in full." McCabe was already reaching for his bag of gear to ditch the flame-print suit. "Almost exactly two hundred miles. We'll have an hour to prep and get suited up."

McCabe assumed command of the back of the chopper, spelling out the game plan for each team member. He stopped in front of Wade last. "Good news and bad news… and good news. Since you've worked the longest day, the rest of the team goes in first. Which means you can rest before the bad-news part." He passed a parachute pack. "Speaking of which, chute up. Because if we can't reach someone, you're jumping in to secure the location and help ride out the storm."

Apparently they might well have to pull out all the stops after all. "And that second round of good news, sir?"

McCabe smiled, his humor resurfacing for air. "The volcano on Mount Redoubt hasn't blown in a year, so we've got that going for us."

------*m*------

A wolflike snarl cut the thickly howling air.

Kneeling in the snow, Sunny Foster stayed statue-still. Five feet away, fangs flashed, white as piercing icicles glinting through the dusky evening sunset.

Nerves prickled her skin, covered with four layers of clothes and snow gear, even though she knew large predators weren't supposed to live at this elevation. But still… She swept her hood back slowly, momentarily sacrificing warmth for better hearing. The wind growled as loudly as the beast crouching in front of her.

She was alone on Mount Redoubt with nothing but her dog and her survival knife for protection. Cut off by the blizzard, she was stuck on a narrow path, trying to take a shortcut after her snow machine died.

Careful not to move too fast, she slid the blade from the sheath strapped to her waist. While she had the survival skills to wait out the storm, she wasn't eager to share her icy digs with a wolf or a bear. And a foot race only a few feet away from a sheer cliff didn't sound all that enticing.

Bitter cold, at least ten below now, seeped into her bones until her limbs felt heavier. Even breathing the thin mountain air was a chore. These kinds of temps left you peeling dead skin from your frostbitten fingers and toes for weeks. Too easily she could listen to those insidious whispers in her brain encouraging her to sleep. But she knew better.

To stay alive, she would have to pull out every ounce of the survival training she taught to others. She couldn't afford to think about how worried her brother and sister would be when she didn't return in time for her shift at work.

Blade tucked against her side, she extended her other hand toward the flashing teeth.

"Easy, Chewie, easy." Sunny coaxed her seven-year-old malamute-husky mutt. The canine's ears twitched at a whistling sound merging with the wind. "What's the matter boy? Do you hear something?"

Like some wolf or a bear?

Chewie was more than a pet or a companion. Chewie was a working partner on her mountain treks. They'd been inseparable since her dad gave her the puppy. And right now, Sunny needed to listen to that partner, who had senses honed for danger.

Two months ago Chewie had body-blocked her two steps away from thin ice. A couple of years before that, he'd tugged her snow pants, whining, urging her to turn around just in time to avoid a small avalanche. If Chewie nudged and tugged and whined for life-threatening accidents, what kind of hell would bring on this uncharacteristic growling?

The whistling noise grew louder overhead. She looked up just as the swirl of snow parted. A bubbling dome appeared overhead, something in the middle slicing through…

Holy crap. She couldn't be seeing what she thought. She ripped off her snow goggles and peered upward. Icy pellets stung her exposed face, but she couldn't make herself look away from the last thing she expected to see.

A parachute.

Someone was, no kidding, parachuting down through the blizzard. Toward her. That didn't even make sense. She patted her face, her body, checking to see if she was even awake. This had to be a dream. Or a cold-induced hallucination. She smacked herself harder.

"Ouch!"

Her nose stung.

Her dog howled.

Okay. She was totally awake now and the parachute was coming closer. Nylon whipped and snapped, louder, nearer. Boots overhead took shape as a hulking body plummeted downward. She leaped out of the way.

Toward the mountain wall—not the cliff's edge.

Chewie's body tensed, ready to spring into action. Coarse black-and-white fur raised along his spine. Icicles dotted his coat.

The person—a man?—landed in a dead run along the slippery ice. The "landing strip" was nothing more than a ledge so narrow her gut clenched at how easily this hulking guy could have plummeted into the nothingness below.

The parachute danced and twisted behind him specterlike, as if Inuit spirits danced in and out of the storm. He planted his boots again. The chute reinflated.

A long jagged knife glinted in his hand. His survival knife was a helluva lot scarier looking than hers right now. Maybe it had something to do with the size of the man.

Instinctively, she pressed her spine closer to the mountain wall, blade tucked out of sight but ready. Chewie's fur rippled with bunching muscles. An image of her dog, her pet, her most loyal companion, impaled on the man's jagged knife exploded in her brain in crimson horror.

"No!" she shouted, lunging for his collar as the silver blade arced downward.

She curved her body around seventy-five pounds of loyal dog. She kept her eyes locked on the threat and braced for pain.

The man sliced the cords on his parachute.

Hysterical laughter bubbled and froze in her throat. Of course. He was saving himself. Nylon curled upward and away, the "spirits" leaving her alone with her own personal yeti who jumped onto mountain ledges in a blizzard.

And people called her reckless.

Her Airborne Abominable Snowman must be part of some kind of rescue team. Military perhaps? The camo gear suggested as much.

What was he doing here? He couldn't be looking for her. No one knew where she was, not even her brother and sister. She'd been taught since her early teens about the importance of protecting her privacy. For fifteen years she and her family had lived in an off-the-power-grid community on this middle-of-nowhere mountain in order to protect volatile secrets. Her world was tightly locked into a town of about a hundred and fifty people. She wrapped her arms tighter around Chewie's neck and shouted into the storm, "Are you crazy?"

"No, ma'am," a gravelly voice boomed back at her, "although I gotta confess I am cold. But don't tell my pal Franco I admitted as much. My buddies can't fly close enough to haul us out of here until the storm passes."

"And who are these buddies of yours?" She looked up fast.

No one else fell from the clouds. She relaxed her arms around her dog. He must be some branch of the military. Except his uniform wasn't enough to earn her automatic stamp of approval, and she couldn't see his face or read his eyes because of his winter gear and goggles.

He sheathed his knife. "Air Force pararescue, ma'am. I'm here to help you hunker down for the night to ride out this blizzard safely."

All right, then. That explained part. It was tough to question the honorable intentions of a guy who would parachute into the middle of a blizzard—on the side of a mountain—to rescue someone.

Still, how had he found her? Old habits were tough to shed.

"Um"—she squinted up at the darkening sky again— "are there more of you about to parachute in here?"

He shifted the mammoth pack on his back. "Do you think we could have this conversation somewhere else? Preferably after we find shelter and build a fire?"

That much she agreed with.

Staying out here to talk could get them killed. For some reason this hulking military guy thought he needed to save her. She didn't understand the whys and where-fores of anyone knowing about her presence in the first place. However, simply walking away from him wasn't an option.

Easing to her feet, she accepted the inevitable, sheathed her knife, but kept her hand close to it. Just in case.

She would not be spending the night in a warm

shelter, curled up asleep with her dog. She would have
to stay awake and alert. With too many secrets, she
couldn't afford to let down her guard around anyone,
and sprinting away wasn't exactly an option.

Her uninvited hero was already taking charge. "We
need to find the best location to minimize the force
of the wind, then start digging out a snow pit." He
had some kind of device in his hand, like a GPS. "I'll
keep the instructions simple, and you can just follow
my lead."

"Excuse me, but I've already located shelter. A cave
only a few yards away." She knew every safe haven on
this pass. She had a GPS too, although it hadn't come
out of her case since she'd left her small mountain community this morning. "But you're welcome to work on
that pit if you prefer."

"Oooo-kay," he said with a long puff of fog. "Cave
it is."

"Follow Chewie."

"Chewie?"

"My dog." She pointed to her malamute mutt, now
sniffing his way westward along the ledge.

The man hefted his gear more securely on his back—
a pack that must have weighed at least fifty pounds.
"Looks like a pissed off wolf to me."

"Then perhaps you need to get out those fancy night-
vision goggles you guys use." She felt along the rock
wall marbleized by the elements. "Sun's falling fast.
Don't lollygag."

His steps crunched heavy and steady behind her.
"You're not the most grateful rescuee I've ever come
across."

"I didn't need saving, but thank you all the same for the effort."

He stopped her with a hand to the arm. "What about your friends? Aren't you worried about them?"

His touch startled her, the contact bold and firm—and foreign. She came from a world where everyone knew each other. There was no such thing as a stranger.

She gathered her scrambled thoughts and focused on his words. "My friends?"

How did he know about what she'd been doing today? She'd been on her own, escorting Ted and Madison to a deputy from the mainland who would take them the rest of the way. He worked for a small county along Bristol Bay and arranged for transportation by boat or plane, even bringing in supplies for them in an emergency.

Had something gone wrong after they'd left her? Ted and Madison were seasoned hikers, physically fit. They'd been frequent patrons of the fitness equipment she kept at the cabin that housed her survival and wilderness trek business. She couldn't imagine there would have been any problem with their trek off Mount Redoubt to rejoin the outside world.

"The rest of your group. In case you were worried—which apparently you're not—they're all toasty warm with dry blankets up in the helicopter on their way back to the resort cabin, probably wishing they'd stayed in California. How is it that you have managed out here so long away from the group?"

Climbing group, from California? He must think she was a part of some other group. Relief burned through her like frostbitten limbs coming to life again. He didn't know about Ted and Madison or the sheriff's deputy, and he had no idea at all why she was really out here today.

She couldn't afford—her relatives back in their community couldn't afford—a single misstep. There were careful procedures for people who left, methods to protect their location. "I've had better survival training than the average person."

And she would need every bit of that training to ditch this hulking big military savior when the time came to escape.

Chapter 2

HE'D RISKED HIS NECK FOR A WOMAN WHO COULD TEACH A survival course at the base.

Wade jabbed a stick into the small fire, stoking it to life. Tough to believe a half hour ago he'd jumped out of an MH-60 with the intent of saving her. Crackling flames created a bowl of warmth and light in their little eight-by-eight cave. Damp logs weren't ideal. They smoked thicker and reeked. But bits of bark and tinder they'd collected off the earthen floor worked.

At least they didn't have to worry about snakes in Alaska—no reptiles, period, because of the cold.

She—whatever her name was—knelt beside her big old dog, brushing icicles from the mutt's fur. He would have offered a hand, but she didn't appear to need his help on any level. He couldn't help but be fascinated by her skills and poise in a situation that would scare the pants off most people.

Too bad they hadn't found her before the storm picked up speed and limited their options for extraction.

His other team members had loaded up the stranded climbers. He'd thought he was in the clear for finding his bunk. Then the infrared cameras had shown another person moving nearby.

They'd tried to get information out of the four rescued men, but they were nearly unconscious and completely incoherent. Franco and McCabe had their hands full administering first aid. There hadn't been more than a second to decide if that additional warm body on the screen was human or not.

A second was all he needed.

Even the slim chance another person was alone and defenseless down there meant he had to try. With the worsening storm, rescue options had been slim.

Seconds after he'd parachuted in to rescue her, *she* had led *him* to this fissure in the mountain wall, with sure and expert footing. Their Alaskan grotto wasn't exactly the Anchorage Hilton, but it beat the time he would spend freezing his tail off, carving out a tiny snow igloo.

So now he would hang out alone with this silently efficient woman for the night, possibly longer if the storm didn't lift. The time would pass a lot faster if she spoke. But tension radiated off her in waves thicker than the black smoke spiraling toward the cave's opening.

Granted, they were total strangers forced into close proximity. It was one thing to spend the night protecting an exhausted victim. Another entirely to bunk down with a healthy female who didn't need anything from him. The long, dark hours stretched in front of him. Awkward as hell if something didn't break the tension.

The stick in his hand glowed. He held it over his head like a lighter.

"'Free Bird,' 'Free Bird…'" He chanted the concert mantra, thinking back to his partying teenage years.

"Pardon?" She glanced at him over her shoulder with blank eyes.

Hazel eyes that shifted from dark brown to golden green in the firelight. A sharp—unwelcome—jolt of anticipation stabbed through him at the thought of seeing more of her.

He pitched the stick back into the flames. "'Free Bird.' The song. If you hold up a lighter and request the song, it's concert code for an encore... Okay, never mind. Explaining a joke doesn't work."

"That's what I hear." She gave him a small, obligatory smile.

Standing, she shrugged out of her yellow and black parka and shook the melting snow free with efficient snaps of the wrist. She spread the coat out flat near the fire to dry, dropping her ski mask alongside. Behind her, the mouth of the cave was an opaque sheet of swirling dark, as if they'd been sucked into a black hole. Just the two of them. And her dog.

And her survival knife, which he'd noticed she never once let out of reach.

She tugged a long braid from the bib of her snow pants. Now that he looked closer, she was younger than he'd initially thought, somewhere in her twenties. Younger than his own twenty-eight. The thick snow and her confidence in such an extreme setting must have led him to jump to conclusions. The wrong ones.

He'd expected her to be tougher, more muscular, rather than a thin and wiry gymnast sort. Her face was pale and narrow with creamy skin and a full mouth that didn't need lipstick to draw his attention. The dim firelight glinted off a long, sapphire blue streak through her brown hair.

Not what he'd expected at all.

"My name's Wade." And he should start ditching his gear to dry too. Should. Would. Soon.

"Hi, Wade."

"And you are?" he asked. Not that she answered. She just kept her back to him as she unzipped her black snow pants, revealing… a hot pink wind suit? Now that was another surprise.

He shrugged out of his parka and draped it over his survival pack. "I thought we should at least know each other's names before we strip out of these wet clothes."

"I promise not to so much as peek." She peeled the outer gear past her bulky boots.

Holy crap, those legs of hers went on forever and ever. He looked away. "Just trying to make some chit-chat to pass the time."

"People who come to this part of Alaska aren't here for the conversation." Draping her clothes, she drifted into his sight line again.

"You have a valid point. Talk about a last-frontier kind of place. I can see the appeal of a getting away from it all for vacation." Except now that he looked closer at her, he wondered if perhaps she had some Inuit heritage… or in this region of Alaska, perhaps Aleut or Yupik. Maybe she'd come from California because of a family tie? His curiosity was piqued.

And yeah, it had something to do with her legs in pink track pants and that funky sapphire stripe in her braid.

What other surprises did she have bottled up inside that killer body of hers? "I'm not asking for a birth certificate or blood type. Just your name."

"Excuse me for being concerned about survival rather than niceties." She tugged off her boots and pulled the liners out to dry.

She was carrying this avoidance a bit far.

Unease shifted inside him. He wished the airwaves were clearer so he could radio back to the base, ask some questions about the mystery woman. But he wouldn't get a clear signal up here until the storm passed.

At least the GPS was working. "You're surprisingly calm."

"Panic is a waste of valuable energy stores. As are tender sensibilities. We both should strip down to our underwear and let any perspiration on our clothing dry."

She unzipped her pink shirt, revealing gray thermal, which went up and off too. Leaving a body-hugging synthetic Under Armour that clearly outlined lush breasts in a sports bra. Then she peeled away her pants and thermals, revealing silky leggings that left zippo to the imagination, God help him.

His mouth dried up. His hands went on autopilot, adding his gloves to the drying gear.

Yeah, he was all about the rescue. He was a professional. But he was also male. And breathing. And wondering what she wore on the bottom. His polypro long johns weren't going to make for much cover if he stared at her any longer.

"Wade?"

"Yeah?" He looked away and draped his wool socks over a pair of stalagmites.

"I have a blanket in my pack. I assume you have one in yours. We should double up and share." She clipped out orders like a drill sergeant. "And don't worry. Your virtue is safe with me."

"Thanks." An unexpected smile curved his mouth. Ms. Drill Sergeant had a sense of humor. Who would have thought that? "We can sit on your blanket and wrap up in mine."

"Actually"—she folded her blanket in half and draped it on the ground—"we should sit on either side of Chewie. He's a furnace and a mighty protector of virtue."

Sitting, she whistled once and Chewie lumbered over from his perch by the opening. The dog settled on his haunches beside her.

Wade eyed the alert canine cautiously as he dropped down beside the hairy beast. "It's not my virtue I'm concerned about."

"Don't tell me you're a cat person." She reached past to secure the crackling blanket around her shoulders with a shiver.

Warmth from Chewie began to heat up their cocoon. His toes started to burn as circulation sped up, reminding him how not funny, not sexy, this night was. Well trained or not, he couldn't afford distraction. Having her turn out to be so competent surprised him. And surprise wasn't good. Her evasiveness began to set off alarms in his head.

He slid a hand free and tossed a small branch onto the fire—their tinder was limited. He didn't want to start from scratch again. "You weren't even winded out there. Most people who come here don't even make it up this far. Work out much?"

"As a matter of fact, I do." Her head lolled against her dog. "I run a, um, gym."

"And where's that gym in California?"

Her mouth snapped shut, her teeth clicking.

"You act like a local, and you have your dog with you. Most everyday folks don't travel here with their pets." The pieces began to come together in his mind. He'd probably pissed her off with his assumption she was a part of the group. "I'll bet you're a guide rather than a tourist."

Looking away, she fished in her pack and pulled out a granola bar that appeared homemade. "You're a regular detective. Maybe I should just stay quiet and you can guess. Yes, in fact, I think that's a great way to pass the time."

"Under one condition."

"That's rich, considering I don't have to tell you anything."

Something was off about this whole discussion. As a teen, he'd quibbled often enough, and his military parents had seen right through it most of the time, not that he'd cleaned up his act until life smacked him upside the head. He'd been hardheaded back in those days too.

Still, he couldn't pinpoint exactly what about this woman didn't ring true. His brain must be numbed by the altitude—or testosterone. "I risked my ass to save your life. You can toss me a bone here. At least tell me what I should call you."

She hesitated for an instant, almost imperceptible. Almost. Her fist clenched around the unopened granola bar. "My name is Sunny."

"Sunny, huh?" Ironic, given her dark and evasive ways. Pointing that out would be counterproductive. He accepted the victory, even if she hadn't supplied a last name. "So, Sunny, back to that whole 'Free Bird' joke of mine, are you not a big concertgoer or am I just that much older than you?"

And why did he want to know her age? Maybe because he didn't want to find out he was hanging out under a blanket nearly naked with a teenager—who happened to also be a mountain guide.

"I'm twenty-seven," she answered simply.

An adult. Thank God. "Chewie's an interesting name choice. Should I keep my boots out of his reach?"

"Actually, he's named for Chewbacca in *Star Wars*." She combed her fingers through the dog's coat. "Steven Spielberg patterned Chewbacca's vocalizing after his malamute. Mine's an Alaskan malamute and Siberian husky mix, and I can hear it every time he 'talks.'"

"My boots are safe then."

Chewie "answered" with a garbled howl.

So she wasn't into concerts but enjoyed old movies. Interesting.

Sunny peeled away the wrapping on a second granola bar. "Here. My hand should have thawed it some by now. It's full of peanut butter, so if you have a nut allergy…"

"I don't. And I've eaten rabbit eyeballs and bugs, which were only marginally worse than the MRE—meal ready to eat—I have packed away in my gear. This will be manna from a goddess." He also had glucose tablets and protein bars, but he would save those for later. He trusted his rationing skills better than those of this woman he didn't know.

She passed one to him. "Rabbit eyeballs and bugs? Interesting. And gross. We can definitely save your MRE for later, if we absolutely need it. Tell me more about yourself."

The storm howled outside while he thought about her none-too-subtle attempt to change the subject. He chewed the homemade granola—not bad, although it could benefit from some chocolate and marshmallows. No harm in telling her why he was here today. It would be a cold-ass, long night if neither one of them talked.

"I'm a pararescueman with the Unites States Air Force. You may have heard the job referred to as a PJ, since we used to be called parajumpers."

"I've heard of it, and I guess the job title says it all, with the rescue part." She stared over her peanut butter snack solemnly. "And in case I haven't said so yet, thanks for risking your life for me."

"Even if you didn't need saving." He could be sacked out in his apartment right now instead of quizzing an evasive woman he didn't have time to date anyway. Besides, if he had this much trouble prying her first name out of her, a phone number was likely out of the question.

"Do you have a husband? Maybe he was with you today?" That would explain a lot about her standoffish attitude. He should have thought of it before now.

"I'm not married."

Okay then. He'd pushed for her age and her marital status. He wasn't fooling anyone, not even himself. She was hot and he was interested in learning more about her, not just to pass the time.

"What happened to separate you from your climbing group?"

—◈◈◈—

Sunny hesitated for a second too long and she knew it.

She should have had an answer ready, but she'd allowed herself to be soothed by the rumble of his voice, a raw sort of sound, as if someone had taken sandpaper to his throat. Unique. Not some generic broadcaster's type, but rather the weather-worn timbre of a man who spent most of his time outdoors in rough and untamed places.

Or up late in someone's bed.

Damn. She shifted under the blanket, too aware of the crinkly coverlet against her nearly bare skin already tingling to life again. She almost blurted how the sorta-afghan felt so different, so alien in comparison to the organic fabrics she was accustomed to.

She should just go to sleep rather than risk saying anything more that could reveal the existence of her community or her reason for being out today. Thank God she'd already made the transfer with the sheriff's deputy. Her two charges would be safely away by now. Unlike her.

The real answer to Wade's question about why she'd been stuck out here? She'd let her emotions get the better of her and indulged in a useless crying jag. Frozen tears had wasted time, costing her precious seconds, which left her here rather than at home in her ordinary, happy loft apartment over her survival guide business.

Happy for how much longer? The fabric of her community, of her family, was fraying faster than the fire ate up the tiny pile of timber.

For the past two years, she'd escorted people off the mountain, people who'd appealed to the town council to leave their small off-the-grid community. Theirs wasn't a cult. People could go.

They just couldn't return or discuss where they'd been. Residents of their little town valued privacy.

For the most part, they were self-sustaining. Wild game and fish were plentiful. Every house had a portion devoted to growing fresh foods in a tiny solar-powered greenhouse. They shared, which usually worked well. Other than the winter where somehow they'd ended up with more canned salsa than anything else.

Money wasn't needed often, but when necessary it came in an assortment of ways over the years—from selling Internet articles to savvy stock market investments that supported green living. Funds went right back into bringing supplies to the community, most of the time with her leading the way for the transference of goods.

And if the council gave the thumbs-up? Her next guide trek would be for her sister's departure. She and the rest of her family would never see Misty again.

Sunny bit her lip hard. She'd let her selfish grief distract her once already today. She scrambled for a simple explanation that would fit what Wade already assumed about her being a part of the climbing group his PJ team had rescued, while still covering her butt if he later learned she wasn't connected at all.

"The snowstorm hit out of nowhere. It's easy to get disoriented." That much at least was the truth. "Tell me more about your job."

And stop asking about her life. Helping her forget the fact that they were both nearly naked under this blanket would be nice as well.

He eyed her over the top of Chewie's head, his cocked eyebrow making it clear he wasn't buying her diversion for a second. And it hit her.

Damn.

Wade was a good-looking guy. His shoulders stretched the blanket they shared with Chewie between them. The thermal underwear he wore didn't leave much to the imagination. She'd seen hard bodies making use of her workout equipment, but this guy had pumped muscles that couldn't be earned with free weights. He was in prime condition, honed to the max.

As if God hadn't already gifted him with enough, Wade had the face of a fallen angel—black hair, dark stubble. Even his nose was long, straight, and perfect.

Apparently he'd never lost a bar fight.

She swallowed down a lump of granola bar and passed him the rest. "Really, I want to know about your job. What pushes a guy to jump out of an airplane into a blizzard? And by the way, how do you learn to do that?"

Eyeing her over the dog's head, he bit off a chunk and passed the nutrition bar back. "We do basically the same training as SEALs, plus we're also trained medics. Our focus is on rescue, military and civilian, in any situation."

It sounded exciting and studly and altruistic, all rolled up into one. She couldn't help but wonder how her brother's life might have been different if he could have been a part of this arm of the military instead...

She shoved away the thought she wasn't even allowed to think, much less say. "What do you mean by 'any situation'?"

"We rescue downed pilots in a war zone. We jump into the ocean to assist astronauts' landings. We work with SWAT teams, the FBI, and such, providing medic support during their training exercises."

"Hairy stuff."

"Not as bad as jumping into a minefield, like my buddy did last year."

"A minefield?"

"My pal Franco was dropped onto a mountain in Afghanistan to rescue a Green Beret with his legs blown off in a minefield. We couldn't risk the rotor wash of a landing helicopter setting off another mine that would take out the whole aircraft and everyone in it. So Franco parachuted in alone. He used his medic training to secure the patient, then the helicopter hoisted them both up." He shook his head. "He didn't even break a sweat."

She considered herself pretty fearless after numerous treks around the mountain alone. She taught courses in survival and wilderness trekking. Yet even thinking about what he described sent her stomach freefalling.

The fact that he told a hero story about his friend rather than bragging on himself impressed her all the more. "Do you and your buddies try stuff like that on a regular basis?"

"It's a kick-ass rewarding job with a kick-ass high," he said dismissively. "What made you come to Alaska?"

The laser focus of his coal black eyes told her he hadn't been fooled by her diversionary questions for even a second. Once he got off this mountain, he would learn there wasn't an unaccounted-for woman in the climbing team. She certainly didn't want to leave him with so many unanswered questions that he started poking around.

If he did, she wanted him to be looking in the wrong direction, to protect the community's location. And most important of all, to protect her brother's identity.

"Guess I should come clean with you."

—⁓—

It was a clean kill.

Flat on his belly, he adjusted the arctic adapter over

his NVGs for a better look at Sunny and her military rescuer. Tough to do in this storm, even with the high-tech gear. But he needed to monitor them from the cover of the tiny snow igloo he'd carved out after offing Ted and Madison.

He didn't want to kill Sunny and the guy as well—unless he had to. It was one thing to take out a couple no one would report missing. Even Sunny's death could be hidden, since nobody in the outside world would miss her.

However, it was another thing entirely to murder a member of the military who couldn't so much as go on vacation without permission. The big guy's disappearance would bring on a full-scale search party where there were too many secrets dumped down the fissures and crevasses of Mount Redoubt. But these next five days were crucial to his mission. Five days until the big pay-off for his real boss over on Bristol Bay. Five days until some of that payoff came his way, more money than he was making at the sheriff's department, and a helluva lot more than he ever could have dreamed of making as a cop writing speeding tickets in backwoods Oklahoma.

Sunny and her "savior" seemed occupied for the moment, hunkered down with the dog between them. His fists clenched around his NVGs.

He really hated her fucking dog.

The beast had never so much as growled at him. But he could see in that canine's creepy almond-shaped eyes—one blue and one brown—how much it wanted to go for his jugular. Someday, he would take care of that freaky beast for good.

Content Sunny wasn't going anywhere for now, he

sank back on his haunches and pulled off his NVGs. Might as well make the most of his time tonight and take care of some clean-up.

He scooped his hunting knife off the ground and swiped the jagged blade through the snow. Blood stained rusty red through the slush. At least this landscape made for a more forgiving killing field than most. Blizzards, combined with repeated thaws and freezes, dispersed evidence. Already, snowflakes muted the splashes from crimson to muddy brown.

Rushing to get back into the pit he'd carved for himself in the snow, he dried the blade that had sliced through flesh just an hour ago. He'd slashed Ted's neck first, taking out the stronger of the two. Madison had fought harder than he'd expected. If she'd been his first kill, she might have actually hurt him.

Instead he'd used the tools at his disposal, sliced her up quickly, then pushed her into a deep crevasse. Her screams had been swallowed by the howling roar of the storm. He'd pitched Ted's body in after hers.

He should have been back at the police station by now, but the storm had trapped him as effectively as it had Sunny. Right now, survival was all that counted. He needed to swap out and hide his bloody clothes before they froze to him. Nobody would come looking for him. He knew the rules. He'd signed on with a secret society of his own that shot deserters. No trial. No questions asked. And his assignment had shifted, once that military guy parachuted into the picture.

Now, he needed to make sure Sunny stayed true to her society's rules and returned to where she'd come from, none the wiser about her friends' fate. She could live a little longer, as long as she stayed on Mount Redoubt and played her part in keeping secrets.

But under no circumstance would she be allowed to leave this mountain alive.

Chapter 3

Wade was a skeptic.

When somebody said they were going to come clean, that usually meant they were about to lie again. So Sunny's vow to share all now—well, he wasn't feeling it.

He leaned forward to warm his hands in front of the small fire—and get a better view of her face around the panting dog between them. "I'm all ears."

They had until morning for her to spin her stories. All night. Alone.

Damn, the flickering firelight showed more than her face. The blanket was stretched to the max from being shared by two people and a dog. The edge gaped, giving a clear shot of creamy cleavage.

Who would have thought a freezing, dank cave could have ambiance? His eyes shifted to her mouth, full lips that Hollywood types would pay a bundle for. Although he would bet his left nut that the mouth on this granola girl was 100 percent natural.

Those lips were also moving as she shared more of her so-called truth, so he needed to tune in to her rather than his blood surging south.

"I wasn't part of that climbing group." Her braid slid forward over her shoulder, swaying. The sapphire stripe danced like the hottest flames lighting the cave. "I live in Alaska and am a bit of a hermit when I'm not working."

"You live out here? Alone?"

Her plait kept swaying and swishing. He couldn't look away from that glistening blue stripe.

"I like time by myself. If I lived in Australia they would call my trips a simple walkabout. Nobody's going to miss me for a few days, and on the off chance anyone does, they will know I can make it out here on my own."

He filed that piece of information away. She wasn't part of the group they'd rescued—that much of her story rang true. Why hadn't she said so at the start? And it didn't escape his notice she still hadn't given her last name.

None of which should matter to him. He'd accomplished what he set out to do. He'd ensured she found shelter through the storm. Another successful day on the job. Another step closer to a Middle East deployment in two weeks. They'd been training hard with mountain exercises in preparation for the rugged and high-altitude terrain of Afghanistan.

Still, Sunny set off alarms in him beyond the sexual draw—which was fierce enough on its own. Could she be a part of something illegal? That would explain her evasiveness. All the more reason to stick to his guns. This mission wasn't complete until he saw her safely deposited into official hands.

"This isn't a walkabout kind of place. You know I can't just leave you here alone. There are rules of safety, and if I leave you here, chances are another rescue group will have to be launched before you make it home."

"You underestimate me."

"I'll be sure not to do that again."

Her braid swished just shy of a stray ember from the

fire. His hand shot out to clasp the plait before it reached the glowing coal.

"Careful," he warned himself as much as her.

The rope of hair was softer than he'd expected for someone who spent so much time outdoors. He'd thought it would by dry and weather worn. Instead it felt as silky as the parachute he'd lost over the mountainside.

He rubbed his thumb along the woven bumps. Touching her this way, such simple contact, shouldn't be so powerful, but it was. His body heated with an internal fire blazing higher than the one in front of them.

"Mine." She grabbed her plait just above his grip and tugged lightly.

"Yes, yours." Still, he held on. He burned to wrap the braid around his hand and draw her closer. To taste those lying lips of hers.

But he wouldn't. Couldn't. "You should get some sleep. I'll take the first watch, then you can tend the fire while I rest."

Wordlessly, she stared back at him as he continued to hold her hair. The fire crackled with settling logs, hissing at the damp tinder. He'd spent hundreds of nights with complete strangers in barracks around the world. This shouldn't be any different. But he couldn't lie to himself.

She tugged her head lightly. "Thanks. I could use some rest before it's time to leave. Now if I can have my hair back?"

He opened his fist and the plait slipped against his palm as she pulled away, silk against his chilled skin. He tucked his hands back under the blanket, now wary *and* turned on. Great.

But damned if he would let anything distract him from his job. The mission was everything to him. He used to be a hardheaded fuckup, right up until the day when he was seventeen, standing on the flight line, pissed off at his mom for making him watch another air show. His dad had been flying in a formation of army helicopters, the same as he'd seen more times than he could count growing up.

Except that time, it had gone all wrong in a blink. One of the choppers crashed in front of all the spectators. In front of him. His mother and sister had started screaming along with everyone else. He hadn't even known he was running toward the flames until hands tore at him, holding him back.

Someone else's father had died that day, not his. His father had landed safely minutes later, but Wade changed. He grew up. No longer could he plow through life doing whatever the hell he wanted. Never again would he be forced to stand helplessly at the sidelines.

He was a rescueman now. And like it or not, this woman was his mission tonight.

Even if he closed his eyes after she woke to take her turn at keeping watch, no way in hell was he going to sleep.

Sunny had stared at Wade's closed eyes for what had to be at least an hour. His breathing was even as he rested his head against his arms crossed on his bent knees, sleeping sitting up. This guy was obviously a pro at catching a nap anywhere, anytime. She'd struggled to get any rest at all, leaning against Chewie.

Wade had apparently learned the skill from his military training. She couldn't sit that still even when she was awake. Her brother had told her once that a fifteen-minute nap in flight could be a matter of life or death.

One more check of Wade's breathing, and she decided to make her move. The sun was just starting to splinter the inky sky. He would wake soon.

It was now or never.

She rested her hand softly on Chewie and signaled for him to stay quiet and still. One careful step at a time, she eased out from under the blanket and into the frigid cave. She shivered at the slap of cold air after the warm cocoon they'd created.

The fire had burned down to a few glowing coals that radiated little heat or light. Rays fingering through the opening gave her just enough illumination to gather her clothes, ease each piece on one leg, one arm at a time. She tiptoed back over to Wade and inched the blanket off Chewie.

God, this was trickier than she'd thought, tucking it against his side before he noticed the canine furnace move away. Wade shuffled, his breathing hitching once, twice, before he settled back to sleep again. Hopefully he was out for the count. She couldn't risk him following her to her home and learning about her brother. And if she went with Wade back to the outside world, authorities could make the connection between her and her brother. This was the easiest way.

Wriggling her toes in her dry but stiff wool socks, she stuffed her feet into her boots and motioned for Chewie to join her. Once they made it out the cave door and melted into the mountainside, it would be impossible for Wade to find her again.

While she had a birth certificate, a social security number, she didn't have utility bills—and neither did her neighbors. Neither did her brother. There wasn't any record of her since her family had moved to the self-sustaining community when she was in junior high school.

There was virtually no paper trail to their town. Some came for the more natural style of living. But she knew all too well that others came to hide. Like her brother. She couldn't let someone she'd only known a few hours make her forget the importance of family loyalty—no matter how compelling that man might be.

If only he would let her just walk away. But this man had come to rescue her off the mountain and she knew he wouldn't stop until he delivered her lock, stock, and barrel into the military's custody.

The sun was rising. The storm had passed. The time was now.

She couldn't resist glancing back for a final look at Wade. His unshaven face sported heavier stubble the same dark shade as his long lashes against his cheeks. Her fingers itched inside her gloves to touch him, test the texture of those lashes the same way he'd obviously lingered over the feel of her hair in his hand last night. She swallowed hard. Damn inconvenient time to find a guy who turned her on, after a three-year dry spell. But delaying would be a frivolous indulgence that would cost her too much. She would not risk losing the chance to say good-bye to her sister.

Steeling her will, she turned away, hand on her dog's head.

"Going somewhere?"

Wade's question stopped her short.

She looked back sharply. Wade stared back at her, wide awake, his muscles bunched.

Her heart lurched. She glanced around the cave quickly, took in his clothes still drying on rocks and stalagmites. It would cost him at least a couple of minutes to dress and he couldn't plunge outside in his thermal underwear.

Decision made, she ran.

Okay, more like she plodded and slid and even skated down the snowy path, Chewie loping alongside. She had to get away. She'd told Wade she would be safe. He'd seen her ability to take care of herself. Why couldn't he accept she could survive out here on her own? She refused to feel guilty for ditching him, but she couldn't climb on board his military helicopter and answer all their questions.

Questions that could lead them to her brother, lead her brother to a court-martial.

Tears stung her eyes for the first time since she'd seen Wade parachute through the storm. She listened for footsteps behind her, but the huffs of her panting dog filled her ears. How far had she run? She'd lost track and was relying on instincts from years of exploring. But she knew better than to let her attention wander. Something she should have thought of yesterday.

Her foot slipped.

A scream burst past her lips before she could hold it back. She scrambled for balance on a loose rock under a knee-deep bank of snow. Her arms flailed for something to grab hold of, but trees were small, scrubby. Not to mention, few and far between. She landed hard on her hip against an icy boulder. An arctic fox darted out and away. The hackles rose along Chewie's back.

She rolled to the side and fell on her butt. Snow edged into a gap in her bib overalls where her coat had ridden up. A critical mistake.

Keep moving. Don't stop. She braced a hand on Chewie's back, found her balance again, and plowed forward.

Every frozen breath stabbed at her lungs, already hungry for oxygen. She glanced over her shoulder. Wade trekked after her, surefooted and gaining fast. As seasoned as she was navigating this region, he was far more adept.

And stronger.

Most would have given out at this altitude long ago. But not him. She had a serious problem on her hands.

The rocky path narrowed ahead. Yes, she was racing in the opposite direction from the pass that would take her to the valley where she lived, but she refused to lead him to her brother's doorstep. And if she remembered correctly, there was another cave to duck into a couple of miles away, which in these conditions could mean walking for hours, but she couldn't dwell on that. Focus instead on the hot springs in the cave ahead, bubbling waters heated from a volcano, which could provide warmth through to her cold core.

Her guilty core.

A stitch started in her side. She forced her feet to move, one in front of the other, even when the stitch turned into a stab. Her legs felt like lead—

Wade tackled her from behind. She slammed into the ground. The weight of him pressing against her back knocked the breath from her. Rock and ice chunks bit into the exposed patches of her face. God, he was solid as a tank.

Chewie's growl echoed lowly in the distance, but for some reason her dog didn't lend a helping paw. The traitor.

"Let me go, damn it." She bucked underneath him, desperate for air and freedom. "I'm not your prisoner. You can't force me to stay here with you."

He clamped his hands around her wrists. "I don't know what you think you're doing or who you're running from, but we can't keep playing this game of freeze tag."

The hell they couldn't. She forced herself to go slack beneath him, making the most of the second to catch her breath, to rest up for her next move. "You're right. It was silly of me to try to get away."

Holding her breath, she listened to him breathing against her ear. The heat of him seeped into her like a furnace against her back, made all the hotter in contrast to the ice under her stomach. They were out here alone at the ends of the earth. No people. Rocky landscape with sparse, low trees. Nothing but miles of barren horizon stretched over water, with hovering clouds threatening and this exasperating man—a *tenacious*, exasperating man who had the uncanny knack of pushing her buttons, which pissed her off all the more.

"Listen, Wade," she gasped, pushing aside the Gore-Tex hood that covered her mouth, "please just let me leave. I do *not* want to be rescued."

"Are you on a suicide mission?" he growled.

"I only want to be left alone." She wriggled beneath him until she faced him, their bodies sealed chest to chest.

His hand gravitated to his hip—to his sidearm. "Are you running from the law?"

Could she bring herself to take the gun she felt strapped to his leg? She shivered. No. There had to be another way for her. She couldn't risk the weapon accidentally going off. She couldn't risk shooting him. He hadn't done anything wrong, only tried to save her.

She thumped his shoulders, once, twice, and again even harder until finally he let her slide out from under him. Not that he took his hard, wary eyes off her for even a second.

Sitting, Sunny dusted off her snow pants. "I am *not* a criminal."

"Does someone think you are?" he snapped back.

She weighed her words carefully. "No one in any law enforcement agency is on the lookout for me." Her brother, however... "Please stop wasting your time on me. Aren't there people out there who need the skills you have to offer more than I do?"

"As a matter of fact, there are. But I don't have the luxury of choosing where I go." He planted his hand on the snow, leaning toward her. "Right now, *you* are my mission."

He studied her intently as a caribou strayed from the herd in the distance. The sun slashed across the sky, reflecting off the snow, and she realized she was seeing him fully for the first time. Yesterday had been overcast with the storm, and the cave had been shadowy at best. The impact of his undiluted stare sent a quiver of awareness down her spine, a gush of longing through her veins.

What if they'd met in a normal setting, on equal footing? What if he'd walked into her business, a newcomer to town looking for a guide to familiarize him with their mountain?

A rustle behind her gave only a second of warning to brace herself before Chewie barreled into her shoulder. His bulk showered a sheet of snow into her face. The frigid splash brought her back to reality. Daydreaming was dangerous. She was a practical woman, damn it. She refused to be swayed by a hot body and intense eyes. And she might not have another chance to escape.

Before she could weaken or second-guess, she shoved to her feet and ran her heart out. A rational part of her brain insisted that she stop, conserve her resources, come up with another story that he wouldn't believe but that would buy her more time. And yet, she couldn't stop running. Something inside her had snapped, until she felt like a frantic ground squirrel on the run from a red fox.

Chewie loped beside her. Her pulse drummed in her ears. A long shadow stretched over her, a man's shadow, closer, closer still. Chewie stopped, howling. But still she ran.

The ground fell out from under her.

Screaming, she clawed at the icy wall. Her feet backpedaled, seeking purchase on ground giving way. Distantly, she heard Wade shout from above. Oh God, she was going to die. Frozen chunks of earth battered her body as she plummeted downward while her stomach rose to meet her throat. There was no way to see the bottom, to know when she would die, to prepare for—

Impact.

Pain splintered through her body. Sparks danced in front of her eyes like a northern lights show on speed swirl. Blood filled her mouth as she bit her tongue. The metallic tang saturated her taste buds with the reminder that thank you, God, thank you, God, she was still alive.

She stared up at the circle of light overhead, not all that far, but whew, how it was spinning. Blurring. Then finally it slowed and she saw Wade.

He scaled down the side without any formal climbing gear.

Holy crap. She'd lived in this area for fifteen years and still she was stunned. Like Spider-Man in camo, Wade worked his way down with just a rope around his waist anchored into the ice above. Closer, closer still, he moved until he dropped the rest of the way, landing beside her with surefooted grace.

His face cast in shadows, he leaned over her. "Are you okay?"

Why hadn't she checked herself over instead of lying here mesmerized by him? She must be more dazed than she'd thought.

She wriggled her toes, her fingers, then sat up cautiously. Chewie whined from above at the edge of the drop-off. The world bobbled, then settled. "I think so. Just stunned."

His head tipped, his face bathed in sunlight again. Fury burned from his eyes as he leaned over her. She scrambled backward without much success, her braid coming loose from her jacket as her head swam.

"Don't try to get up yet, not until I can check you over more fully," he commanded.

She'd forgotten about his medic training. Wow, they could use a guy like him where she lived. The silly, unattainable thought made her realize just how scrambled her brain really was by the fall.

Silent, brooding, he knelt beside her, his face taut with anger. He stripped off his outer gloves until he wore what appeared to be thin pilot's gloves. One limb at a time, he moved her legs and arms, working them back and forth, side to side. The feel of his hands on her body, even through layers, unsettled her, stirred her. Sure, he was doing the whole medical thing and no doubt he was mad as hell. He wasn't doing anything different from how she checked people over during a trek if they pulled a muscle.

Still, somehow she knew. This was different.

He ended by placing his hands on either side of her face and staring into her eyes. Checking to see if her pupils were even and not blown, undoubtedly, but still the fierce focus on her made her ache in a way that had nothing to do with the fall.

Wade leaned closer. "No more running. This insanity stops here, now."

"What are you going to do?" she gasped out in tiny bursts of white, most of the air still punched from her lungs after the fall. "Toss me across your shoulder and carry me down the mountain caveman-style?"

A tic flicked the corner of his eye. His hands fell away. "I can't leave you out here to die." He stood, extending a hand. "And believe me, if I go back empty-handed, there will be search teams."

She clasped his fingers and rose slowly until she stood in front of him. "Tell them you found a bear, not a person."

"There aren't any bears up this high. I do not lie." He squeezed her hand lightly, purposefully. "And I really hate it when anyone lies to me."

He was a second away from insisting on answers. She knew it. Could see it in his dark, demanding eyes. Answers she wouldn't—couldn't—give him. But how could she keep those words from falling from his mouth when it was just the two of them out here alone together?

Completely alone.

A tempting possibility tickled at the back of her brain, a way of shutting him up right here and now. There was no chance their worlds would cross again. No chance she would ever know how things might have been had he simply walked into her life one day, asking to take a tour around the terrain, maybe even flirting a little. Things weren't that simple for her.

And suddenly she was certain of exactly how to distract him. At least for a few minutes. One kiss, to silence his questions and answer one of her own. This was her one chance to know if the attraction was real.

And hopefully for her peace of mind, the kiss would suck.

~~~

What the hell?

Wade stood stunned with Sunny's mouth pressed to his. But surprise shifted fast to hardcore need. He pulled away, only an inch, but enough to see her, to figure out what kind of crazy getaway plan she had in mind now, even when there wasn't a chance in hell she could scale her way out of here without him right there with her.

She looked up at him with wide hazel eyes that should have been vulnerable, scared, or even angry. But instead stared back at him with an answering heat that felt so damned good as it radiated from her and into him.

It could be a ploy. But she was damn willing. He was at his wits' end and she wasn't going anywhere. He had nothing to lose by caving in to a need that had ridden him hard all night.

Wade sealed his mouth to hers again.

His arms locked around her and he clamped her close, near enough to feel the generous swell of her breasts under the parka. Her leg was wedged between his and he shouldn't be able to feel jack with so many layers between them. Shouldn't. But could.

Her thigh pressed right against his swelling erection. Damned inconvenient time to get turned on. Really turned on. Arousal fed off the adrenaline pumping through him, devouring like a parched beast falling into an oasis.

He angled his mouth over hers, his tongue plunging deeper, tasting, stroking, stoking need higher and hotter. Her braid brushed against the back of his hand. He clasped the thick mass and wrapped it round and round his hand, binding them closer together as they stumbled back against the ice wall.

She tasted like peanut butter, crisp snow, and pure sex. Her tongue touched his without hesitation, met and thrust. He searched her mouth as she battled to explore his first. She kissed the same way she did everything else, with energy and confidence.

Her gloved hands pressed his head for a fuller meeting, then grasped at his shoulders, and God, he wanted to feel her bare fingers on his skin. Yeah, this was crazy and he was going on fumes after yesterday's training mission then parachute rescue, followed by a long night sharing a blanket with Sunny, nearly naked. This was a more twisted and demanding exercise than even crazy-ass Major McCabe could come up with.

Images of Sunny's mile-long legs walked through his memory, reminding him of just how wild she'd driven him, stripping last night. The back of his eyelids were hazy pale pink with the image of her thermals, which molded to her body and hinted at flesh tones. Legs and curves and breasts, every inch of her was right there for him to taste.

He wanted to blame the mountain air for this insanity, but he knew full well what he was doing and he wanted more. Which was impossible for about ten reasons right off the top of his head, starting with the layers of clothes and their location. He wasn't a monk by any means, but he'd been a while without sex and the grinding need to be inside her broadsided him.

Then reason whispered through the sex-crazed fog. She had to be setting him up. The passion wasn't real— not for her anyway. She must be using her body to get something from him one way or another. If not at this moment, then to lure him into a false sense of security for when they climbed out.

His mouth stilled against hers and he eased away, just an inch, enough to see her without levering off her body in the narrow mountain gully. She stared back at him with what looked like confusion, but he knew better than to trust her. Everything she said and did was part of some game to hide a deeper agenda.

The uncertainty on her face, real or faked, faded. As determined as she was, she might even try to knock him out. Or worse.

The possibility that she might actually try to kill him splashed cold water all over his libido.

He locked her wrists with his hands to keep her still until he could clear his mind enough to think logically. Except he slowly realized she wasn't moving after all. Her whole body was stock-still, her eyes wide as she gawked past his shoulder. Her confusion had turned to something that looked a helluva lot like horror as she kept her eyes averted, staring down. Yeah, he was pretty upset at himself too.

Except something about the way she peered downward made him want to look too. Was this another trick? He firmed his hold on her wrists. Warily, he tracked her gaze to the patch of slushy earth beside his boot.

A dead face stared back at him through the ice.

Chapter 4

SUNNY SCREAMED.

Horror raked up her throat as dead eyes peered at her through a thin sheet of ice and snow. Not just any eyes. Madison's eyes. The woman she'd escorted through the pass just yesterday.

She clasped her throat, right where the gash gaped across Madison's severed carotid. The dead woman's blonde hair fanned around her. The fatal wound was outlined in crystallized drops of frozen blood, as if rusty red tears wept from her neck.

The screams kept coming and she couldn't make them stop even as each panicked wheeze froze in her lungs. Wade clamped a hand over her mouth just as he'd covered her lips with his moments ago in that unwise, out-of-control kiss.

Oh God, they'd been kissing beside a dead body. Nausea gagged her.

"Careful," he said softly, urgently. "Too much noise could cause an avalanche."

His whispered warning launched hysteria at the possibility of being buried alive—with Madison.

What had happened? Where was Ted? And the sheriff's deputy? Questions dog-piled inside her, shredding through her already raw emotions with vicious teeth.

Her brain went into hyperdrive. Ted and Madison must have been caught in the storm too. Although very clearly she'd been murdered. By whom? A squatter? And where were Ted and the deputy?

God, if she'd thought to look for Ted and Madison the minute the storm started, maybe she would have found her before this.

Or she could be right there under the ice, waxy and dead just like her friend.

Hysteria bubbled until her cries gurgled, much like Madison must have choked on her own blood.

"Sunny? It's okay," he continued softly, sliding his arm around her shoulders. "It's all right. I know the first time you see a dead body it's scary as hell. I wish I could say it gets better, but it doesn't. You just learn to hold back the reaction until the crisis passes. And we need to do that now. We need to function so we can get out of here."

She forced herself to take slow, even breaths, to push cold oxygen and reason to her stunned brain. "Okay. I hear you."

"Good, now we have to get out of here and make our way to a better pickup zone so my team can bring us in. Then we can notify the authorities about this person so they can work on an ID and notifying the family."

He didn't realize she knew Madison. Her secret was safe for a while longer… Except she needed to know about Ted and the deputy, no matter the cost. "What if there's someone with her? Shouldn't we look around?"

"On the off chance? Even though a rescue team could get us out of here, it's a volatile place to hang out." He looked at the frozen face, then around the narrow crevasse about twenty feet from the edge above. "She was probably with the original group we rescued. They were so disoriented when we rescued them we never could get a solid count as to whether it was four climbers and a guide, or four people total."

He squinted up toward the horizon, his face alert. "And if that's the case, then we need to be careful, because there's a murderer out there somewhere."

Her teeth started to chatter from the cold and fear. The fall too, maybe. But her body was definitely going into shock.

He squeezed her shoulder. For comfort? More likely to make sure she couldn't get away. "Come on. She's not going anywhere, and we need to think smart."

She couldn't hide or play word games anymore. Not with Ted's life at stake. "I know her. She's not with the other team, and she must have been murdered recently. Sometime after yesterday morning." She swallowed hard. "I do guide work and I was out helping her meet up with another, uh, guide today. She had a partner, Ted."

Her voice cracked with emotion. Damn it, she was stronger than this. But the exhaustion, the horror of seeing Madison, thinking of her friend's dream to attend college, remembering how she'd always made homemade granola for the whole community at Christmas… It was all too much.

Wade stared into her eyes for four toe-numbing seconds—deciding if she was a party to this horror?—before shaking his head. "Right. You're good at making crap up, but I'm not letting you run again. If there's someone else out there, then my team can track him."

"But what about Ted? The deputy?"

"My first priority is to get you out of here alive. Now let's go." He pulled a knife from his boot and began carving a toehold out of the ice.

"I'm not a child."

"I noticed," he said, then continued without missing a beat. "We need to haul our asses back up out of this gorge. Are you going to help me dig out some handholds or not?"

"You're right. I'm sorry." She pulled out her survival knife.

"Shit."

His curse stopped her. "What?"

He slapped a hand against the ice, his shoulders braced in resignation as he looked down, giving her only a scant second's warning before he said, "I think I just found Ted."

Misty sat cross-legged in front of the computer screen at Sunny's place, wondering how long it would be before she could email with Madison or Ted. The computer booted up—God love the hydropower from the volcanic hot springs that generated electricity whenever the solar panels were drained due to longer nights.

Internet access wasn't widespread around here. Satellite connections could be iffy, depending on the weather. But thanks to a deal Sunny had cut with the sheriff's office, they had Internet at her business and at the library that also served as the school. On the rare occasion when there was some kind of hookup or membership fee or info required, Deputy Smith helped them out. He was a good guy that way.

Since her older sister was running behind, their brother had opened today, and he would rather work out than play on the Internet. Which left Misty free to use one of the two computers tucked by the snack counter that served muffins and granola.

The bright gym full of windows was just coming to life with the early-morning crowd. The metal grate was still rolled down in front of the juice bar, but the Everett twins—Flynn and Ryker—lumbered out of the locker room without speaking, ready to pump iron after their early start running snowplows.

Over on the small stage, Lindsay, the substitute aerobics instructor, toyed with the sound system, increasing the bass reverb until the floor buzzed under Misty's feet. Lindsay—a former classmate—was also a first-year art teacher at the village school who taught first grade all the way through to twelfth. And as if that wasn't enough, she was four months pregnant with her first baby by the younger Everett twin. Lindsay's life was moving forward, while Misty's stagnated.

She spun her seat back toward the computer, away from Lindsay's growing tummy.

Still no messages on the computer. Bummed, she tugged at her purple hemp sweater, wrapping it closer around her in the chilly gym. It was probably too early to expect anything from Madison, but Misty couldn't help watching, wondering, hungry for anything about how someone from here would adapt to the world outside. A world she would be joining soon.

Madison had promised to update her, even send photos of their new place once they got settled. When community members left, they always sent messages at first, but the notes faded away over time as they got wrapped up in their busy new lives.

She wouldn't be that way, though, once she left. Even if

she couldn't come back, she had to hear about her family's lives and she hoped they would want to know about hers. She would never stop praying that they would join her.

Or at least understand her reasons for leaving.

The cursor blinked on the computer screen. Still no new messages in her mailbox. It would probably be a while before they got their place set up, but they'd promised she could stay with them. Ted's family had money. They would be so happy to have him back in the family fold, they would probably do anything he asked.

She resisted the urge to cross her fingers under the table. She was an adult now, for crying out loud. Twenty-two years old last week. Able to go out on her own.

It was rare to have community members leave twice in a week. For the most part, people were happy here. Decisions to live off-the-grid didn't come lightly. There was a lot of preparation to do ahead of time, things to learn. Although in her case, she'd been a kid.

So there was a whole other aspect of facing the unknown beyond their mountain valley.

Would it be like on television? With so many satellite channels to choose from, she felt like she had a solid image of the outside world—they weren't hermits here. Just insular. She'd soaked up reruns of everything from *Sex in the City* to *Law & Order* to *True Blood*.

Everything moved so fast, so bright. She couldn't wait to be a part of it all. She couldn't wait to meet him, Brett, face-to-face. She tapped in the Web address for the online dating site… and oh God, he was online, waiting for her just like he'd promised.

The instant message icon blinked. Her heartbeat sped up a notch.

Brett: Morning, beautiful.
Misty: Less than a week til we meet in person.
Brett: Reservations r made.

Her shadowy reflection on the screen grinned back at her. He'd promised to take her to Prince William Sound for a day cruise where they could see orcas, porpoises, eagles, otters, and puffers together. Next February, he would take her to the Fur Rondy in Anchorage, billed as the largest festival in North America. In March, they could watch the Iditarod dogsled race finish.

The way he talked about being together nearly a year from now gave her hope she hadn't dared store up in a long time. Together they would experience the adventures she'd been craving since her illness.

Misty: Just want to see you in person rather than pictures.

Although his profile photos showed a megahot thirty-nine-year-old guy. Photos of Brett standing beside a Cessna. Brett holding up a string of fish with his parka open to reveal a broad chest. Brett in a suit, holding his niece during her baptism.

The images came together for an athletic, sensitive man with a sexy groomed beard. She couldn't believe she'd found him online. He said he worked long hours as an airplane mechanic. Couple that with the higher male-to-female ratio in Alaska, and he'd decided to give online dating at try.

Brett: Feels like I know you already. Can't wait to
hear your voice.

Her hand flew to her throat, a nervous habit she'd
picked up around four years ago. She chewed her bottom lip, deciding what to say next.

Misty: Sorry it's taken me so long. Can't be helped.
Leaving my hometown is… complicated.
Brett: Alaska is a big state. We'll work it out.

No kidding. Alaska had a landmass the size of Texas,
California, and Montana combined. Sometimes she felt
absorbed by the vastness of it all.

As much as she wished to be from somewhere else,
she'd been up-front with Brett about living in America's
last frontier, telling him their remote town had post office box numbers for emergencies. This wasn't a cult
with freaky rituals, just a group of people committed to
living off the land as much as possible.

Actually, she looked forward to carrying a lot of that
knowledge and mind-set with her out into the world.
Not that she was rejecting her hometown, merely embracing a new one because there were limitations to
living here. She forced her hand away from her neck
and back to the keyboard.

Misty: What if you're disappointed by me?
Brett: Not possible.

Misty: You don't know all the problems that come
with being with someone like me.

The cursor blink, blink, blinked so long, her heart sped faster. A message popped up.

Brett: Do you want to back out on meeting?
Misty: No! Just afraid you'll be sorry.

The cursor blinked and blinked as she waited for his answer. Finally…

Brett: Sometimes you gotta take a leap of faith.
Either you're in or you're not.
Misty: I'm only scared.
Brett: Don't want to frighten you. Trust me.

Trust. It seemed like all she did was trust other people to lead her through life. She wanted to be in charge for a change, no longer the absentminded tomboy, the needy sister. Rather she would be a take-charge woman.

A hand tapped her on the shoulder.

Gasping, she jolted. Even four years after losing her hearing, she still wasn't accustomed to the shock of having someone sneak up on her. She was getting better at coping strategies, like feeling a slight tremble in the floor or gust from an opening door, but she'd apparently let herself become too absorbed in her online conversation.

Thank God for her sister's dogged insistence on expanding their Internet capabilities, because here, at least, Misty had no limitations.

She spun, careful that her back covered the computer screen, and found her older brother with his wife. Astrid stood closer, while Phoenix hung back by the door with his year-old son strapped to his chest in a BabyBjörn. An image of Brett holding his baby niece flashed into her mind. She wanted that for herself, and that wouldn't happen for her here.

Take charge. Pioneer her own future. She mentally recited her new mantra.

She held up a hand asking them to hold on for a second and turned back to the computer to type.

Misty: Gotta sign off. More later. Love.

Love. She shivered. Could she love someone she'd never met in person?

As she turned back to Astrid, Misty scratched her neck, not because of any itch but to gauge her voice by the vibrations against her fingertips. "Yes?"

Astrid dropped into a chair beside her, her face scrunched with worry and exhaustion. The former New York teen model wore her platinum blonde hair in a lop-sided ponytail and her gray sweatshirt was dotted with what looked like pureed carrots.

The new mother had left behind a potential seven-figure career and fame ten years ago to join their community. "Have you seen Sunny?"

"Not since she left yesterday." One hand still against her throat, she fidgeted with her own shoulder-length brown hair. Would Brett prefer it longer? Chemically highlighted? Maybe even with a bold steak of color like Sunny's? "But you know how she is."

"Damn." She hitched the quilted diaper bag onto her shoulder, always careful to keep her face toward Misty for lip-reading. "I was hoping she could take my lunch shift at the snack bar so I could take J.T. for his well-baby checkup, and Phoenix has a class to teach."

Clinic appointments were tight since one of their nurse practitioners had left last fall, determined to become a doctor. What a loss that she couldn't come back. The rigidness of the city council's rules made her want to scream. Silently of course.

"I can take your shift. I promise to be extra careful in taking the orders, no mistakes, even if I have to make them write down what they want." She was weary with everyone cosseting her. She'd worked so hard to accommodate for the deafness that had resulted from a fierce case of meningitis, and still everyone babied her.

Her smile wobbly, Astrid hugged her hard and fast, diaper bag swinging around to thump them both. The scent of baby clung to her sister-in-law's clothes. Did she even know how lucky she was?

Pulling back, Astrid scrunched her nose. "Sorry. I forget sometimes. I just wanted to say thank you for helping, and I wish there was some way to pay you back."

Hopefully Astrid could help Phoenix understand why she had to go. It was so much easier for Sunny to stick it out here. She had options.

When the boundaries of their community became too constrictive for her, she hiked into the mountains, teaching survival courses. Camped. Kayaked.

But Sunny wouldn't miss saying good-bye. Of that Misty was sure. If only Sunny could be the one to escort her out instead of their brother—their half brother, rather. Phoenix's biological mom had died when he was two, then their dad remarried...

Misty watched him stride away and sit on a stationary

bike, baby strapped to his chest while he started his workout. Phoenix didn't talk much, but he was a good father. She couldn't remember a time when her brother hadn't been quiet, almost like a ghost from one of their grandmother's Yupik legends.

Astrid waved a hand in front of her eyes, snapping her fingers. Misty jerked and turned fast.

"Sorry. I was daydreaming."

Facing her, Astrid tapped the top of the computer. "You never have to worry about bad breath with an Internet boyfriend."

"Not funny."

"But true." She leaned closer to clasp Misty's hands. "You can do better than this."

"Here? With all of a half dozen guys that are even remotely appropriate for me to pick from? No thanks."

"Lindsay's brother Jayden would treat you like a queen. He's obviously adored you since he got here two years ago."

"Be real. He adores my boobs." She clapped her hands over her D-cups, which had filled out by junior high. "He's never even looked me in the eyes once. Not to mention, he cheated on his last two girlfriends." An unforgivable sin in her eyes. "He's just running out of women to screw over, since he's plowing through the females in this town so fast."

"Okay, you could have a point." Astrid tugged a bib apron from her backpack and slung it over her neck for her breakfast shift at the shop. The oatmeal-colored fabric hid the carrot stains and transformed her into a professional barista.

Misty helped her wrap the tie around twice until she

could knot it in the front. "And seriously, what a dumb ass. This is such a small community, it's not like anything's a secret. Did he actually expect to get away with it? Twice?" She gave the knot a final tug, her hand gravitating back up to her throat. "I can't hide here forever. I want a life like other people have. Like you have."

Astrid's face lit with the sympathy that was all too common around here since Misty's illness, looks she could only erase if she left here. Her parents were dead now, gone in a car accident. Her brother was married with a family of his own. Sunny had her business.

There was nothing left to keep her here. Why couldn't they support her need to start her own life? She would honor their decision to keep this place quietly under the radar, but it was their choice to cut off contact with everyone else. Her going didn't have to be the end of their relationship.

But she was willing to accept those consequences if that's what it cost to leave. To have access to medical technology that would never reach this far. She didn't blame her parents for the meningitis caught and treated almost too late.

But she wouldn't let anyone keep her from the surgery that could restore the hearing she'd lost.

Tears stung her eyes and she massaged her throat to check for vibrations and make sure no sob sounds slid free. How much longer would she be able to talk understandably if she didn't get a cochlear implant? How strange did her voice sound already after almost four years without hearing herself?

She studied Astrid's mouth but she wasn't speaking, her lips didn't move. Even though Astrid was good about keeping her face where Misty could always see it during conversations, so much was still lost in translation. Lip-reading only worked for about 50 percent of the words, even though she was meticulous about watching not only the lips, but also the tongue, teeth, cheeks, and neck, as well as facial expressions and gestures. It had been so damn exhausting at first on top of the grief.

So many sounds she'd taken for granted before and now missed with an ache so deep, she felt a part of her life had been amputated. Maybe if she didn't know what she was missing... Maybe...

Unable to hold back the flood of emotion, she shot to her feet. "See you at lunchtime. I gotta go."

Misty snagged her parka off the back of her chair and raced for the entrance by instinct, her sight blurred, further locking her away in a world with limited senses. She slammed through the front doors and burst outside, leaving behind the musty, sweaty scent of the gym. The crisp outdoors enveloped her, the smell of the pure mountain air even more intoxicating since she'd lost her hearing. Still, it wasn't enough to replace what had been taken from her.

Blinking fast and swiping an arm across her cheeks, she cleared her eyes until Main Street—the only street, really—took shape again. Stores and homes were built in tiered levels, notched into a ridge, conforming to the natural dips and rises of the mountainside. Her parents had owned the whitewashed building across and at the end of the road and she still lived there with her brother and family since their parents had died two years ago.

Twenty-two and still living at home, unlike Sunny

who had a loft apartment in the log cabin that housed her business.

She stepped out onto the road and felt the vibration under her feet. She looked up sharply just as a rusted Reva screeched to a halt an inch away from hitting her. She held up a hand in apology to the electric car's driver.

Come summertime, snow would melt away to open bike trails for even more traffic. Frozen lakes would thaw and fast fill with kayaks. But she wouldn't hear the gurgle of the water or the laughter from the boats.

It was a perpetual vacation, and some thought she was crazy to leave. She already planned to search out a more open community after her surgery. Surely she could find one, with over two hundred thousand families living off-the-grid in the United States these days.

Surely Brett would join her.

Hands stuffed in her parka pockets, she tromped through the sludge on the sidewalks. Why did it have to be such a big deal because she wanted to leave, to have surgery, to have a future with Brett? He could come here, but that still wouldn't help her, not in the way she needed. It was so unfair that life made her choose between being with her family and regaining her hearing.

She thought of the chubby-cheeked nephew she would never see grow up. Adult choices sucked. Not that she really had much of a choice. She had to leave this place to receive a cochlear implant, and the longer she waited, the tougher those good-byes would become—and the lower her chances of success would be with the procedure.

The local doctor assured her she was a good candidate. She'd been born with her hearing, only losing it nearly four years ago during the bout of meningitis. While they had a hospital here, the facility wasn't specialized enough for the procedure.

She had no choice but to leave, and leave soon. Even though Sunny was the best guide, there were others who could escort her down. Still, Misty couldn't bring herself to leave until Sunny came back. She had to say good-bye to her sister.

And then she would follow Madison and Ted's path out of this place forever.

Brett downloaded the data received during the latest chat with Misty. Sometimes things were just too easy. He had Misty right where he wanted her, and his hired help from the local sheriff's office was taking care of the messier details on the mountain. He was perfectly positioned halfway between civilization and no-man's-land.

Clicking through the commands to file and save, Brett finished with a final tap, then spun in the leather chair to face the four-paned window. From his third-floor tiny office in the Alaska Peninsula Power Plant, he could overlook Bristol Bay in the distance, imagining it feeding into the Bering Sea. Fishing boats dotted the thawing waters along the peninsula that led to the Aleutian Islands.

And here he sat, in the perfect position to use the untapped potential of one of those islands. Far enough away from the scrutiny of major cities like Anchorage or Fairbanks, but not completely isolated on one of those godforsaken islands.

How naïve for Misty and her friends to think they

could live off-the-grid as if the rest of the world didn't exist. The world was too global, even in the remotest corners of Alaska. Those who grabbed control first, those who created opportunity out of even a barren wasteland, the kingdom builders like himself… They would survive in the end.

Above all, Brett was a survivor.

Communicating with Misty had offered the perfect means to install keylogger software into her computer, which in turn spiderwebbed into the community's mainframe. The inside contact would be sure they couldn't run the kind of advanced scan needed to detect the program.

Every keystroke made on their computers was logged and sent in daily emails to Brett. No one slipped anything past the keylogger. Printouts were made and checked for cooperation, for dissent. There was no room for mistakes.

The insular community had been all too easy to infiltrate, manipulate. What would young Misty think if she knew her own little society was corruptible? He'd only needed to figure out which ones to tempt with the promise of feeding an ecoterrorist agenda. Those corruptible few were the truly bloodthirsty ones, as the world would know four days from now.

How easy it was to fool people through a computer. With an Internet connection and some help from his hired goon in the sheriff's office, Brett could pretend to be anyone on this end.

Even Ted and Madison.

Chapter 5

SUNNY JAMMED HER FOOT INTO THE TOEHOLD WADE HAD carved out of the ice wall. Gut-gnawing terror fueled her determination. Her muscles strained and trembled as she clung to a tiny crinkle overhead, eyes locked on Chewie leaning over the edge, barking furiously. Panicked paws shifted and twitched, sending small snow showers down on her head. She'd stuffed her bulky overgloves into the bib of her snowsuit. Cold penetrated the thin undergloves, which were waterproof but not nearly as warm. A minor inconvenience, when she thought about her two dead friends below.

Her hand slipped.

Wade palmed her back and wedged his shoulder under her butt. How he managed that while keeping his own balance climbing, she couldn't imagine and didn't have time to ask. Ted and Madison lay lifeless twenty feet below, and since there was no sign of a third body, she had to wonder. Had the deputy gone for help and been killed? Was he out there now? Or oh God, could the deputy have killed them? And if not him, then someone else who might still be nearby?

She shivered and secured her grip with fingers so frozen they were stiff and numb. She refused to slow Wade down. She'd already done enough damage, bringing him out here with her during her reckless dash to escape. But if she hadn't, then Ted and Madison's bodies may never have been found. The people at home might never have known they were dead, since there wouldn't have been anyone to report them missing. The only hint of their disappearance would have been the lack of emails, which would be easy enough to write off as making a clean break. God, it was too easy for a person to fall off the face of the planet.

But then wasn't that what her family had made a point of doing, severing all ties with civilization?

So close. She was so close. Only a few more inches.

Slapping an arm over the edge, she hauled herself upward, groaning at the effort, afraid she wouldn't be able to pull her own weight. Her arms trembled, and her toes cramped.

Chewie stretched over, his jaws open. His fangs flashed in the early-morning sun. *Snap*. He sunk his teeth into her parka, tugging, yanking with just the extra help… she needed until…

Sunny hitched a knee over the edge. Growling with exertion almost as loudly as her dog, she levered herself over and rolled away flat on her back. Exhausted. But she couldn't afford to rest. She scrambled to the edge on shaky legs and reached for Wade in case he needed help.

Wade vaulted over the edge, landing beside her, crouching on one knee. She should have known a superhero wouldn't need her help. Hysteria welled in her oxygen-deprived brain.

She flung herself around him, clinging to life and vitality, grateful to be alive. So damn glad Wade was alive as well, that he hadn't been harmed chasing her into whatever the hell had happened below. All the ache and want she'd felt for him during that insanely impulsive kiss roared to life again, catching her unaware when her defenses were down. Her already rattled world had been shattered in less than a few short hours. Now all she could think about was broad shoulders and how much she wanted to wrap herself around all that strength until things righted again. How totally anti-her. She wasn't the clinging-vine sort. Was this how Stockholm syndrome worked? Yet she couldn't deny her nerves tingling to life like thawing after a deep freeze.

A bit mortifying though, as Wade was certainly only pausing to give her enough time to catch her breath before they moved on.

Chewie nudged her shoulder just as Wade cupped the back of her neck, staring into her eyes. Checking her pupils again?

He squeezed once reassuringly before tugging her hood up. "We can't afford to rest." Unspoken was the horrible threat that there could be a killer lurking nearby. "Do you need me to carry you?"

"No, no…" She pushed herself onto her hands and knees, then rose. "I can do it."

"Good. Make sure you keep up." He pulled the fat gloves from her overall bib, the backs of his fingers brushing quickly along the top of her breasts. "My team will be using my locator beacon to search for us," he said, the last part loudly. As if announcing it to anyone who might be listening? "And I want to position us in the best possible place for extraction. Are you sure you don't want me to carry you on my back? The faster we move, the sooner we're out of here." He held up the gloves.

She stuffed her hands inside, fighting for enough oxygen to level her out for travel. "Lead. I'll keep up."

With a curt nod, he started away from the hole in the earth. Away from Madison and Ted's icy crypt. Her foot sunk into a deeper drift and she struggled to stay upright, not to lag, her eyes locked firmly on Wade's broad back. Stride by stride, he guided her down the rugged slope. Chewie loped behind her as if protecting her back.

A scant scattering of stunted conifers dotted the landscape the farther they descended. Not dense, towering pines like in other parts of Alaska. The wind was too fierce here for that, snapping off tops of taller trees. Tearing at her every step until she feared the roar could blot out warning sounds. At least the barren landscape made it easier to scan for threats, human or otherwise, as they neared brown bear territory and the end of hibernation.

Watching Wade's measured, steadied steps, she didn't doubt that he could have carried her down the mountain pass just as fast. She was holding him back, but he wouldn't leave without her. He'd made that clear.

Time to commit to getting off the mountain, even if it meant stepping into the outside world. She would face whatever else came her way—

A buzz vibrated the air by her ear. Then another. Chewie's growl overrode the wind just as Wade turned back toward her.

"Gunfire!" He yanked her arm and tucked her behind him as he zigzagged to the left.

Bullets spewed against a lone tree ahead, splintering frozen bark left, then right. Her hand in Wade's, she trailed him, racing, scanning, finding...

A man stood on top of a boulder a football field away,

rifle on his shoulder. She hesitated, stunned. She'd suspected, but still, to see the sheriff's deputy, Rand Smith, peering down the scope of a rifle rattled her.

He fired. She shrieked once and ducked, bracing for the impact of the bullet.

Wade yanked her down behind a short, fat tree. Panic kicked into overdrive. No matter how well versed she was in mountain survival, she was really out of her element now. Her body had been pushed to the edge of endurance, and fear sent her teeth chattering in a way that had nothing to do with cold.

Bullets zinged off the trunk, two in a row, *pop, pop*. Snow from the branches spewed in chunks. She grabbed Wade's parka and pressed closer. A sense of their life and death stakes tangled up with a bizarre mess of want and fear until she desperately needed to hang on to the one familiar person in a world flipped upside down. The deputy dropped to his stomach and took aim again.

"Chewie?" she whispered, looking around frantically, then calling louder, "Chewie?"

Zing. Another bullet ricocheted off a pile of rocks at the base of the mountain.

Wade shoved her to the ground and dropped on top of her with an "Ooof." Anything that hit her would have to go through him. Except he didn't flinch, so she hoped, prayed, he hadn't been hit. The bullets kept popping, echoing around the narrow crevasse in the mountain. Snow and ice chunks battered down around them, clinking off Wade's backpack.

His hand slid from her and to his waist. He pulled out a gun, an ominous black pistol. He held it up, but for some reason, he didn't shoot. Not that she intended to question anything he did right now, because he was the one keeping them alive and *she* was the one who'd screwed up again and again.

Faster and faster the mountain rumbled, until she realized.

Deputy Smith wasn't trying to shoot them. He was trying to start an avalanche and collapse the walls on top of them.

Wade was running out of options fast.

The bastard lying belly down on a stretch of ice kept shooting at them, and while Wade had a clear shot, more gunfire could risk setting off an avalanche, since he had the foothills and overhang above him. A few more yards and they would have been in clear open space—clean pickings for the gunman. But he also could have gotten off a shot of his own. Wade gripped the barrel of his 9 mm. He hoped he wouldn't have to use it, but if the man came closer, he wouldn't have any choice. He just prayed the snowy overhang would hold until the chopper arrived.

"Come on, come on, come on," he mumbled softly.

He kept his body between Sunny and the bullets. Snow and chunks of ice thudded and stabbed downward, faster, thicker. He hunched around her, tighter. Adrenaline seared his veins until he could almost feel his near-frozen toes thawing.

"Wade"—Sunny gripped his jacket—"any ideas? What do you need me to do? We can't just stay here like sitting ducks."

"I agree." Another shot echoed. An icicle stabbed into the earth an inch away from his head. Shit. He rolled to his side, tucking Sunny behind him. A second fell. Fire flamed through his shoulder. He fought the urge to shout, to roll to his side and clutch the wound. "Now would be a good time to say if you know of any secret caves."

"Sorry." Her breath caressed his neck. "It's flatland ahead and nothing that I know of back the way we came."

He needed to decide fast. Wait until the other guy ran out of bullets. Or shoot back. The flat terrain ahead of them that appeared so starkly majestic at other times looked damn barren, open, and dangerous right now, empty except for the crouching gunman.

And a tiny speck on the horizon.

His heart rate ramped. A chopper. His. Theirs.

The rotors growled louder, closer, until the gunman's head popped up. He bolted out and tore off running, long strides lumbering through the snow too fast and far away to catch even if he could, which he couldn't—not with Sunny to look after.

Wade jumped to his feet, dragging Sunny up with him. Ignoring the blazing pain from his shoulder. "We need to book it."

Still, he kept his eyes glued to the guy even while racing to the open area. The beacon in his boot would direct the helicopter even without radio contact. Rotor wash stirred up a hurricane of snow around them.

"My dog!" she screamed. "Chewie!"

Chewie leaped from behind a tree, loping across the ice toward them.

"We won't leave him," he shouted back.

The chopper engine grew louder, the winds swirling harder. The helicopter sprayed bullets into snow near the deputy. The rifle fire stopped abruptly. A curse whispered on the wind as the guy bolted to his feet and sprinted away. Part of Wade burned to chase the bastard down and pound the shit out of him. But getting Sunny the hell out of here had to take priority. They would deal with the gunman later.

Wade grabbed her hand and ran harder, trudging through the snow toward the clearing. The helicopter hovered overhead. He pumped his hand, signaling for them to drop a line, which was faster than waiting around for a landing.

The cable descended with a treble hook seat rather than a basket. Wade hefted Sunny onto the seat and strapped her in before she could ask for help. Much like his mom, who had found it faster to do something herself than to explain. Now his mother could barely feed herself because of her battlefield injuries.

Thoughts of how he hadn't been there to help those closest to him threatened to rattle his focus, and he of all people knew how important attention to detail was in his job. Wade hooked himself to the same cable, facing Sunny. He grabbed the dog by the collar and hauled him into his lap, arms around the furry beast.

The cable yanked, went taut.

He looked down, the ground spinning below but clear enough to see the gunman scrambling to take cover near a snowmobile. Wade hooked his arms tighter around the dog, his grip slipping, slick.

Slick with blood.

———— ~~~ ————

Sunny huddled in a blanket in the belly of the helicopter while some guy in cammies pulled off her boots and rubbed her feet back to life. Her frostbitten skin flamed with returning sensation as she sipped the lukewarm cocoa someone else had thrust in her hands.

Still, her teeth chattered in the aftermath of their ordeal, the cold—being shot at. The sheriff's deputy had raced away on a snow machine. So far as she knew, there wasn't anything they could do to catch him, and she doubted he would be moseying into work, not since he must have seen them hauled up into the military chopper.

Her hand fell to rest on her dog's head, taking reassurance in his presence. Chewie stayed tight against her side with a blanket draped over his back, covering all that gooey mud she'd only briefly seen on his side before they'd hauled her in.

She'd never ridden in a helicopter before. She had vague memories of riding in a plane before her parents moved to the Aleutian Islands, but that had been so long ago and perceived in a child's mind as a smooth bus ride through the clouds.

This… This was loud, musty—and invigorating. The rotors overhead roared as they cut the air.

And the men.

A half dozen men in military survival gear packed the back of the aircraft. They appeared to all know each other. He'd said he was a pararescueman—a PJ—for the Air Force. Could this motley crew be his team?

An odd assortment. Not quite what she would have expected. They had a ragtag quality until you looked closer and caught the laser-sharp eyes, the obvious strength and agility. Still, different… She squinted in the shadowy confines for a better look at each of the men, people who could well decide the future of her family. But nobody wore a blazing red sign blinking "Weakest Link."

Wade shouted over the roar of the engine. "Mark the spot. There are two dead bodies down there."

"Say again?" The oldest of the group leaned forward, his face hardening.

"Two bodies. Under the ice."

Sunny wrapped the blanket tighter around her as images of Madison and Ted's waxy death masks marched through her brain.

The older man, who seemed to be in charge, swept a hand over his face before continuing, "There's nothing we can do for them now except find their families and make sure they get a decent burial."

"Appears they were murdered."

"Damn. Okay, location noted. But we need to get you patched up first." The guy waved over a lumbering hulk of a guy. "Franco, you got this?"

"Roger that, Major," Franco answered, peeling off gloves and cracking open a first aid kit more tricked out than anything she kept at the gym. "Cuervo, could you rig me some light?"

A guy wearing a name tag that said Jose James leaped to his feet, and suddenly a spotlight clicked on, clamped to one of the pipes running along the side. The blazing illumination pointed at Wade revealed…

Oh God.

She saw the dark stain on the shoulder of his parka. She gasped, horrified. She reached out to touch his knee, surprised at how automatic her response was. But they had bonded on that mountain, no doubt. Wade had saved her butt all too thoroughly for her to pretend she didn't care what happened to him now.

Although what exactly had happened, she didn't know, and clearly there were others here better equipped to tend his injury. Why hadn't she seen it before? Her mind raced back to the dark ooze she'd seen on him and Chewie and just assumed it was mud. Guilt pinched. She'd been so busy thinking of her own survival she hadn't even noticed.

She yanked the blanket off her dog and frantically searched through his fur, checking him over for any sign of injury. Chewie pawed her hand and tried to shove his nose into her drink. Finally, satisfied there was nothing she could detect, she shifted her attention back to Wade.

Across the helicopter, Franco snapped on gloves, setting out what looked to be antiseptic, clamps... and she couldn't tell what else, because her stomach started roiling. She wasn't the queasy sort. It had to be the adrenaline dump on top of her exhausted body, but she couldn't imagine going to sleep now.

Especially when she didn't know the severity of Wade's injury.

Franco held his gloved, sterile hands up for a second. Then proceeded to peel away the thick snow gear one layer at a time, until Wade sat bare chested. Her breath hissed inward at the expanse of muscled strength—and his unflinching expression. Perspiration and empathy trickled down her spine. His jaw might be tight, but otherwise he showed no reaction to the blood oozing from what appeared to be a bullet wound in his shoulder.

Cricking his neck, Franco tossed aside the scissors, hacked-up parka, and shirt at his feet. "Looks like the bullet just grazed you, but I'm going to need to check to be sure. Are you up for that now or do you want me to slap a bandage on until we can get you to an ER?"

"Take care of it now," Wade growled without hesitation.

His muscles flexed and tensed. She'd seen a lot of men who took care of themselves in her line of work at the gym, but Wade's body was a honed, peerless machine. And as gorgeous a specimen as he was to look at, she'd experienced the benefits of all that training first-hand, so she wasn't looking at him like some ordinary groupie might. She admired him with a fierceness as raw as the rest of her emotions today.

Given her wound-up condition, she burrowed deeper in her seat to make sure she didn't fall over if she passed out. The last thing she wanted was to divert any attention—any help—away from him. The next part happened so much more quickly than she'd expected. At a time like this, she could easily picture these guys working a medical crisis in battle under fire. Fast. Cool. Efficient.

He'd told her they were medic trained. But seeing that in-the-field training in action was another story.

The guy—Franco—pulled out forceps and gauze, then proceeded to swab the injury with copious amounts of antiseptic.

Unbidden, the memory of their kiss blasted into her brain. Hot. Needy. Far too urgent for her liking. She'd never responded to a man on such a visceral level before. It made no sense. This whole nightmare made no sense. But the reality of it still made her tremble, and that kiss was like the stable core of an ordeal that had thrown her hard off course.

Tamping down the memories, she focused on Wade.

Franco pulled out two syringes and began making injections around the wound. Numbing and antibiotics, most likely. Sunny's fingers dug into the empty cocoa cup, anticipating the hurt even though it wasn't her own.

Seconds later, the military medic picked up some other silver tool that looked a little too torturous for her piece of mind. "I'll make this check as fast as I can."

"Stop explaining and start doing."

"Roger that. I'll start on three. One. Two." He probed with gentle yet lightning speed, fresh red blood trickling down Wade's chest.

"Shit!"

Franco slapped a wad of gauze on Wade's shoulder, clearing away the fresh blood. He then looped two stitches through before Sunny's heart rate even returned to normal.

"Done, pal. Now quit your whining around the pretty lady. She's going to think you're a wimp." Franco sank back on his heels, peeling off his bloodied gloves and pitching them on top of the bloodied gauze. "You're lucky it's so cold out. That slowed the bleeding."

Lucky?

In comparison to Madison and Ted, they were. But she kept thinking of that bullet tearing through Wade's shoulder, an injury that happened because he'd been protecting her. She was so used to looking out for others, this felt… strange.

"Ma'am?" A masculine voice pulled her eyes off Wade. "My name's Major McCabe. You can call me Liam, or some folks call me Walker, like *Walker, Texas Ranger*, because I used to be an army ranger. Now isn't that convoluted?" he said with a smile meant to put a

person at ease, to distract from the horror of how close
Wade had come to having a bullet pierce his heart.
"Here's more cocoa for you and water for your dog. Can
I get you anything else?"

Her brain turned sluggish from exhaustion and she
scrambled to think. Her stomach grumbled an answer
for her. "Some kind of PowerBar would be good, if you
don't mind."

"Coming right up. It's military issue, which means
it tastes like crap on cardboard, but it'll do the job."
McCabe hunkered down in front of her, blocking her
view of Wade. "Are you okay?"

"One of your buddies asked me that right after you
pulled me up. I'm all right. Shaking, but okay." Her
brain cleared and she realized she needed to let them
know. "There was a third person with Ted and Madison.
A sheriff's deputy."

"Yes, Wade told us."

"He did? I don't remember…"

"You've been drifting in and out. You've been
through a lot. You should rest for the next hour until we
land. There's nothing more you can do."

And she realized he'd handed her the perfect out.
She could pretend to be addled by altitude sickness. For
the first time in her life, she would be the helpless one.
And there was only one person in this new world full of
strangers she could even consider trusting.

Her eyes fell on Wade, pale but steady. If only she
could be so sure she could trust herself when it came
to him.

Chapter 6

Towel wrapped around his waist, Wade stepped out of the shower at the squadron locker room. Back at Elmendorf Air Force Base for only a couple of hours and already the mess on that mountain seemed a world away.

Sunny seemed a world away even though she was only next door in the women's locker room. In the shower. Shit.

He worked his aching shoulder on the way toward the lockers, past the stalls, sandals slapping against the slick tile. The low hum of voices echoed in the steamy space, water still running behind him from McCabe finishing up. As he approached, the voices stopped.

Team members were scattered around the room, familiar as ever. As was their curiosity. They all could have been dressed and gone by now, since their part of the mission was complete. He, on the other hand, still had briefings left with the base officials. Jose "Cuervo" James pulled on a marathon T-shirt. Marcus "Fang" Dupre, already dressed, worked a Sudoku puzzle, not even hiding the fact that he was killing time waiting to grill him. Only Gavin "Bubbles" Novak halfway managed to hide his interest—grim as ever. But then he always stayed more on the periphery, packing and repacking his gear, cleaning his gun.

Wade plunged deeper into the room to his locker and grabbed a fresh camo ABU—airman battle uniform—crisp and new, replacing the BDUs they used to wear. Good God, how much money was spent every time the uniforms got changed. Again.

And yeah, he was cranky.

He still faced at least a couple of hours' debriefing on what he and Sunny had uncovered out there. "What? Are we in high school or something? You guys all but said, 'Hush, here he comes.'"

Chuckling, Franco reached into his locker for a pullover sweater, his part done for the day, no need for his uniform. "Did you keep your shoulder dry like I told you?"

"I went to the same medic training for six months at Fort Bragg just like you did, smart-ass." He stepped into his ABU pants, for once grateful that he spent so much time at the base, he had uniforms to spare in the squadron locker room. Reaching back into the locker, he almost managed to suppress a wince at the tug to his shoulder. A T-shirt was definitely out of the question. He yanked off the button-down blouse—why the hell did they call it a blouse? Like it was some silky woman's shirt rather than a camouflage jacket.

Battle boots next. He dropped to the bench, glad for an excuse to sit so the room would stop spinning. "I know how to take care of myself."

"Then next time you can patch yourself up, princess." Franco sat next to him, lacing up his own hiking boots. "Hardship duty, dude, being holed up with her for two days."

He kept his mouth zipped. His old man would be proud of his self-control these days.

Jose slammed his locker shut. "Ah, he's embarrassed.

It *was* chillier than usual. This cold-ass tour of duty can be hell on a guy's ego, what with shrinkage and all."

If only that had been the problem. It may have been cold as hell out there, but that hadn't stopped him from almost losing his objectivity over a woman he barely knew. Sliding the last button through, he flinched at his own lack of control.

Laughter fading, Marcus closed his Sudoku puzzle book, studying him through narrowed eyes. "You hurt yourself out there worse than you're saying?"

"Jump out of a plane, you're gonna be sore." He dismissed the worry fast. "But then you guys wouldn't know that, since you were back here playing Xbox."

Gavin looked up from cleaning his gun, one eyebrow raised. "Cranky, cranky, are we?"

And he was. Not because of the injury. Or because of the bodies they'd discovered, although that definitely cast a huge dark cloud over the day all on its own.

He was edgy and cranky because he was all but chewing nails over how bad he wanted a woman who'd so far refused even to tell him her last name.

Marcus set aside his Sudoku book. "Maybe you should give that last girl you dated a call, the one who worked at that diner across from your place. What was her name... Katie... Kimmy..."

"Kammi," Jose sighed reverently, hitching a Nike running bag over his shoulder. "That was one smokin' hot babe. Still don't understand why you let her get away."

Wade smiled tightly. "Feel free to ask her out anytime. I hear she's working the lunch shift now."

Not that he was keeping tabs on her or any of his other exes. He just wasn't the get-serious kind. Most women he'd gone out with over the years didn't have the patience for his kind of workaholic devotion to the job.

A door across the room creaked open, and he welcomed the distraction from discussion of his dating history. A fresh recruit airman stopped just inside. "Sergeant Rocha?"

Wade pushed to his feet, buttoning the cuffs on his uniform. "That would be me."

"The lady from the mountain, Sunny Foster, she's asking for you."

Whistles and wolf calls came from his buds, but he didn't even rise to the bait. He was too focused on what the airman had said.

Foster.

Funny how one word could change everything. Her name was Sunny Foster. Apparently the pimply faced airman had better luck getting her to talk than he had.

Of course now that the authorities were involved, her secretiveness would have to come to an end. A good thing. Except he could only think of the flash of terror in her eyes he'd seen, once she was inside the helicopter. Only a quick moment of vulnerability, but he hadn't doubted what he saw. He didn't know why, but he knew he couldn't leave her alone and defenseless.

The urge to protect powered his feet double time across the tiled floor.

As Sunny waited in the small conference room, walls lined with framed lithographs of military aircraft throughout the years, the full impact of her situation washed over her.

She was at least six hundred miles from home. She had no clothes. No money. No way to contact her family, other than the Internet. And she couldn't leave without Chewie, who was currently being looked over by the base vet who took care of military dogs.

Even her clothes were borrowed, jeans and a sweater loaned to her by a female clerk in the squadron who was close to the same size. The jeans fit, although the sweater was snugger than she was accustomed to. Homesickness enveloped her like the track suits she wore to work. She missed her home, her job, her routine. Most of all she missed her family.

They must be freaking-out worried by now, especially Misty. And there wasn't a thing she could do about it.

Sunny tugged the lip balm from her pocket—yet another thing she'd had to accept for free—and slicked it across her cracked, dry lips. God, it sucked to be so at the mercy of others. She was an independent business-woman in her community. None of which apparently meant a thing outside her boundaries. Now she had to figure out how to get back, a logistical conundrum.

It wasn't as if she could say, "Hey, could I hitch a helicopter ride back home?"

Round and round she turned her Styrofoam cup of coffee on the table in front of her. A dozen black office chairs—the kind that spun—were placed around the table, all empty except for the one she sat in. Waiting.

A computer sat on a lectern and a telecon screen hung from the ceiling, but they weren't any good to her with their blank screens, certain to have security codes.

The door clicked, giving a second's warning some-one was about to enter. Spinning her chair toward the entrance, she held her breath, not sure what to expect from this evening. She'd asked to see Wade…

And there he was, filling the doorway with his familiar broad shoulders and indomitable will. But Wade also looked different, more unreachable. It had to be the uniform, because his eyes were the same.

He wore camouflage pants tucked into combat boots, a maroon beret tucked in his thigh pocket. His hair was shorter than she'd realized before, but then he'd worn his hood most of the time. And he was clean shaven now. He'd been magnetic, virile, commanding during their survival trek, but now she saw—holy crap—he was poster boy handsome.

A lean face with strong cheekbones, perfectly sculpted like some hard-as-stone statue. Yet his perfection was offset with just the right masculine rough edges, his windburned skin, even his calloused hands, gave him the appeal of a man who could protect, survive.

Win.

Her eyes settled on his mouth, chapped like hers, yet somehow that hadn't hampered him in the least when he'd kissed her on the mountain. The time seemed so surreal now, a world away.

The air went heavy and awkward. She hated feeling out of her element. She searched his face for signs that he might be downplaying his injury, the memory of all that blood still too fresh in her mind. Dark circles marked under his eyes, but other than that he seemed steady, focused. On her.

She gripped the arms of her chair. "How's your shoulder?"

"Sore, but livable." He wheeled out a chair and sat

beside her. "I won't be jumping out of planes for a while, but I should be back to work in the field in a week or so."

"Good, I'm glad to hear that." Her fingers itched to touch him, just his knee, so close to hers. "I wouldn't want you to suffer because of me."

"I'm just glad that deputy is a crappy shot." A smile crinkled the corners of his intense brown eyes.

"The day could have ended so much worse." She tugged at the hem of her sweater, swamped with memories of what it had been like in the cold and snow with Wade lying on top of her. Praying they would make it out of there alive.

She shook off the wave of intense feelings, focusing on more practical concerns. "About tomorrow… I need some help in figuring out how I'm going to get back home."

"Major McCabe is looking into that now. It may take a few days to find a mission already slated to go to that region, but once we do, we can put you on the aircraft. You'll just need someone to pick you up. Or you can arrange for private transportation faster. Your call."

Leave tomorrow or wait around for days? Days when her sister could be planning to leave. "I think I need to look into those speedier arrangements. And what about that deputy who shot at us?"

"Authorities here have notified the sheriff there, his boss. They're already sending a scouting party for him and the bodies. They'll want to take your statement over the phone today before you leave."

"Of course. Whenever they're ready." She struggled to push aside years of suspicions hammered into her head, the mantra repeated by her parents to be careful who she trusted. There were people out there who would shut down their community if they could, would take away their home and shuffle them back to a more congested area where it was "easier" to track their activities. But what other option did she have if she wanted justice for Madison and Ted than to talk now?

"Afterward, I can help you make arrangements to fly home." Wade continued, "I could drive you to an airport."

Now wouldn't that have made things easier? Too bad there would be no record of her existence in any bank in the world, let alone access to a credit account. "I was only planning to go on a mountain hike. There aren't exactly any places that call for a MasterCard or Visa there. And my family doesn't have reliable phone service. Um, sorry, but where I live is pretty remote."

"As are a lot of places in Alaska." He leaned back in the chair, watching her as if waiting for her to say more. When she didn't, he continued, "So? What's the plan?"

"I don't know," she finally admitted. "I don't know who to trust and what's the right decision."

"I'm not sure I understand what you mean."

"I'm sorry." She shook her head, sweeping her hair back, the length still damp from her shower.

His eyes tracked her, stayed on her hair. She forced her hands back to her lap.

"Can I trust you?"

"I don't know. Can you? On the one hand, I did save your life. And on the other, I'm a guy you've just met."

Somehow the way he left the decision up to her put her more at ease. "For now you're a better option than some folks I've known a lot longer."

Like the deputy who'd played duck shoot with them

earlier. My God, she needed to warn so many people in her community who trusted that man.

"It would help if you told me what you're talking about." He leaned forward, elbows on his knees, muscular arms straining the sleeves of his uniform.

She stared into Wade's eyes, the same steady gaze that had gotten her safely off a mountain and away from a madman. Taking a deep breath, steadying herself, she needed to reach out to him again if she wanted any chance of warning her sister.

"Call me a paranoid, off-the-grid kook who sees conspiracy theories everywhere, but I just can't shake the weird feeling that the deputy's actions have to be a part of something bigger." She didn't trust the local sheriff's department now, not when she knew how many friends Rand had back home. The corruption had to go deeper. And if it did, the military's phone call to his boss wasn't going to save Misty. "Otherwise it just doesn't make sense for him to kill two people."

She hoped he wouldn't think she was crazy. She needed him to believe her. And sitting so close to him and confiding her deepest fears, she realized she needed *him*. All those raw feelings he'd stirred inside her back on the mountain came roaring to life again now, like frostbitten toes recovering sensation with a vengeance.

"He could have had the hots for the woman." His shoulders shrugged, his chair nudging closer until she could almost feel the body heat radiating off him. "It could have been an assault situation gone over the edge. Then he came after us because we found the bodies. He was probably trapped out there in the storm the same way we were."

"That all makes sense, I guess." She held ultrastill. A move away could well relay how much his presence affected her, and she wasn't sure if she wanted to take that step or not.

"Actually, I didn't come up with the theory myself. That's what his boss seems to think happened. Apparently Rand Smith had been talking about the woman around work for quite a while."

Could be, but it still felt… off. She'd been with Ted and Madison when they'd met with the deputy and she hadn't gotten that vibe at all. Of course nothing felt normal right now, and Wade's presence scrambled her already shaky senses. "I should give my statement while things are still fresh in my mind—and before I pass out. Are they coming in here or do I go somewhere?"

"You'll call from here. It'll be a video-con, so it will be like a regular face-to-face interview."

She drew in a shaky breath. "Okay, I can handle that."

"Afterward, I'll make sure they give you quarters to stay in for the night." He reached into his pocket. "You'll need some cash for incidentals."

"No!" She placed a hand on his arm. A jolt of awareness sparked up her fingertips, tingling all the way into her arms. Ignoring him wasn't working, but that didn't mean she would lose sight of what she needed to accomplish tonight. "Can we please just go somewhere else?"

"We?"

His body tensed. Their eyes locked. Heat spiked in the room. Or was it just in her bloodstream?

"Honestly, after all I've been through recently, I really don't want to stay here alone." She tried to think of a reason why she wouldn't take the offer of a free room just because it happened to be on a military base that totally freaked her out. She downplayed it with "Gotta confess, the base is rather overwhelming. I've had a scary couple of days and thought... Maybe I could stay at a hotel. I'll pay you back with interest. But I need to get off base. All the noise and people are like a steamroller to my senses when I'm used to the closest neighbor being a mile away."

He shook his head. "Those close-by people also bring security, and until I know what the hell was going on with Deputy Smith, I'm not going to feel comfortable with you out there unprotected."

"How about I stay with you then," she blurted in desperation.

His eyes blinked wide for a second before his expression went neutral. "How do you know I don't live here on base?"

"You're not married, so you can't have one of the base houses... Well, unless you're a Catholic chaplain—then you could live on base alone." She couldn't help but grin. "Are you a priest?"

"Not by a long shot." Leaning back in his chair, he folded his hands over his chest, his smile a hint wicked.

Heat singed her ears. "Didn't think so." God, she liked his smile. "And since you're not a freshly recruited E1 airman, you can't live in the airman's dorms. So I can only conclude you do not live on station. Have I covered everything?"

"You know a lot about base life."

Her insides chilled. Why was it so easy to lower her guard around this guy? She would do well to remember that around him, and without question, he was her best bet for a ticket off this base until she could figure out what to do next. So she needed to rein in the rogue attraction where he was concerned. "I had an uncle in the service. So can I stay at your place or not? I saved your butt on that mountain, after all, by showing you that cave."

"And I saved your butt when the guy was shooting."

"That you did."

He angled forward again, so close she thought for a second he was going to kiss her. Which would only complicate things.

"I didn't mean—"

"I know," he said simply. "Yes, you can stay at my place if you wish. It's small, but there's a bed and a sofa."

A sigh shuddered through her long and hard, her relief almost overriding her body's reaction to watching his lips wrap around the word *bed*. One hurdle taken care of. And if she could keep her wits about her, she had a place to stay and access to a computer that was less likely to be monitored. And although that kiss still hovered unspoken in the air between them, he'd offered a sofa rather than assuming she wanted to jump in bed with him.

Now if she could only be so sure she could hold strong against sliding into the comfort of his arms to calm her soul and fears.

Brett fought the urge to fling his BlackBerry across the room, smack between the eyes of the mounted reindeer head.

How in the hell had that deputy—Rand Smith—screwed up so completely? It was such a simple job. Take out two people with an entire, deserted wasteland to dispose of the bodies. He'd thought having someone from the local police department on his payroll would make things easier, not harder.

Pacing, Brett restored order to his office, to his world. He dropped a stray pen into the pewter holder, thumbed a fingerprint from a glass whale paperweight his wife had given him to commemorate their fifteenth anniversary. Everything he did was for her, and had been since the day he fell hard and fast for the flame-haired, fiery-tempered woman on a charter fishing boat.

He'd left Montana for Alaska looking for opportunity and adventure, and he'd found Andrea. Everything he did was for her, to give her what she needed.

For the past two and a half years, that tiny, secluded town had offered a perfect—and lucrative—conduit for smuggling people, intelligence, and even weaponry in and out of Russia. He could stash them there until the time was right to make the next move. And never had a package promised to be more profitable than the explosive surprise in the works three days coming.

One pacing step at a time, he steadied his heart rate and his focus. He could make this happen. He *needed* to make it happen for Andrea. His knuckles skimmed the top of a honeymoon photo snapped on safari in Africa. With the larger payoff in the works, he could give her a future with more magical times like that.

He set the frame in place, carefully angled in the collection lined along his windowsill. Now was not the time to draw attention to this corner of Alaska. Mistakes were not tolerated by his new business associates, and his gut clenched over the possibility of Andrea being widowed.

The most expedient way to keep a lid on this? Let Rand think he was regaining favor with a last chance opportunity to off Sunny Foster, a woman who now knew way too much about the world outside.

Then he would stage Rand Smith's death to look like an accident, while planting some love letters from Madison on his person. Loose ends tied up neat and tidy.

He reached for the phone to call his wife. Damn right, people would do anything for love.

Walking up the narrow stairwell to Wade's home, a third-floor apartment, Sunny couldn't shake the sense that she'd missed something crucial back at base. She'd given her statement to the police about what she'd seen. She'd explained simply that she escorted small excursions leaving an off-the-grid community on the Aleutian Islands. Luckily—and a little surprisingly—the interrogator on the other side of the phone line hadn't pressed.

They hadn't been able to hold the video conference as originally planned, due to a storm that rolled in through the islands, scrambling the satellite feed. The techies had tried for ten minutes, but only received blurry reception, so they'd opted for phone lines, which worked well enough with only the occasional crackle. Thank God, that was out of the way. Now she could focus on contacting her family.

Then what? She would be alone with Wade in his apartment. Adrenaline and want and a thousand other confusing emotions scrambled through her brain. She didn't know what she felt anymore.

She only knew she had to reach her sister, and Wade

was the one person she even halfway trusted out here. Not that trust had anything to do with how she kept checking out the taut curve of his backside in uniform as he led her up the stairs.

Chewie's nails clicked on the scarred wooden steps as he followed her. The base vet had given him a clean bill of health. And now she owed Wade even more.

Stopping outside the thick oak door, he pulled out his keys, unlocked two dead bolts before opening up. He spread his arm wide. "Welcome to my garret, sweet garret."

"Thank you, really. You're being so generous." Careful not to brush against him, she strode past into his one-room studio apartment, sprawling and rustic.

Thick maple beams stretched across the slanted ceiling, all natural and light. Chewie lumbered past slowly, nose to the ground, sniffing as he explored the new space. The apartment itself was full of typical guy furniture, a fat brown sofa and huge recliner. An over-sized television with a flat screen took up half a wall. She'd seen some like it in movies, but had never used one. Most of the appliances where she lived were older and simpler, requiring minimal power. And they always used fireplaces and wood stoves.

Apparently, so did Wade, if the massive stone hearth was anything to judge by. Chewie padded over, hunkering down to stare at the bear rug with a low growl. Finally, her dog surrendered and flopped into an exhausted heap with a hefty sigh.

Wade flipped a switch, activating track lighting along the angled ceiling over the kitchen. "Help yourself to anything. The cabinet under the little island there has standard snack crap, chocolate chip granola bars, Pop-Tarts, and such."

Best as she could tell, all sugary. Not much of a gourmet or health food aficionado, but somehow it made her smile all the same. Then she saw what she'd really come here for.

His dinette table sported a computer and a printer rather than dishes or even a napkin holder. Her fingers curled into a fist to resist the temptation to type away right now. Only a minute or so more and she would be able to contact her family.

She traced the edge of the dark wood table, nostalgia blindsiding her. Meals were a big deal in her family. She pressed her fingers against the ache in her chest. The skylight and wall of windows gave a sweeping view of the breathtaking Alaska Range, reminding her all the more of her family, her home. God, she loved this place, a photographer's dream. A place where people were just as welcome in jeans and mukluks as they were in diamonds and furs.

And suddenly she realized. "I don't know where you're from."

"A little of everywhere." He dropped his green bag of gear by the sofa. "My dad was an army warrant officer, helicopter pilot. Mom was an air force reservist, a medical technician on C-130s outfitted as hospitals."

"You're a military brat times two."

"Needless to say, we moved around."

"I imagine your parents are proud you've continued in their footsteps." Her father had never said anything against his son. But there were days…

"So my dad says. But I sure gave them a few gray

hairs back in the day." He walked past her almost touching, electrifying the air on his way to the stone fireplace. "I was a hardheaded hell-raiser in high school."

"What made you change your ways?"

Kneeling, he tossed two logs onto the grate. "Oh, the hardheaded part is still alive and well. Ask anyone. As for the hell-raising?" He arranged kindling with knowledgeable precision. "Let's just say it ended the day I witnessed a helicopter crash. As I watched the rescuers in action, I knew right then what I wanted to do with the rest of my life."

She sensed there was more to the story, but he didn't seem open to sharing as he kept his back to her, striking a match. "What are your parents doing now?"

"My parents have retired to Arizona, where my dad plays a lot of golf and my mom, um, shows off pictures of their grandchildren."

"Grandchildren?"

"My sister and her husband have two kids, a boy who's five and a girl who's four."

"Those are sweet ages. My nephew is only a year." Unable to look away, she watched his big capable hands stoke the logs with quick efficiency. "His name is J.T. Most days I get to spend extra time with him, since we have a day care at the gym that my brother uses while he work—"

She stopped short before she spilled her whole flipping life story. What was it about this guy that made her babble on?

Glancing back over his shoulder, Wade stared at her so long she looked behind her… and found nothing.

"Do I have something caught between my teeth?"

He shook his head, dusting bits of bark from his palms as the logs crackled with building heat. "Nah, I'm just enjoying the view. And before you get nervous or offended, I'm about ready to fall on my ass from exhaustion and blood loss." He winked. "I'm not a threat to your virtue any more here than I was in the cave."

All the same his words stirred images of what they could have done in that sprawling bed of his two steps up under the skylight.

When she looked back, he'd opened a drawer on the dresser, all the wood light colored with a simple sealant over the natural maple.

He pulled out a couple of perfectly folded items. "T-shirt and drawstring exercise pants for you to sleep in." He tossed the pile on the counter, the words AIR FORCE stamped in blue across the front. "I'm gonna change into some sweats, in case you were wondering. And I'm gonna clean up again. The shower at base was rushed, to say the least. After I finish, we can talk about where to go next in the morning."

He was making it too easy to lie to him.

"May I use your computer?" She scooped up the large T-shirt that smelled like him. "I need to email my sister so she can let my family know I'm okay."

"Of course." He leaned in the open doorway to a roomy bathroom with a spa shower.

She hauled her eyes off the glassed-in shower and the steamy fantasies it evoked. "Thanks."

At least she didn't have to explain the whole phone issue in detail, how they had local telephone service available, but long-distance connections were harder to come by. And most people didn't want either.

Being out here, things that had once seemed normal now seemed... not so normal. "Thank you. I won't monopolize it."

"I'm good. I won't go through withdrawal if I go another hour without checking messages." His smile squeezed the guilt inside her all the tighter.

He closed the bathroom door behind him and she rushed to the kitchenette. Dropping into the chair, she stared at the keyboard and screen for a minute to familiarize herself, then logged on to her community's home page.

> Sunny: Misty? Are you there?

She watched the cursor blink, blink, but nothing happened. Her sister must have left the computer logged on while she stepped away.

> Sunny: Wanted 2 let U know I'm okay. Got caught by the storm. Safe in Anchorage. Have help from guy who rescued me. Will b home soon.

The next part was tough and didn't seem right to pass along in an instant message.

> Sunny: See my email. Have sad news 2 long to explain here. Love U.

Composing that email was even tougher than she'd expected. Breaking the news of a death this way was unimaginable. But she had to be sure Misty did not leave with the deputy. Heaven only knew why he'd gone off the deep end, but she'd be damned before he got near her sister. And she wasn't trusting the sheriff to do the job for her in a timely fashion. The deputy was in law enforcement too, after all…

God, she sounded like a paranoid conspiracy theorist.

She logged off. There was nothing more she could do tonight. Even if she found a way to magically get back to the Aleutian Islands before morning, she was simply too dog-tired to start the climb home. Hopefully tomorrow, in the broad daylight, she could construct a logical plan to return as quickly as possible.

The back of her neck prickled with awareness, the sense of being watched. She pivoted in her chair fast to find Wade standing in the bathroom doorway again, sweatpants slung low on his narrow hips. Curly dark hair sprinkled along his chest up to his shoulders—and a small strip of gauze over his stitches, not larger than a Band-Aid. Yet a few inches lower and he could have been dead.

His eyes were surprisingly alert for a person who'd been through so much, and right now his entire attention was focused on her. "The bathroom's all yours."

Her throat went so tight she had to force words up and out. "Thanks, uh, I insist on taking the sofa, since you're injured." She grabbed the T-shirt off the counter on her way. "So don't even try to argue some he-man chivalry stuff."

She charged toward the bathroom, needing to put a door between herself and Wade with no shirt. Too late, she realized he hadn't moved.

"If you say so," he answered simply, looking down at her as they stood chest to chest in the narrow doorway.

"Thanks." The lone word came out breathier than she would have liked, but then she didn't seem to be in control of much about herself around this guy. "For the shirt and the Internet."

"So you *were* able to send an email to your family." He appeared relaxed. In no hurry to step away from her.

Her throat went dry as dust. She edged back half an inch, the doorframe not budging. The scent of his soap was so vivid she could almost imagine what his skin would taste like if she were to…

She cleared her throat and willed her heartbeat to conduct business as usual.

"I did send a note, thank you. I worry though, about it getting through, since the connection can be spotty, depending on the weather. Hopefully everything will be fine for me to leave in the morning." What should have filled her with relief also brought a strange kick of regret over saying good-bye to this man. "I guess I should get some sleep."

He caught her arm as she started to turn, his touch sparking off a delicious reaction inside her. "I just have one more question for you."

Oh God, how could she have let her guard down so quickly? "What would that be?"

"Why did you kiss me out there?"

Chapter 7

FINALLY, HE HAD SUNNY FOSTER OFF HER GAME. FOR ONCE, he'd surprised her. Standing in the doorway to his steamed-up bathroom half-dressed wasn't the smartest way to approach her about the way they combusted around each other. But hell, nothing about the past few days was normal, even for a guy like him who faced the unexpected on a regular basis in his line of work.

He let go of her arm and knuckled back a strand of her silky hair over her shoulder. Strands glided over his fingers, hooking and catching on calluses the way she snagged his attention. Gone before he could catch hold.

She didn't so much as take a step away from him, but her pupils widened with awareness until her eyes were nearly midnight black. Steam clung to his body, fogged up his insides, disarming him from the core. Who was he kidding, she heated him through and through by simply standing in front of him.

"So, Sunny, why did you kiss me up there on the mountain?" He flattened his hand to the doorframe to keep from gathering up her hair in his hands and burying his face in the mass of it all, aching to bury himself in her.

She chewed on her bottom lip. Even coated in ChapStick, it was still raw and a little cracked from their time exposed to the elements. "The way I remember it, *you* kissed *me*."

Her accusation lacked the boldness of her usual speech pattern. Damn it, she recalled that kiss in every bit as much detail as he did.

"Right, that I did. Because I was feeling the attraction between us as strongly as I know you did. Spending the night together in the cave, so close and aware of your every move, damn near going out of my mind wanting to see if your skin felt as soft as it looked."

The memories sent an intoxicating bolt straight through him, his groin tightening inside low-slung sweatpants.

She boldly stared him down, even though he was half-dressed. "The way I remember it, we had a wet, smelly dog between us and you were pissed because I didn't faint at your feet with gratitude when you parachuted through a snowstorm all macholike to rescue the 'helpless' damsel."

He grinned, scratching his bare chest absently. "You think I'm macho."

"I think you were crazy to kiss me out there."

His gaze settled on her mouth. "Then you were equally crazy, because I recall in great detail how you kissed me back."

Her shoulders stiffened, her eyes defensive. "I may have been caught up in the adrenaline of the moment."

"Maybe. And yet here we are talking an awful lot about kissing."

She jabbed an angry finger at him, stopping just shy of touching his chest. "I wasn't propositioning you by asking to come to your place."

"I didn't think you were." He was quite clear she had some agenda hidden inside that mysterious mind of hers. "Although you're awful trusting, coming here."

"If you planned to assault me, you had plenty of

opportunities out there." Her throat moved in a slow swallow as she shivered, rubbing her arms. "And plenty of chances to dispose of my body."

He couldn't resist touching her, comforting her. He cupped the back of her neck and massaged lightly, letting the mass of her silky hair engulf his hand as well as his senses. "There's nothing we can do about that tonight. Put it out of your mind."

"I wish I could." She swayed toward him, her eyes open and sharing the hurt inside her for the first time.

The medic, the part of him trained to heal, was drawn to her, nudging aside other more primal wants for the moment. "Come on. Let's see if I can find something more substantial than a sandwich."

And in order to see to those needs, he should get his hands out of her hair and his eyes off the sweet curve of her breasts. He angled past and away.

―――∿∿―――

Sunny watched Wade walk away from her, his big, honorable, sexy body leaving her aching. No simple sandwich could satisfy the hunger inside her.

She truly hadn't asked to stay at his place with the intent of seducing him. But come morning, she would have to leave here and she would never see him again. Her life would go back to the way it was, with her narrowly focused world, a life that had seemed infinitely satisfying before these past days with Wade.

That safety, security, comfort had been blown to hell with a simple glimpse of frozen faces through the ice and she needed something, she needed this man, this chance to escape from it all, before reality intruded tomorrow.

Tomorrow, when she would have to disappear on her own, without the military's help that would undoubtedly be bureaucratically slow. Wade might well be grilled about where she'd gone on his watch, but she'd drawn the deputy and heaven only knew what other kind of trouble to Wade. The best she could do now was stay away from him. It was safer that way, especially when she was still so unsure about the reason for the attack on her, on Ted and Madison, in the first place.

But for now, for tonight, she would steal what moments she could with Wade before she undertook the biggest risk of her life to return to the village and warn her family and friends.

Sunny flattened her hands on either side of the bathroom doorway and called out as he sauntered toward the kitchen, "I realize that I kissed you back on the mountain. And I enjoyed it."

She'd never seduced a man before. Her scant sexual history hadn't given her much in the way of an education, practice, or even confidence. But the way Wade stopped in his tracks encouraged her.

Deep in the far corners of her brain, the part of her that never forgot to keep her barriers up, she knew this wasn't wise. Being together wouldn't come without repercussions to her life, perhaps even to her heart. She wasn't being fair to him with all she held back. She wasn't the sort to let things go so far, so fast, but these weren't normal times and she didn't have all that much experience to draw upon. There weren't a lot of men to choose from where she lived. A couple of dates in high school, none that went too far, as she was still adjusting to the sudden shift in her life.

Then her rebellious years hit. The time when she couldn't bring herself to leave her family, but kept hoping they would get so angry with her they would ask her to go.

She'd speed-dated a dozen guys in her community and slept with three of them, but the experiences hadn't been particularly satisfying, more like an exercise regimen that exhausted her body, gave an outlet for frustration, but left her yearning for a shower afterward. She'd carried too much anger and resentment to be focused on the moment or the person, and was horribly unfair to the man on another level.

After that, there wasn't anyone to date who wasn't somehow connected to that time.

But that felt so far away right now as she stood with Wade in his studio apartment. Still, he kept his tensed back to her for five thumps of her heart, three slow rises and falls of his broad shoulders. Then he pivoted on his heels to face her.

His eyes crackled with a fire as hot as the flames in the hearth. "Believe me, I noticed you were kissing me back."

"And it's something I want to do again."

One dark eyebrow arched in surprise. "I concur."

Only he could make such a clipped, military-style response sound totally loaded with sexuality. Her whole body burned with the need to press against him, full-out, no barriers, skin to skin with nothing between them, not even the ghostly shadows of their two very different worlds.

She moved to him or he walked to her. She couldn't remember who took the first step, and it didn't seem to matter once her mouth met his. As her arms locked around his neck, his hands cupped her bottom and lifted her against him. Her breasts flattened to his chest, her nerves flaming to life as she tasted him, aching to devour the moment. She'd lived so much of her life in control of her world, of her body. Right now she didn't feel in control of a thing. It was all about feeling. Exploring the hard planes of his muscles. Savoring the scent of his freshly washed body. Luxuriating in the knowing caress of his lips shifting to her ear, to her neck, then nudging aside the collar of her shirt to taste her shoulder.

Without lifting his kiss from her body, he backed her away from the bathroom. But not toward the bed as she expected, was prepared for mentally, emotionally—physically. Instead, one step at a time he inched her toward the flickering fireplace, stopping at the bear rug in front of the stone hearth.

She scaled the expanse of his chest with her fingers, only pulling her hands aside long enough for him to peel her T-shirt up and off her body. As her clothes fell away, his sweatpants hit the floor, she couldn't help but think how they were dancing through a strange echo of how they'd undressed in the cave. Except her hands were on him, his were on her. Intimately. Experiencing all the places they'd only eyed before.

A rustle from across the room pulled her attention briefly away as she glanced over to find… Chewie huffed and curled up in a corner of the kitchen by his water bowl, presenting his back firmly to them. Ignoring or pouting, she didn't know, but since he seemed settled either way…

Sunny looked back at Wade standing gloriously naked in front of her, bathed by the firelight from the grate and by moonlight from the window overhead. His body was honed and solid. But more than his muscles held her attention. The complete and intense concentration of his deep brown eyes, zeroed in on her, made for heady stuff.

She forced herself to look away from his mesmerizing gaze back to his body. He had a deep tan that spoke of time spent outside of Alaska.

"A month in Guam," he said, as if reading her mind.

She could picture him on the beach in swim trunks, plunging into the surf, droplets glistening off his skin. She had a sudden deep hunger to walk barefoot on a beach. She had a vague memory of playing on a California shore during a family vacation. Most of all she remembered the sun, so brilliant she had to squint, the beach so very different from the Iowa cornfields were she'd been brought up. Was it her imagination that daylight was so vividly stronger then? Or was she allowing the clouds of their family secret, of her sister's pain, to darken the already dimmer Alaska days?

As fast as the memory rolled over her she pushed back the tide. She wanted to be part of the here and now. Nothing else.

Cautiously, she sketched her fingertips just shy of where the bullet had grazed him. "Your shoulder?"

"Is fine. I've been hurt worse on a fishhook." He turned his face to kiss her wrist, then nuzzled the throbbing pulse until her heart rate spiked.

Her eyes threatened to flutter closed and she forced herself to think, to speak. "You're on painkillers. You might hurt yourself without realizing it, or maybe you're not clear on what you're doing, what *we* are doing."

He cupped her face in his hands. "Believe me, I'm completely clear. I've been injured far worse than this, and the one pain shot they gave me back in the chopper has long worn off. In case you haven't noticed, we aren't doing anything." His touch trailed from her face in the lightest of caresses, over her shoulders, and down her arms to clasp her wrists. "Yet."

Desire thickened the rush in her veins. Why was she arguing against something she wanted so much?

Raising one of her arms upward, he nibbled along her inner arm, upward. He drew her arms around until he pressed her palms to her breasts. "I'll be careful, God knows, I'll be careful, because the last thing I want to do is make you turn away."

Ever so slightly he increased the pressure on her wrists until she touched herself more fully against the ache. Her nipples hardened against her palms in an unmistakable message of her arousal.

Was he doing it to show her how much she wanted him? She didn't need the reminder, but it was also tougher to resist when faced with her own obvious need. While she knew the texture of her own body, she'd never touched herself this way in front of a man before and the forbidden air of it, the voyeuristic way he watched her fingers on her skin, ratchetted her bliss to a higher level.

Just as she felt his hands on hers, guiding her touch, she could also see the reflection of their bodies in the skylight windows, with the inky night for a backdrop. She couldn't miss the way her body curved around his, the way they fit together as if they were made for each other.

Light from the hearth superimposed itself over their bodies sometimes, twisting and flickering, presenting a picture of her going up in flames with him. And God, that was just about right.

Clasping her wrists, he guided her, gently lifting the curve of her breasts, his head dipping as he took one already taut nipple into his mouth. Tasting, tugging, while still steering her hands in a tantalizing massage. He aroused her with his mouth, with the way his pseudo touches directed her hands against her skin.

A low moan slipped from between her lips, the already tight thread of pleasure pulling, increasing until a tingling built between her legs. Moist and achy and needing. Him. Inside.

Soon.

Arching her back, she pressed herself deeper, more firmly into the sensation of his mouth, her own strokes, letting him know she could take—she wanted—more. His gentleness was admirable, considerate, and not entirely necessary right now. She needed to soak up all she could from the night and this small window of time together.

She freed her hands from his and grabbed his shoulders, angling her hips against his, pressing the thick rigid length of his erection against her stomach. He throbbed a burning imprint on her skin, making her catch her breath with need. She sunk her fingernails into his shoulders and murmured her pleasure, her desires. And bless him, he was an attentive man. He increased the friction of his teeth and tongue from one breast to the other until she writhed to get closer, hooking a leg around his, pressing her core to the raspy length of his leg.

Sunny trailed her fingers down his neck, between his ribs, lower until she reached his six-pack abs and the tip of his erection, hard and sleek against his stomach.

Encircling him, she swept down and up, learning the steely feel of him, soon to know him all the more intimately. She stroked the length up, down, and again, her thumb working over the tip, smoothing the moist bead with each caress.

Groaning, he clenched his teeth, his head falling back, his eyes closed tight. A surge of satisfaction pumped through her. She reveled at bringing him even a measure of the pleasure he gave her.

Already, this time with him, the feelings, the sensations, were so much more than anything she'd experienced. And how much more waited for her. Her thumb glided over the swollen head. He growled low in his throat, burying his face into the curve of her neck. Heated breaths grazed her skin, warmed even further her overheated flesh.

And just that fast, her knees gave way to the compounded pleasure. Wade guided her downward, settling her fully onto the bear rug. The fur brushed her hypersensitive nerves with thousands of tantalizing strokes. The silky glide sent her back arching, her arms splaying, as she breathed deeply as if to inhale the moment. The scent of his soap mixed with the smoky outdoors air from the fireplace until it seemed his place and her world blended.

Kissing his shoulder, she urged him to roll to his back. "I know you're a superhero and all, but popping a stitch would be a serious mood buster."

"You have a point," he conceded, finally relenting and allowing her to guide him the rest of the way to recline on the deep brown rug. "Feel free to take over, but no more playing. I'm on the edge and I want to bring you there with me."

Excitement, anticipation, and a near painful need surged.

She straddled his hips. Her fingers lightly traced the lines of his washboard stomach, grazing the hard line of his arousal again and again until he clamped a hand around her wrist and eased her away. He wasn't fighting fair. She slid her other hand between them, cupping the weight of him until his jaw flexed from restraint.

Again, he stopped her caress and she started to protest. Then with his other hand, he clapped a condom into her palm.

She recognized an invitation when she saw one.

Hands shaking, Sunny tore the packet in two and sheathed him, lingering at the base until he gripped her waist. Unceremonious. Strong. Certain.

His fingers slid over her stomach, dipping lower until teasing between her legs. His callused fingertips, his circular pressure, had her swaying.

"Okay," she gasped, "I'm in charge, right?"

"Yes, ma'am, totally in charge." He slid a finger inside her, then a second, crooking until he found…

"Um…" She gasped, feeling more and more out of control by the second but not in the least interested in telling him to stop the delicious pressure in exactly… the right… spot. She sighed, moaned, rocked to increase the sensation, bringing her so close to completion.

His hand slid away and she gasped, nearly cried out over the loss, but before she could form words, he hooked an arm around her waist. The fire in his eyes echoed the one in the hearth, the one even deeper in her belly. Wade guided her over him until he nudged against her with a muscular grace she'd seen on the mountain, and now she was benefiting all the more.

She was hot and damp and ready for him. So much so, her skin felt tight and itchy, as if she would explode from the need expanding inside her. The whole experience overwhelmed her, so very different from the fumblings from her past that left her achy for more.

He filled her, stretched her—eased her. Muscles bulged in his arms as he lifted and guided her hips. His lean athleticism sent a tingle through her veins. She knew the dedication that came with building a body like that, and a shiver of excitement tingled up her spine.

The rug was silky and sensual under her knees. What would it feel like to stretch out completely here? The thought was almost enticing enough to give it a go, but the promise of stretching out on Wade was even more tempting.

Her hair slithered forward over her shoulders to spill across his chest. He plucked at the sapphire streak in her hair, skimming it between his thumb and forefinger with a slow tug, drawing the hair as taut as the pleasure inside her. Then his hand slid behind her neck, her hair tangled around his fingers as he cupped her head, urging her toward him until she sprawled on top of him, bringing her mouth to his.

He teased at the seam of her lips and she opened for him, taking his tongue into her mouth as totally as she welcomed him into her body. He thrust again and again with bold confidence. He took her every bit as completely as she took him. The sex was raw and physical from a man who was more than her match yet never used that strength for anything other than her intense bliss.

The bristle of the hair on his legs brushed a sweet

abrasion along her calves. And his chest, the whorls across his pecs, abraded against her nipples, teasing the ecstasy tauter, tighter inside her. He made love with total physicality, using every part of his body to love her. His mouth cruised her neck, her earlobe. His fingers found the most sensitive pressure points. Alternately lighter and stronger touches found erogenous zones in places she'd never expected. He must be putting that medical training to good use and she couldn't bring herself to regret his calculation for even a second, since it brought her closer and closer to release until...

She plunged over the edge, freefalling into gripping spasms tightening through her again and again. A moan built in her throat and tore free. Echoed in her ears. Resonated inside her as he thrust, pounded, drew out her orgasm until she thought surely that was all. But as his hoarse shout of completion ripped through the air, a fresh bolt of pleasure shuddered through her already exhausted body until she melted into a limp mass onto his chest.

More than anything, she wanted to stay tangled up in the moment with the warmth of each other and the fire, the sensuous brush of the fur rug, and Wade against her. She wanted to linger, draw in the scent of them together, musky and mingling with the hint of smoke. And she would, for a few more stolen hours.

Panting from the exertion, the sheer power of the pleasure, she slid off him and onto her back. Gusts from the heater stirred the fur against her skin. The sleek pelt teased her all over, from the side of her cheek to the flattened palms of her hands to the lingering moist heat between her legs.

As the perspiration dried on her naked flesh she couldn't ignore the truth. She'd just experienced the best sex of her life.

And after tonight she could never see him again.

He could see the dim light in the third-floor apartment window, but not much else since they'd drawn the shades.

Keeping surveillance, Deputy Rand Smith ducked down in his crappy rental van. But then what vehicle didn't turn into rusted-out shit eventually around here? He'd come up to Alaska from Oklahoma, hoping to make some serious money working security shifts in the oil fields. Fat chance. He hadn't been able to land anything other than a near-poverty-wage deputy job in a tiny-ass town on Bristol Bay. He couldn't get hired anywhere civilized like here in Anchorage or Fairbanks or Juneau. He hadn't even been able to save enough money to get back home…

Until Brett had approached him about pulling some private security hours over at the Alaska Peninsula Power Plant. His whole life was turning around now that he was making the kind of income he deserved. He wouldn't screw this up. He wasn't a loser like his drunken father always said.

Rand sipped his fourth cup of coffee to stay awake and keep warm. He was running on fumes after traveling all night from the mountain, flying to make it to Anchorage, but his options were fading fast if he wanted to stay alive. And he did. There was no running away from what he'd joined, with smuggling terrorists and weapons into the U.S. With big payoffs came big risks.

And people like Brett and his Russian mob associates killed those who failed very, very slowly.

He had his orders. Make sure Sunny Foster never led anyone to her mountain village. Brett needed that unknown patch of earth as a hiding place. Kind of like laundering money through businesses, he laundered people through that community, solidifying their new identities.

Having Sunny out in the open endangered all of that. The second she stepped away from her hulking military bodyguard, a gun to her side should silence her until he could stash her in the back of his rental van. Then, she would die.

But he wasn't like Brett and his "associates." He would at least make sure Sunny's death was quick. The same way he'd done for her friends on the mountain.

Enjoying just watching Sunny breathe, Wade rested on his side, propped on an elbow. With his other hand he skimmed his fingers along her arm as the early-morning sun streaked through the window. There was good sex and great sex. Then there was sex with Sunny, which took great to a whole new level.

He hadn't been alone in the feeling. He could see, feel, hear her response each time. The power of it still echoed in his memory, and he wanted her again, something he couldn't imagine easing up anytime soon.

Problem was, he'd seen the barriers returning to her eyes before she'd drifted off to sleep on the rug beside him. They'd never made it to the bed. He'd pulled a blanket and a couple of throw pillows from the sofa rather than disturb her, then started his vigil watching over her in between catnaps. The warmth of her naked body, every curve fitting against him, made him want to stay awake and catalog the feel, the scents. Somewhere around four in the morning, her dog had curled up on a corner of the blanket, staring him down with those two different colored eyes, daring Wade to make him move.

A sigh slipped from her mouth a second before she stretched, her feet inching out from under the wool blanket he'd picked up at an Inuit festival last summer. Sunny's lashes fluttered open. She stared around the room with disoriented eyes until her gaze landed on him and cleared. Strange how a person could smile and frown at the same time. He stared back silently, waiting to take his cue from her.

She looked away first. "You should be resting. You've been through a lot, parachuting out of a helicopter, rescuing me, getting shot."

"Grazed. And are you telling me to go to bed?" His knuckles detoured over her stomach. "As long as you join me, I'm game."

She laughed, a forced sound that didn't come close to filling the space between them. "That would necessitate walking, and I don't think I can manage that just yet."

"Then we can stay put right here." He stoked the embers in the grate and tossed on another log before reclining back with a barely disguised wince.

The need for sleep clawed at him, but he couldn't rest until he could be sure she would still be around when he woke up. As if he could anchor her here a while longer, he draped the Inuit blanket over her again to cover her escaped toes. The wings of the raven woven into the print seemed to wrap around her protectively, the way he burned to do.

Settling beside her, he curled an arm around her waist. "I make amazing chocolate chip pancakes."

She laughed again, more freely this time. "Sounds positively... unhealthy."

"Whipped cream and all, which is not limited to use on the pancakes. I have a sweet tooth."

"I noticed from your kitchen." Sunny captured his hand, her thin fingers linking with his with surprising strength. "I have to go, you know that."

Yeah, he'd gotten that vibe and didn't like how much the thought of her leaving unsettled him. "You're a bit underdressed and most of the world's still asleep. We may be in a town bigger than yours, but we're still not in the City That Never Sleeps."

"Huh?" She gave him a blank look, her hazel eyes uncomprehending.

"New York City... the City That Never Sleeps... Never mind. Explaining jokes doesn't work." Just like the whole "Free Bird" moment back in the cave, it was as if she had holes in her vocabulary.

"Point made. We're in Alaska." Her words were hurried, embarrassed almost. "The pace is slower. This whole huge state is like a small community."

How secluded was her mountain town? "And where exactly in Alaska would you be from, in case I wanted to call you for pizza and a movie?"

She sat up abruptly, blanket clutched to her chest. "I don't think that's such a good idea." She held out her arm for Chewie to sit beside her, her fingers disappearing into the dog's black-and-white coat. "Unless

I misunderstand, your job takes you away most of the time, and even when you're around, dating me? Well, the commute's a bitch."

"Hey, I'm only talking about a date. And as for the commute, doesn't everyone around here hitch rides on all the little planes like they're buses or taxis?" He wasn't in the market for anything long-term, especially not with a deployment to Afghanistan coming up soon. He tugged a strand of her hair, the same chestnut brown, rich color of the woven blanket. "Why don't you leave it to me to decide if I can handle the trek? Starting when I take you back."

"You aren't going to go with that 'You're my mission' line again, are you?"

"That would be pointless."

"I'm glad you understand." She tipped her head, easing her hair from his hand, her emotional walls all too clear.

"So you want me to do what, exactly?"

She studied him warily, her eyes as narrowed and standoffish as the dog's. "I do need help, obviously. There should be money wired to me by the morning. That's why I needed to use your computer. So it's only a matter of finding out which bank to go, which will be in an email."

"And if the money's not already there this morning?"

Her hold tightened around her dog's neck. "I don't want to borrow trouble. Let's wait and see."

Frustration chewed through him, damn near buzzing in his ears, louder and louder. Until he realized his cell phone was vibrating on the kitchen table. Ignoring the call wasn't an option. It could be work, and if he had to leave, she wouldn't even be here when he returned.

Damn it all. For once he didn't look forward to the rush of a new mission. He shoved to his feet and padded barefoot and naked across the room. He couldn't even take heart in the fact he felt Sunny's eyes following him every step of the way.

He snatched his phone from the table, and sure enough, a number with a prefix from the base flashed across the screen. "Sergeant Rocha speaking."

"Wade, my friend." Major McCabe's voice filled the earpiece with none of his normal lighthearted humor. "You'd better sit down. The National Guard just checked in after retrieving those two bodies."

"And?"

"There weren't just two bodies."

His gut clenched. His eyes shot to Sunny. "How many?"

"Thirteen, for now, including the pair you found. But there could be more. They're still scouring the site. And every one of them was murdered, throat slashed."

The memory of Ted and Madison staring up sightlessly through the ice slammed through his brain. He plowed a hand through his hair and wondered how to break this news to the woman staring at him intently from across the room. The woman who would be devastated when she found out the news. "Thanks for letting me know."

So he could make damn sure Sunny didn't take off on her own once that cash transfer came through.

"This isn't just a courtesy call," McCabe continued. "Since you're involved, Special Agent Lasky with our OSI is working with local cops. We need for you both to come to base to look at some pictures, see if she recognizes any of the faces."

His eyes raked over her protectively and he balked at the notion of exposing her to more violence, putting those images in her brain forever. She stared back at him curiously, her arms still around her dog's neck, the blanket draped over her. He wanted to freeze this moment, because without a doubt, he knew in his gut that life was about to go to hell hard and fast.

And while he couldn't protect her from she was about to see, no way was he letting her out of his sight.

Chapter 8

MISTY TUGGED THE ZIPPER ON HER BACKPACK AS SLOWLY as she could. Not that it made any difference. Her sister wasn't going to walk through that kitchen door this morning. Sunny wasn't going to insist she eat some whole grain tofu crap for breakfast so that Misty could fake fits of gagging.

It was time to leave. She had an appointment set up with a specialist. She couldn't afford to wait any longer.

Her brother would take her. Still, she hated being a burden on her family, an adult woman still living with her brother and his family in their perfect house with gingham curtains and cast iron cookie molds decorating the walls.

Hugging the pack tightly to her empty stomach, she forced her eyes to stay well off the old upright piano against the far wall.

The floor vibrated under her feet, signaling the approach of someone entering through the mudroom, and for a second her heart sped up with optimism. A heartbeat later, before even turning, she realized the steps were too heavy, the vibrations too strong for someone her sister's size. She only knew one person with just that gait.

Pivoting slowly—she still battled problems with inner-ear problems affecting her balance—she found exactly who she expected. *Flynn Everett*. The older of the Everett twins. The single one.

The one who'd had a crush on her since the ninth grade, when the teacher made them lab partners.

Silently—duh, when was anything in her life anything but silent anymore?—Flynn filled the doorway from the mudroom, wearing jeans and a yellow cable-knit sweater, his parka hanging open. His hair was a darker shade of blond these days, but just as thick.

Her fingers fisted at her side with the memory of the coarse strands gliding over her frantic hands while they made out in his truck. Sometimes he'd climbed inside her lilac purple bedroom in the middle of the night and they would make out. A couple of times they'd come so close to having sex. God, she'd loved him back then, with all her heart and hopes.

Until he'd cheated on her at the end of their senior year, when they'd been days away from graduation. Days away from having a future of their own. What a dumb ass Flynn had been to think anyone could get away with screwing around in this tiny, gossipy community. It was almost as if he'd wanted to be busted.

As if he'd wanted out of the relationship with her.

An unhealed ache settled in her heart. God, couldn't he have just asked for his promise ring back?

Only weeks later, she'd caught meningitis and foolish, foolish girl that she'd been, she hadn't wanted to live. Her sister had blamed the local hospital, but Misty knew she'd wanted to die. She'd let her illness progress too far, too fast, before telling her parents, because she'd simply wanted to curl up and let go.

But she knew better now. Sure she'd been hurt over Flynn's defection, but they'd just been kids and he'd just been another boy trying to get laid. She had a fighting spirit these days and nothing he said could make up for that betrayal.

If he'd even meant the apology he poured out when he visited her in the clinic hospital, an apology she'd barely been able to register as her fever soared. He'd likely just felt guilty more than sorry. And soon after, she hadn't been able to hear his apologies any longer. The guilt in his eyes, however, increased tenfold.

The thought that he might pursue her out of remorse and pity made her shudder in disgust even now. She'd drawn her boundaries fast back then and stuck to them over the years as their paths inevitably crossed at the gym, the grocery store… pretty much every day and everywhere in such a small town.

She planted her hands on her hips and stood proud in her kitchen, more than a little happy she wore a body-hugging turtleneck sweater. He'd always liked her in green, said it reminded him of summer. Damn.

"What are you doing here so early?" She formed each word carefully, determined not to let him feel sorry for her, praying her voice didn't sound too strange.

"Sunny isn't going to make it back in time to escort you down the mountain." He walked closer, careful to face her, always vigilant about making it easier for her to read his lips.

His lips…

The first she'd kissed.

A mouth that had once explored every inch of her body, bringing her pleasure in every way possible without actually going all the way. Back then he'd had a mustache, not much of one, but enough to tickle her. She'd thought it was such a turn-on. But she'd been determined in those days to wait for marriage—only to have him screw her best friend. Former best friend. June had come crying to her, pretending she felt guilty, sobbing about how she just couldn't stay silent and let Misty keep dating someone who would cheat on her.

He hadn't just kissed her. He and June had impulsively had sex in his parents' empty house.

Misty's hand twisted around a strap on her backpack until her fingers numbed. She'd prayed so hard her friend was lying. Then she'd confronted Flynn and quickly read the guilt on his face. He hadn't denied anything, only asked for forgiveness.

Four years had passed and looking at him still made her physically ill. And the irony of it all? She couldn't turn away to hide her face while continuing the conversation.

"Flynn, are you trying to make me wait, too?" Part of her wondered if her sister had done this on purpose to delay her leaving town.

"You want to go? I'm here to help. I'll lead you out. My truck can plow through faster. I can drive the whole way if the weather holds, and hike with you just as Sunny would have if the weather doesn't cooperate. We're talking two days together, max, until you get to civilization. Once I know that you've got boat or plane transportation the rest of the way, I'll back off." Warily, he stepped deeper into the kitchen, wiping his boots just like old times. "I'm the best, other than Sunny, and she's so damn beyond normal, my brother swears the government implanted a compass in her brain."

She fought the urge to laugh. She'd always enjoyed the way Flynn could poke fun at his younger brother's obsession with conspiracy theories. But now wasn't the time to get sentimental about the things she'd once liked about him. This was about carving out a future for herself, a hearing future with Brett. "Phoenix will take me."

"We all know he won't want to risk exposure," he said, and they both knew he didn't mean exposure to the cold. "Especially not now that he has a kid."

She didn't like to think about her brother going to jail—or rather to a brig. She also didn't like to think about why he'd made the choices he had in the first place that led him to hide out here. The present, their lives, had been formed by decisions made too long ago to regret and rethink now.

"I can manage without you. I don't have to go far. Someone is meeting me on the other side." She threw that last part out on purpose to hurt him.

And she struck pay dirt.

His big round shoulders braced, his chest expanded— and a flash of hurt spiked through his ice blue eyes. Unmistakable. She was an expert at reading people's expressions these days, her other senses intensifying once her hearing was taken. He grabbed for the edge of the piano to steady himself—her old piano.

Okay, she'd wanted to hurt him and had succeeded. The victory vibrated hollowly inside her.

Flynn glided his thick gentle fingers along the piano's keyboard, pushing ivory soundlessly as he walked closer, his mouth forming, "Who?"

"What?" she asked. Even knowing she'd read his lips correctly, she needed a second to think. Her reactions were jumbled. She forced her mind to center on that picture of Brett holding his niece so tenderly.

"Who. Is. Meeting. You?"

He not only spoke but his hands spelled out each letter. She'd almost forgotten how in the early days after she'd gone deaf he'd taught himself to alphabet sign as well as some general ASL from the Internet. He'd even shaved his mustache to help her read his lips better, a mustache he'd been so proud of growing, laughing over how finally people could tell him apart from his twin brother, Ryker.

Thoughtful though the gestures had been, it wasn't enough to make up for what he'd done with June.

"A man." She met him face-to-face, the scent of his morning workout still clinging lightly to the air. "I've moved on."

Still he didn't touch her. "Which one of the men who left?"

She realized he thought she'd hooked up with a former resident, perhaps through their Internet contact. Perhaps it was best he continued to think that. Explaining to him how she'd fallen for someone she'd never met in person suddenly sounded silly, and she couldn't bear it if he laughed at her.

"You threw away the right to know anything about my personal life." Her nails bit into her palms so deeply, she realized that in her anger she'd forgotten to gauge the hum of her vocal chords as her mouth worked, neglecting to manage the awkwardness of a voice she could no longer hear.

Flynn nodded once. "That's true, but it doesn't stop me from worrying about you." He backed a step, continuing to speak as he faced her while making his way to the door. "I will be out front waiting in the truck, and you can be damn sure I will be with you every step of the way until I'm sure you're safe."

At the last word, he turned away, cutting off any chance she had to argue as his departing footsteps vibrated through the floor, clear up into her angry heart.

———————

Brett thumbed the earbud in more securely as he slid from the driver's side of his SUV, outside the power plant. "It's your family causing the problems. You take care of it."

"Misty insists on leaving," his contact answered through the satellite phone line.

"And you know what will happen to her if you allow that." Did he have to spell out everything to these idiots? "If you want to keep her alive, make her stay. You need my help to carry out your mission. I can only provide that if your community stays airtight. I'm not interested in risking jail time. Now decide how important this operation is to you."

"I'll stop her." The answer came fast, breathlessly, the sound of music and an exercise instructor echoing in the background. "She won't get off the mountain. We can proceed as planned."

Extremists could always be counted on to do anything for their cause. It was almost too easy to play off their fanatical leanings, too easy to mislead and use, to let them think this was only about blowing up a power plant.

"That's better," he said, nodding to two employees taking a smoke break outdoors, making the most of the fickle April weather bringing a warmer day. "We work well together because I can depend on you."

"What about Sunny?"

He weighed his words carefully while waiting for a moose to clomp lazily across the parking lot and disappear into the trees.

"I'm sorry. I truly am, but you know the rules," he continued, tucking into the back entrance, bypassing the front desk and his busybody secretary, Donna, on his way to his office. "Her leaving the community is unfortunate, but our success depends on protecting the anonymity of your group. She can't be allowed to go back and forth. She's made connections outside. She'll want to stay in touch—she could talk."

She would tell people in the community what happened to Ted and Madison. His whole operation depended on keeping the others calm, having them believe they could actually leave anytime they wanted.

"There has to be something you can do."

Damn it, he didn't have time for this crap. He entered his office and closed the door tightly behind him. "If you truly feel that way, then I'll find someone else to—"

"No, I understand." The fanatical fire for a cause would make a person sell out their own family.

"Good. We're on the same page then." And as long as he perpetuated that feeling, the mission would move along smoothly. He angled past the only chair in his cramped office and sat behind the desk. "You'll make your mark. You'll make a difference."

Everyone wanted to think they could change the world, reshape history, coerce others into believing the same damn things they did.

Idiots. The smart ones—people like him—figured out which side had the most money and shouted, "All in."

Not that he had any interest in sharing his own phi-
losophy and diluting the money pot. Let the activists
blow up this power plant two days from now to make
their statement. It would divert attention from his work,
from the package coming through. The big payoff that
would make it possible for him to deliver the treatment
Andrea needed.

Three days until completion of *his* mission.

While Alaska was reeling from the explosion of a
major power plant, struggling to heat homes, he would
smuggle in his largest group of people yet—terrorists
making their way into the U.S. across the Russian bor-
der. The Aleutian community provided the perfect out-
of-the-way place to stash them, giving them a chance
to test out their newly acquired American accents and
knowledge until such time they could be assimilated
into sleeper cells in the lower forty-eight.

Not everyone who left the community died. Just the
ones who weren't on his list of new Americans, international spies blending into the middle-class mainstream.
Not that the individual on the other end of the phone
knew all of those details, rather just assumed the "new-
bies" were a part of their own ecoterrorist cause, reaching out across the country.

"Listen, maybe I can make an exception in Misty's
case, because of her medical condition," he pacified…
he lied. Stroking his beard, he spun his chair around to
look out the window over the thawing Bristol Bay, past
the fishing boats. It was almost as if he could see them
on their island mountain as he looked down the Alaska
Peninsula that led to the Aleutians.

"All you have to do is make sure Misty doesn't leave

for a little while longer. Just keep things calm for now and we can revisit the subject later. How does that sound?"

"Okay, I can tr—"

The rest of the words got lost as Brett's office door burst open. Heavy oak creaked the hinges as the secretary he shared with three other employees poked her head inside. "Mr. Livingston?"

His sat up straight fast. Donna knew to interrupt him only if his wife had an emergency.

He covered the mouthpiece of his phone, dread already gelling in his gut. "I assume this is important."

"It is," Donna said excitedly, her chin bobbing with agreement and a barely restrained need to speak.

The woman's helpless, giggly act grated on his last nerve. His wife was so damn strong. Even locked inside her broken body, Andrea never complained, still embracing life head-on.

Brett spoke into the cell phone. "I'll have to call you back."

He disconnected and turned his focus back to Donna. He raised an eyebrow, signaling his impatience.

"One of our friends from the police station told me to let you know something on the hush-hush." Donna was allowed to assume they had an in with the station because of the power plant being a high-value target for attack. "They're calling in the National Guard, something about a serial killer's graveyard on a mountain."

―⁂―

"Why are we going to base?" Sunny asked for the third time since he'd told her they needed to throw on their clothes ASAP and meet with the military security police.

Not that he'd answered her the other two times, beyond saying it had to do with the search for Ted and Madison's bodies. She wouldn't have gone anywhere else with him, otherwise. She'd been away from home long enough. But the need to find out more about Ted and Madison's disappearance was too strong for her to bail out now.

Clothes tossed on haphazardly, she thrust her arms into her parka and followed him down the last flight of stairs leading out of his top-floor apartment. Chewie's paws *click, click, clicked* double time behind her.

"Wade?" she demanded for the fourth time and counting.

He zipped his parka without missing a step on his way toward the looming front door ahead. "It will all make sense when we get there. I don't want to give the wrong impression until we have all the facts."

Dim morning sun filtered through the frosted glass around the door. A second-floor resident in the restored house peered out into the hall, a woman wearing a man's bathrobe. The door closed quickly as the disheveled lady ducked back inside.

Enough. Breathlessly, Sunny stopped on the bottom step, gasping in air cooler than the apartment, but nowhere near what they would both face outdoors.

And wasn't that a metaphor for this whole moment? She had one chance, one second, to segue herself from being a part of the amazing connection they'd shared upstairs—and bursting out into the cold harsh reality. She'd experienced a once-in-a-lifetime night with him, and while she'd known it had to end, it was being stolen from her too quickly, too abruptly.

Chewie stopped alongside her by the rows of brass mailboxes for the apartments above, his furry bulk offering unfailing support as always. "Damn it, Wade, do you really expect me to follow you without question?"

He pivoted hard and fast, his face tight. "If you want unconditional honesty and explanations, then that street runs two ways, baby. Feel free to join in."

His words smacked her with their fierceness—and truth. She was holding back, expecting things from him that she wasn't willing to give in return. And right here, right now, as she stared at his strong and honorable face she wondered if maybe, just maybe, a decade and a half of silence could be shared.

As the scent of bacon and eggs from a nearby breakfast wafted into the empty hall, she swallowed hard, trying to find the words. She hesitated an instant too long.

Wade nodded shortly, pulling his hood up. "That's what I thought." He threw open the door to a covered walkway connected to the stretch of garages. "We need to leave."

Her feet leaden with regret, she started after him. By the time they finished on base, the money would have been wired from her brother. The gym provided a cover of anonymity for him in transferring funds. She'd hoped to spend the morning losing herself and her fears with Wade in his bed, maybe in his shower. But that wasn't going to happen.

She braced herself for the first blast of morning air as she stepped outside. Chewie whimpered beside her.

Her gloved hand fell to her dog's head. "I know, buddy. It'll be okay."

Waiting by the garage as Wade rolled up the door

and headed in to warm the engine, she looked up at the morning sky to blink away surprising tears. Blues and purples blurred together as the morning fought the night for dominance. The world was waking slowly around her with the echo of engines running, other dogs barking in the distance. The scent of coffee carried from the mom-and-pop diner across the street. A snowplow chugged and she stepped out of the way to avoid the slosh of sludge.

The world was so damn normal. Busier than her kind of normal, but still… Things felt safe here. Nice.

Chewie whined again, tugging on her jacket, pulling toward the house again.

"I know it's cold. We'll be in the truck in a minute. See"—she pointed—"here comes Wade now."

The midnight blue Chevy backed from the garage, stopping, idling. Wade launched out of his side and walked to hers. The quaint, gentlemanly gesture stabbed at her already tender heart. She started toward the vehicle.

Chewie growled lowly, a feral, fierce sound she'd only heard once before when she'd come across a baby bear by a melting pond. Muscles bunched under his thick fur with only a second's warning that he was about to—

Bolt.

Her dog raced across the icy road in a blur of black-and-white. Straight toward a man across the street, an anonymous blob of parka with a huge hood shading his face as he stood in front of the diner. He looked like countless other people bundled up, but the full facial covering seemed suddenly sinister.

If Chewie attacked—her sweet gentle pet that had never hurt a soul—he might well sign his own death warrant.

"No!" she screamed for her dog, to the man, desperate to stop the horror unfolding inexplicably before her. "Chewie, come!"

A car turned the corner by the diner, fishtailing, sliding straight toward her dog. Without thinking, she shot forward, her boots slipping, but she wasn't going down. She waved her arms, trying to snag the driver's attention, warn her dog, do something to stop this nightmare from unfolding.

Two big hands—Wade's—stopped her short and she toppled backward into the slush, helpless to do anything but watch as he sprinted forward, toward her dog. In front of the car. The world merged into sounds and shapes.

Squealing brakes.

Chewie's cry.

Wade's big body diving through the air toward the dog.

He knocked Chewie out of the way just as the bulk of the rusted red sedan blocked all else from sight as it slid sideways. Out of control. Careening straight for the man in the oversized parka. The scream froze in Sunny's throat as she stared across the street at the terror-filled eyes of a man realizing he was about to die.

The eyes of a man she knew.

Chaotic noise echoed, crunching metal and the horrible sound of flesh meeting death as the sedan flung the man's body into the air before crashing through the facade of the breakfast shop. *Then silence.* Across the street, Wade unwrapped himself from around her dog. Thank God, thank God, both still alive.

Her eyes darted to the middle of the road where the other man lay, his legs twisted at an unnatural angle, his hood back. His face was clear. She sunk onto her haunches, stunned, horrified. It hadn't been her imagination. She stared in shock at the familiar face, the last one she expected to see ever again. Only a hand's reach away from her lay...

The dead body of Deputy Rand Smith.

Chapter 9

Rolling to rest against an icy stop sign, Wade shook his head clear. Adrenaline stinging his veins, he scoured the growing crowd for Sunny. Her dog's heart pounded steadily under his hand as the mutt sat up carefully. No blood. Just chunks of snow in Chewie's fur. Not surprising, since Wade's cheek stung from contact with the ice.

He worked his own shoulder gingerly and all seemed intact as he shoved to his feet, still searching the swelling throng. And there she was, holding onto a telephone pole, pale but in one piece. He reeled with relief.

Thank God. He hadn't realized until that moment that his heart was lodged somewhere in his throat. He never, never lost his edge in a crisis. His job demanded cool and calm. He forced his pulse to steady.

The wrecked car jutted from the mom-and-pop diner, steam from the hood encompassing the scene. Bricks and glass littered the sidewalk. People poured through the door, pulling on coats, some crying.

Professional instincts kicked in. He needed to check for injured bystanders. Onlookers had circled in the middle of the street, usually a sign of something bad. He shouldered through the gawking throng, parting the crush one determined step at a time.

"Coming through. I'm a medic. Step aside, please."

The wall of people parted to reveal… a man in

massive snow gear lying on the iced road. The individual appeared to be in his thirties, and not likely to get any older. His neck and left leg were twisted at an unnatural angle.

And the corpse's blue eyes stared sightlessly at the morning sky. Damn. Wade dropped to his knees to check for a pulse, already knowing he wouldn't find one. No matter how many times he faced death, it still resonated in his gut.

Even CPR couldn't bring this one back.

Shooting to his feet, he shifted his attention to the vehicle in the diner. Two people were closing in on the teenaged driver already stepping out of the car, one of the individuals wearing a firefighter's uniform. The firefighter must have been having breakfast before or after her shift. Either way, the gangly teenage driver—who ironically didn't appear to have a scratch on him—was being taken care of.

Now that the pressing need for action had passed, he wondered. Why had Chewie run toward this guy? Wade stared closer at the face and while something tugged at him, he couldn't place where he'd seen the guy before.

Sunny's hand fell to rest on his shoulder, jolting him. He clasped her hand before turning.

He stared up, into her horrified eyes. "Sunny?"

"The deputy who shot at us"—she pointed toward the lifeless body on the road—"on the mountain. It's him."

The deputy? What the hell? They were hundreds of miles away—and an airplane ride to boot—from where they'd seen him last on the mountain. Why would he be here, across the street from where Sunny just happened to be staying, unless he was tracking her?

Wade's gaze zipped to the lifeless man who shouldn't even be in this region at all, much less hanging out a few yards away from Sunny. "We need to get to base and talk to the OSI, now. Remember the thing I said you needed to know?"

He certainly couldn't tell her about the newly discovered icy graveyard now, in public. Soon though. Because something bad was going on, something big and far-reaching, for this guy to come all the way here after them.

"Of course"—she clasped his hand—"you're right. Let's get Chewie and go." She paused, then shot to her feet again. "Chewie? What's the matter boy? Chewie!"

The rising panic in her voice alerted him a second before he looked back over his shoulder to find the massive dog limping toward Sunny with determined, loyal—painful steps.

With a killing field of faces to identify, a dead body in front of them, and now an injured pet to care for, Sunny wouldn't be leaving for the Aleutian Islands anytime soon.

This day had gone from bad to insane.

An untasted mug of coffee clutched in her hands, Sunny sat in a sterile interrogation room at the military base's Office of Special Investigation with her interrogator—Special Agent Steve Lasky. In his fifties, the agent had a shaved bald head, piercing eyes, and nicotine-stained fingertips. As best she could tell, the Office of Special Investigations—OSI—was an air force branch of military intelligence. Since Wade had become involved in the incident on the mountain, the OSI entered the ongoing investigation.

Along with how many other law enforcement branches?

Jotting notes on an old-school steno pad, he sat across the table from her, his black suit coat sliding open to reveal his gun in a shoulder harness. From what she'd seen, it seemed to be a fifty-fifty split in the OSI of uniforms and civilian clothes.

He caught her shift in attention to his weapon and eased his jacket back over the gleaming silver gun. "And you were chosen to escort the couple"—he referred to his notes on the steel table—"Ted and Madison for what reason?"

"I'm the town's guide. I also offer survival and fitness training." This tiny room with no windows and recycled air threatened to choke her. "Hiking, trekking, mountain climbing, riding snow machines… It's what I do."

"Right…" He made a note, absently patting his jacket as if looking for a pack of cigarettes. "And all of the other people, you were their trail guide as well?"

"Some, not all. Depends on the weather. I do the walking and snow machine escorts. When the weather permits, the Everett brothers drive their snowplow down the trail."

"Everett brothers?" He glanced up.

"Twins. Flynn and Ryker." Big blond lugs with smiles as wide as the Alaska landscape. "Their father heads the town council." With every word she felt like a Judas sharing all their names, exposing their town, but good God, who could ever have imagined such a large-scale horror?

Lasky nodded toward the TV screen bolted to the

ceiling. The screen, now blank, had scrolled morgue shot after morgue shot earlier, each one a horrifyingly familiar face. "I need to know exactly which ones you escorted and which ones they drove out."

She weighed his request and decided that much she could do. Hopefully, the more she complied, the less he would delve into other areas of their lives.

Image after image of frozen, lifeless faces reappeared on the screen until all eleven plus Ted and Madison were lined up together like a page in a tragic school yearbook. "Ted, Madison, Cheryl, Gregory, Lee, Hope went with me. June, Rose, Marvin, George, and the three O'Brien brothers rode with one of the Everett twins."

And others had left, close to as many as filled the screen now, their faces unaccounted for. Were they frozen out there too? What else would the National Guard uncover?

The coffee mug rattled against the metal table as her hands trembled harder.

Agent Lasky shoved his chair back. "That'll do for now, Miss Foster. If you'll sit tight, I'll be back in ten minutes or so." He started for the door.

"Am I under arrest?"

He glanced back over his shoulder. "Why would you ask that?"

"Because it feels like I'm being held prisoner here."

Those too-perceptive piercing eyes had her fighting the urge to fidget in her seat.

"We ruled you out as a suspect early on. Your survival knife doesn't match the wounds. And all the cuts were made by a right-handed person." He nodded to her hold on her mug of coffee. "You're obviously very

left-handed, something we determined the second we
had you sign in."

His words reassured her and chilled her at the same
time. Everything he'd said and done had been an interrogation technique. What else had he ferreted out of her
without her realizing it? "Thank you. I think."

"You're welcome. You're free to go. With Deputy
Smith out of the picture, there's nothing to fear. Is there?"

God, she was beginning to really hate those open-
ended probing questions of his. "I appreciate your help,
Agent Lasky."

Scratching over his cigarette pocket again, he nodded brusquely. He opened the sealed metal door with a
sinister hiss, leaving her completely alone in the freaky
small room.

Could the deputy really have been a serial killer as
Agent Lasky seemed to believe? If so, how had he figured out where she was, much less followed her all the
way to Wade's so quickly?

The car crash appeared to have been an accident at
least. The driver of the car shouldn't even have been
behind the wheel at fifteen years old. He'd said Chewie
running out in the road freaked him, then he'd lost control of his car and hit the deputy.

The deputy, someone in uniform she should have
been able to trust, had pretended to be her ally for the
past two years as she passed over dear friends into his
care. God, was there anyone she could she trust anymore? Certainly not some slick-suited agent she didn't
even know.

Acid frothed in her stomach as she thought about
how close her sister had come to being among those

dead faces. What if Misty tried to strike out on her own before she could get back? Sunny pushed aside her coffee. She couldn't risk putting anything in her stomach anytime soon. At least the deputy had been stopped, and their friends would receive a proper burial. If he'd acted alone as the authorities seemed to believe, her sister was safe.

However, the longer she sat here, the more she feared there could be something more, some terrible threat still lurking in their closed-off community. Sure, those dead bodies, the retrieval, the questions, would eventually lead authorities to investigate her village.

But she was more concerned with the here and now.

Lasky had requested she stay silent about everything for forty-eight hours while they looked into the matter further with the Alaska police and National Guard searching the area. They wanted to keep a lid on things so as not to create widespread panic and miscommunication of details.

Where did that leave her?

No way in hell could she just sit around on her hands waiting, hoping nothing bad would happen. She was a woman of action. Yes, she could email her brother a warning, but she couldn't simply hope that email arrived in a timely fashion. How often had she seen a post come in three days after it had been sent? At least she knew email was working somewhat, since he'd sent word about the money transfer and a contact number for a flight home.

Her eyes darted nervously toward the one-way window. In the spooky bowels of a military intelligence unit, it felt as if they could hear her thoughts as well as watch her every move. Were there body language experts on the other side of that pane of glass, reading her nerves, sensing her need to run?

Was Wade there?

Everything had happened so quickly once he'd told her they needed to go to the base—ASAP. He'd scooped up her dog so carefully, so tenderly, her heart squeezed in her chest. She'd raced after him, half expecting police to tell them to stop, but apparently the injured pet had provided enough reason for people not to question their leaving.

On the drive over, Wade had called the base. From the one-sided conversation, she could tell he'd phoned his friend McCabe, the one who'd cracked jokes in the helicopter the day they'd been rescued. Wade had asked McCabe to arrange for the base veterinarian to meet them and attend to Chewie while he and Sunny spoke with OSI Special Agent Lasky.

She hadn't wanted to leave her dog for even a second. But now she understood all eleven reasons why.

Her eyes shot back up to the screen, filled again with rows of small images, all the dead faces together. Right now, this was bigger than her brother. She couldn't risk just trusting on faith that the deputy was a random serial killer who only targeted people from her community. This had become life and death important.

Not only could her community be in danger, but they wouldn't even see the threat coming. They'd grown so comfortable in their utopia, thinking they could live alone and free of the rest of the world, peacefully close to nature. But they had been targeted like fish in a barrel and the local police had just let it happen.

She had such warm memories of growing up off-the-grid, but they were souring in a hurry now that she could see they'd never really been as isolated as she'd imagined.

The fairy tale was over. Going it alone hadn't worked for her thus far.

And there was only one person she could even consider trusting to help with her single chance at warning the community—warning her sister—before everything blew up in their faces. She needed Wade to go with her. She'd never seen anyone navigate the harsh Aleutian terrain as skillfully as he did. She was smart enough to know she'd need help getting back in, and Wade was just the man to offer it.

Afterward, they could go their separate ways.

Staring at Sunny through the one-way mirror felt like an invasion of her privacy. But Wade couldn't force himself to look away.

Special Agent Lasky—a guy with a shaved bald head and spooky, all knowing eyes—had gone to verify the names she'd supplied for each of the bodies, her skin turning paler with each person identified. People from her community. It had taken all his restraint not to burst through that door and cover her eyes against his shoulder, to shield her from the horror no one should have to see.

"I'm so screwed," he muttered under his breath.

Liam McCabe leaned into view. "And not in a good way, I take it?"

The major tugged his uniform, obviously having

rushed over on the weekend in a hurry. A host of dead bodies buried in ice would speed up any morning ritual. At least the slower weekend pace afforded them some privacy in the tiled hallway.

"Not funny." Not even the best-delivered punch line could pierce his dark mood today. Too much danger was skating too close to Sunny. "What if her dog hadn't taken off at that moment? What if that bastard Rand Smith had gotten his hands on Sunny while I was backing the truck out of the garage? Damn it"—he thumped the wall beside the mirror, the framed photo of the base commander rattling—"I should have seen something like this coming. I should have protected her."

"Ah…" The major leaned closer. "So that's the way this rolls with the two of you, is it?"

He ignored the not-so-subtle hint for more information. "How's her dog? How's Chewie?"

Seeing the furry mutt's stoic attempt to hobble back to Sunny in spite of the obvious and extreme pain had been moving as hell. That kind of devotion was rare.

"The vet took an X-ray. No broken bones—"

Wade's fist unfurled against the wall. "Some good news at least in one helluva day."

"Amen to that." The major scrubbed a hand over a couple of razor cuts along his jaw from a hasty shave. "But there's definitely a sprain, perhaps even a tear in a tendon. He said the dog will need crate rest for at least a couple weeks."

"How was Chewie? Did he seem stressed over Sunny not being with him?"

"He seemed to remember the vet from before, which helped keep him chilled."

"That's good."

Relief sucked the air right out of him. For the dog—and for Sunny, who would have been devastated if anything happened to Chewie. Her bond with the animal couldn't be missed. Only once he'd told her about the discovery of the additional dead bodies had he been able to pry her from her pet's side.

Fast on the heels of that image, a damn selfish thought slithered through his brain. Now she would have to stick around for at least two weeks. No way could Chewie make it through a mountain pass in his condition.

Heavy footsteps sounded in the hall, jerking them both alert and upright until Hugh Franco rounded the corner in uniform, although it looked like he'd slept in the thing. "Damn, Brick, can't you stay out of trouble for even twenty-four hours? I couldn't believe it when McCabe called me."

Wade thumped his fist to his heart. "Your compassion overwhelms me, my friend."

"Hey, I don't roll out of bed this early for just anyone." He pulled his sunglasses from his head and hooked them on the neck of his wrinkled ABU jacket. "How did it go with the OSI? Any leads?"

"Two agents grilled me, picking apart every word looking for leads that so far I'm not seeing." He didn't like having his time with Sunny splashed all over some official report, but her safety was most important.

"And their theory?"

"They say it's too early to have any definitive answers, yada yada, the sort of evasive responses you expect. But they suspect a serial killer scenario. They're investigating how Smith made it all the way here, and why the hell he was standing around right outside my place. We're too far from her home and his for it to be coincidental."

Wade looked from Sunny back at his two closest friends on the planet. Men he would trust to have his back in a bar fight. Men he would trust with his life.

Men he would trust with Sunny's life.

"I just want to get her away from here," Wade said. "You know? Use some of all those leave days I've built up and give her a chance to decompress until they sort things out. God forbid there should more to this than Lasky and the rest are considering." The farther he got her away from here, the better.

And he knew how to do that too. He had the survival training, the specialized skills, to fall off-the-grid in ways her community couldn't even begin to fathom.

Franco's smile flattened in a flash. "Whatever you need for her, we're here."

An uncomfortable silence settled at the intensity in his voice, an understandable intensity. Franco had lost his wife and daughter years ago in a freak plane crash. He'd fallen apart and almost got psych-evaled off the team. Somehow he'd pulled it together enough to function, to work, but there was an edge to everything he did now.

And when it came to protecting women and kids, he was damn near superhuman.

McCabe cleared his throat. "So, Brick, did you jar anything lose when you tangoed with that car this morning? Do you need me to check out those stitches?"

"All two of them? I'm okay, just a little road rash from when I hit the ground." He worked his arm, the ABU rubbing across abraded skin. "Shoulder's sore, but manageable."

McCabe studied him through narrowed eyes as if deciding on whether to insist on checking him over. "You've had some kind of target on your back since you met this woman. What's she mixed up in?"

His defensive hackles rose. "There are a lot of reasons people go off-the-grid."

Franco's grin returned, half-wattage but powering back to life. "Yeah, just ask Henry David Thoreau."

The major snorted. "Who knew you were a literary scholar?"

"I even read books without pictures."

"Somehow I didn't peg you as having *Walden* on your nightstand."

Franco's smile held for a few seconds before he looked back through the glass again, where Sunny turned her full mug of coffee around and around on the table. "I'm not angling to start a book club here. I'm just saying that I agree with our buddy the major. Your girlfriend seems to be mixed up in some bad mojo."

He'd wondered the same, but hearing it from someone else? Wade couldn't stop the defensive comeback. "I'm waiting to hear what the OSI's peek into her past has to say before passing judgment, thanks…" Oh, and uh… "She's not my girlfriend."

How junior high–like did that sound? And shit. His neck was hot, as if he was blushing or something. Must be more road rash. Yeah, he was going with that.

McCabe didn't look like he was fooled for a minute. "Whatever." His forehead furrowed and he thumbed the crinkles between his eyebrows as if battling a headache. "No matter how it looks, I have my doubts about the serial killer theory."

Damn. Just what he needed. More affirmation of his own concerns. Because Wade had learned one hard-and-fast truism over the years. He could always count on the instincts of his team.

His gaze landed on Sunny, on the vulnerable curve of her neck and the bold brace of her shoulders, with long brown hair cascading down her back. Damn straight he had to get her somewhere safe, and soon, although he suspected persuading her would take some major maneuvering. Whatever it took, he was sticking to her side.

Details first, however.

"Hey, guys, I do need a favor." He hooked an arm around each man's shoulder, McCabe on one side, Franco on the other. "Which of you can dog-sit a seventy-five-pound husky mutt on crate rest?"

Sunny was ready to jump out of her skin.

If they didn't let her out of this teeny-tiny room soon, she would lose it. *Seriously* lose it. Lasky may have said she was free to go, but there was still the technicality of getting through that freaking metal door. She never would have thought herself claustrophobic, but after so long living in the wide outdoors, this interrogation cube on a military base with fences and guards... She shuddered.

The soundproof walls were closing in on her faster and faster by the second. More than her hands were shaking. Her teeth chattered. She was trembling from the inside out.

The thick metal door opened with a hiss. She jolted in her seat, almost toppling the cold metal chair.

God, had they vapor-locked her inside this room?

She righted her chair just as Wade strode through the yawning portal. His big, muscled body filled out his camouflage uniform with invincibility. She never would have guessed just yesterday he'd suffered an injury that would have sent most people diving for bed rest for at least a week. She also barely recognized the uninhibited, wildly passionate lover of last night. The man before her was all military precision and rigid focus.

Wade whipped out a steel chair from the other side of the table and turned it smoothly around, sitting, resting his forearms on the back. Waiting for him to speak, to take her cue from his tone, Sunny stared at him, but he didn't say a word. Just watched her through his chocolate brown eyes, the same eyes that had devoured every inch of her naked body by firelight on a bear rug. She wanted to return to that pocket of time, to that accessible, sensual man rather than this remote wall of cool professionalism.

But she knew it was impossible. Things had changed irrefutably. She didn't have the time or luxury of indulging in an affair with Wade.

Sunny nudged her coffee aside, liquid sloshing over the side. "I want to go home."

Still he didn't speak. Muscles twitched and bunched under his uniform until the camo pattern along his arms took on a serpentine life of its own while the man himself still sat stone-still.

She dabbed up the spilled java with a napkin before leaning forward, elbows on the table. "You don't look surprised."

"I'm not," he said simply, voice gravelly, the only

outward sign of all the physical strain his body had endured over the past few days. "Although I don't think it sounds like such a good idea."

"Agent Lasky said I'm not under arrest. Is there some law enforcement mandate for me to stay in town?" Panic seeped into her, claustrophobia spreading. She felt as if she were talking to a brick wall.

"Of course not. But it wouldn't hurt to keep a low profile for a while, until things clear up and we can be sure you're safe."

Low profile? "That's what I said. I want to go home."

"You aren't hearing me. You need to stay clear of anything associated with your village until we find out for sure exactly what happened to your friends." He covered her hand with his, his skin callused, his touch warm and familiar. "Sunny…"

She chewed her bottom lip, the barely banked fire from last night rekindling inside her. "What?"

He leaned closer, his back to the one-way window. "Let's go off together," he said softly, low and gravelly with unmistakable desire. "We can forget about everything else except each other, being together."

His whispered words tempted her as much as his touch. And that was a lot.

She had to strengthen her resolve. There was danger out there threatening her family, her friends, and she couldn't turn away. "I have to go home."

One dark eyebrow cranked upward and his hand slid from hers, cool air chilling her skin and deeper.

"Okay," he said slowly, although his face turned stony again, not offering much encouragement that he'd actually conceded. "You'll need to stay in contact for the rest of the investigation. Can you do that from your middle-of-nowhere town?"

They had a satellite phone, not that anyone had picked up when she called the number. That happened sometimes, depending on the weather. She would figure that out when she got home, once she talked to her brother, hopefully her sister too. "I can arrange it when I get back."

"Nuh-uh." He shook his head. "They're going to want your contact information. Hell, I wouldn't mind a little of that myself." Irritation flashed through his eyes, the first sign of any real emotion since he'd walked through the door. He thumbed up another dry napkin and slid it across the table. "I'll even settle for your number and address scrawled right here."

Were there people out there listening to their conversation? Was he acting as some kind of interrogator, in spite of his understated sexual overture? She chilled from the inside out even in the heated air wafting from vents above.

"I know this is getting out of hand." She plowed her fingers through her loose hair and wished for a hair tie, a way to control something in her out-of-control world. "Can we talk on the way over to see my dog?"

"Of course." His face relaxed a little for the first time since walking into the room. "Discussion would be a good thing."

So he could change her mind? Not gonna happen, but it wouldn't hurt to let him think he had a chance, especially if it would get her out of this white-walled cell.

"Yes, let's go now, please." She reached across the table to clasp his hand, to regain some kind of connection, even if it couldn't last. "Have you heard anything from the vet?"

"As a matter of fact"—his brow furrowed so deeply her gut lurched in fear—"the good news is there are no broken bones. But it appears Chewie has a sprain or a torn ligament."

Her heart lurched, then settled. *No broken bones. No broken bones. No broken bones.* Those blessed words kept ringing through her head, easing the knot in her gut enough that she could hear Wade continuing to speak.

"I'm sorry I didn't do a better job at protecting him from the car and the fall."

The earnest regret in his voice softened her. "You saved his life. I know that. I just need to see him." She needed to bury her face in his familiar coat, reassure herself he was all right. She pushed back her chair, metal scraping against tile. "Where exactly is he?"

"The vet here on base is caring for him. I'll take you there." Wade stood as well, still towering but not as remote and intimidating as when he'd first stepped in the room, which made it easier for her to say what she needed to tell him.

"Good, then I can collect him on my way out."

She tamped down the regrets over closing the door on her time with Wade. She didn't have any choice. Her brother needed her. The whole village needed a warning.

And she needed this man. "Because I am going home, and I want your help getting there."

Chapter 10

DOUBLE-CHECKING, FLYNN SHUFFLED THROUGH THE survival gear packed in the cab of his truck. Even though he knew he hadn't forgotten anything. But he needed something to occupy himself while Misty said good-bye to her family twenty feet away.

Freeze dried food. Check.

Matches in waterproof container. Check.

He'd never expected a second chance with Misty. He hefted her backpack into his truck cab along with his own while Misty hugged her brother, sister-in-law, and nephew outside their home—her parents' old house.

Arctic mittens, snowbibs, shoes. Check.

Signal mirror and flares. Check.

His hands slowed on maintenance items for the truck as he peered through the windshield. He couldn't count how many times he'd walked up those steps to her whitewashed home built into the side of a mountain.

During high school, he'd been as comfortable there as in his own house, until her brother had ordered him never to set foot on their property again. Her brother hadn't spoken to him once in the four years since then, when he'd forcibly removed him from the porch with a punch that stayed imprinted so firmly on Flynn's memory he resisted the urge to wince even now.

Tent. Check.

Sleeping bags. Check.

Phoenix wasn't looking at him in any welcoming way now either, but he hadn't booted him out of the driveway—yet. It was clear he didn't want his sister to leave, but was beginning to realize the Foster family stubborn streak ran through every member.

Misty cuddled her nephew, the baby's cheek to hers. The kid was so darn cute with that crazy mop of dark hair that almost looked like a wig on a child so young. Misty held him with such confidence and ease, adjusting his tiny earmuffs shaped like dog faces.

For once, Flynn allowed himself the painful luxury of just looking at her. Her hood was back, the wind lifting her wispy, soft hair.

She'd kept it short in high school, but these days wore it blunt-cut at her shoulders with bangs across her forehead. Simple and sexy. She wasn't as flashy as Sunny, who wore bright colors and dyed streaks through her hair. Misty was… Misty. Quietly pretty and soft, with curves and a gentle smile that lit up the place more than any big show.

Her laugh carried on the morning breeze. Yeah, she sounded different these days, more and more so the longer that passed without her hearing her own voice. She'd lost so much and he didn't know how to make it right.

Flynn's dad told him some days just sucked and a guy simply had to get over it. Problem was, for him, every day sucked since he'd screwed up his life four years ago. He still didn't know why he'd cheated on Misty. Hell, he'd loved her. He still loved her so much it hurt to look at her holding that baby and smiling at her family—never smiling at him anymore.

Used to be all he thought about was getting her naked and burying himself inside her. Now all he thought about was how damn bad he wanted to touch her hair. Even hold her hand.

Shit. He was a sap.

Flynn stuffed the gear into the space behind the front seat before backing out of the truck cab. He slammed the door on his truck and walked around the front, sidestepping the snowplow attachment that would make their trek down easier.

His already aching gut churned all over again. He'd lived his whole life in this place. Never stepped foot out and never wanted to. But here he was, driving Misty.

He skimmed his finger along the neck of his sweater. Agoraphobia threatened to choke him. From leaving home? Or from losing Misty? He refused to let his emotions yank him around and wreck his life again. He pushed through the freaked-out feeling and tuned into the family farewell.

Astrid scooped her son from Misty and hugged her with her free arm. "Be careful, sweetie. Be happy." After a second hug, the former New York model brushed away tears, then clasped her baby boy's wrist. "Wave bye-bye to Aunt Misty."

Sweeping her toddler nephew's hood back into place, Misty kissed his chubby cheek a final time. "Be a good boy for Mama and Daddy." Her words fogged puffs into the cold air. "I promise to try to come back and visit after my surgery."

Her jaw trembling with emotion, she clasped her locket, the one he knew held photos of her parents.

They'd been so disappointed when he and Misty

broke up… and then the rumors started from June's telling everyone all about their "night together"—more like a half hour.

Not that he blamed June. He had been every bit as much at fault. She'd been so upset over the gossip, she'd finally left town two years ago. As June had said, she felt like the woman in the book they'd read in high school, *The Scarlet Letter*. How could she bounce back from stealing the deaf girl's guy?

He hadn't liked the way she labeled Misty, but he understood her point.

Phoenix stepped away from his wife and closed in on Flynn, his face unreadable. Flynn braced his shoulders for whatever the guy had in store. He just hoped it didn't involve a fight. He didn't want to subject Misty to that, but he wasn't taking another punch lying down.

Her brother jabbed his thumb toward the other side of the truck, gesturing for Flynn to join him by the weather vane topped with a metal bear.

Flynn kept his back to Misty so she wouldn't be able to read his lips. "I don't want a scene in front of Misty or your wife and kid."

"I agree," Phoenix said surprisingly, the mountain wind muting and tearing at his words. "If you really care for her, convince her she doesn't have to go." He leaned in. "Even with her hearing back, she's not going to fit in out there. She's been gone from regular society for too long."

He could see the logic in Phoenix's reasoning, but if he went that path, he would lose any chance with her. And he had to be honest with himself.

"I'm sorry, dude, but I can't do that. This is what she

wants. You know how it is when a woman has her mind set. If this were Astrid, could you tell her no?"

Phoenix closed his eyes and scrubbed his hand over his cold-chapped face. "I don't even know why I'm still discussing it. I just wish she could have waited, at least until Sunny gets back, but my baby sister is the stubborn one in the family."

He understood well how deep Misty could dig in her heels.

Checking over his shoulder quickly, her brother tucked his hand into his jacket and pulled out an envelope. "Here's some cash for the road."

"No, really, I can handle this." He wasn't wealthy, but he made a decent living. Or at least it seemed so here. "There's plenty of snow in need of plowing, and my brother and I are the only game in town."

"Take it. This is no time to let your pride get in the way. This is about Misty." He thrust the envelope into Flynn's hands. "Take care of my sister."

Flynn closed his fingers over the money. Holy crap, the stack was thick. Even if it was all small bills, there had to be a lot of cash here. And it did bite his pride harder than the slice of winter's worst storm.

But Phoenix was right. This wasn't about them. It was about Misty.

"I won't let her out of my sight," Flynn vowed to her brother and to himself. Regardless of whether or not she let him back in her life, he would make sure she had the future she wanted.

"Good, good…" Phoenix nodded, staring at his sister with obvious emotion in his eyes.

And with reason. In all probability he would never see

her again. Hell, there was a strong chance Flynn wouldn't be able to return either, if he had to follow her too far out into the world. To date, no one had come back once they left. That was made clear by the village council. They asserted if they allowed free flow in and out, before long, uncommitted people would corrupt their way of life.

Flynn skimmed his finger inside the collar of his sweater again, struggling for breath, and praying he would be able to hold strong on his promise to see Misty safely down the mountain.

Failing her again wasn't an option.

Snowflakes swirled in front of his windshield.

Wade gripped the steering wheel of his Chevy truck, cranked into four-wheel drive for the ice-caked road leading to the tiny port town. He'd spent the whole drive over trying to persuade Sunny to abandon this crazy-ass decision to go home immediately, but she dug her heels in deeper and deeper, refusing to discuss running off with him for a week of nonstop sex.

And her request that he go with her? She couldn't be serious.

They'd been driving for hours from Anchorage to the small airport on the Alaska Peninsula where Sunny intended to catch a flight across Bristol Bay to the island. Alaska was all about the flying. Small planes made the state accessible year-round in a way that would otherwise be a helluva lot tougher over snowcapped terrain. At any other time he would have welcomed the notion of tackling the Alaskan outdoors with a woman who enjoyed the landscape as much as he did.

But not today, and they were almost to the airport. Almost out of time to persuade her to stay well away from home while the OSI and the police did their job.

Well, except for her injured dog.

When she'd visited Chewie and heard he had to stay on crate rest, she'd panicked. She'd quickly realized her dog couldn't make the trip up the mountain. Even with most of the trek done by plane and snowmobile, there was still a substantial pass to be tackled on foot.

She'd actually discussed a sled option with the vet, but thank goodness the doctor had stressed the importance of keeping Chewie calm and still. Bottom line, the best thing for the dog was to stay in Anchorage, on crate rest. Since Chewie had seemed comfortable with the vet, she'd forged ahead.

Hell. He thumped the steering wheel, then ignored Sunny's frown.

Even if he could persuade her to stay for a couple of weeks, it wasn't as if they could launch some kind of relationship, with his deployment to Afghanistan looming. Even once he returned to the U.S., he faced a transfer to a new base.

He spun the steering wheel, cranking the truck into the parking lot outside the small brick building alongside a single landing strip. There was so much about this woman's life he didn't understand, yet he knew every inch of her body. Intimately. And he wanted more. More of her. More time with her. Even if that meant following her up the mountain?

Damn, but he was in a crappy mood. He grabbed for his Snickers bar tucked in one of the cup holders, tore off a bite, and chased it down with a swig of coffee, lukewarm and bold.

Sunny eyed his half-eaten candy bar with obvious disapproval as she finished off a bag of granola, her eyes darting intensely. For the first time he considered how everything must look in comparison to an off-the-grid community on an Aleutian island. Could that also have something to do with her decision to leave so abruptly?

If so, understanding her better could give him some insights to change her mind.

He draped his wrist over the wheel. "Culture shock, huh?"

"A little." She crumpled the bag of half-eaten, store-bought granola she'd purchased with money from the wire transfer from her family. She wouldn't even let him pick up the tab for her freaking lunch.

"Anything I can do?"

"It's not like I've lived in an Amish community all my life." She cocked an eyebrow, some of her old spitfire spark returning. "We have electricity, running water, cars. It's like living in a small town, which sums up Alaska in a lot of ways. And I run a gym. I'm a successful businesswoman."

"I didn't mean to sound condescending."

"Try uninformed," she snapped.

"And you're touchy."

"I'll grant you that one. It's been a scary day. I've lost friends I didn't even know were dead," she said, avoiding his gaze. She reached into her backpack and pulled out a rubber band she'd bought when purchasing the granola. "And you might laugh, but I'm worried about my dog."

"I'm not laughing."

"Your friends, Liam McCabe and Hugh Franco, they'll really check on him, just because you asked?"

"Just because I asked. You could say if Chewie's with me, then that makes him officially one of our pack."

"That's nice, really nice." Her eyes fell away, shifting to stare out the window. "They must think I'm a freak."

He pulled the truck into a parking spot, jacked it into park.

"Since when do you give a damn what other people think?" His hand gravitated to the shiny blue streak through her hair, hesitated only an instant before stroking down the length slowly, very slowly, taking his time to touch her. He wouldn't waste a second of what could be his last chance with her.

Her throat moved in a long swallow, her chest rising and falling faster. "Maybe I care what you think."

She swayed closer to him, the first sign she'd given him that she felt the same connection from last night, the same regret that it would end so soon.

He reached toward her hair, carefully, waiting for her to object. She eyed him warily, but stayed quiet. The snow and slush and slow-motion world outside faded as the truck cab narrowed to just the two of them. He moved closer and slicked back her hair in his hands, the long silky strands gliding across his skin, reminding him of the way it brushed across his chest as she moved over him.

Holding her hair back with one hand, he extended his other palm for the rubber band. "I think you're a fascinating, incredibly competent woman."

"And hot, right?" She dropped the hair tie into his grip.

"That goes without saying." He slid the purple band around her ponytail, and while the job wasn't perfect, there was something definitely sexy about the low-slung hair gathered slightly to the side.

All the more sexy because every time he looked at it, he thought of his fingers in her hair, his right to touch her. The way she granted him that right without pulling back. It was something to hold on to in a day where frustration chewed through him over saying good-bye, over the secrets she still held.

Her lips parted.

He waited for her, taking her with his eyes while he waited for her to take him right back.

"Wade?"

"Yeah, babe?"

"Babe?"

"Sorry. Gorgeous babe?"

She rolled her eyes. "Have you ever had a moose burger?"

Not the pillow talk he was expecting, but then when had this woman ever done the expected? He gathered her ponytail in his hand. "Can't say that I have."

He lost himself in the slide of her hair between his fingers while waiting to see where she would go with this line of conversation.

"Moose burgers are amazing. They have less fat, with the gamey kick of deer, but the high-quality taste of a prime cut." Her eyes held his, unflinching as they sat mere inches apart in his truck cab, connected by his hold on her hair. "There are no artificial growth hormones. It's healthier all the way around."

"Makes sense."

She reached toward him slowly, deliberately, almost touching, then her hand shot past him to snag his candy bar and pitch it in the tiny trash bag. "You shouldn't eat so much crap."

Okay, he was having serious trouble following her train of thought. Had seeing the pictures of all those dead friends rattled her seemingly unshakable grip? "What does the fat content in my diet have to do with anything?"

"If you come home with me, you could have a moose burger at my place."

Her question stunned him silent. She was really, no shit, inviting him to follow her to the inner sanctum of her sacred little community.

Suddenly her conversation made perfect sense, a simple offer in keeping with the more subdued tone of the day. Once that settled into his brain, he realized... Finally, she'd made a real step in admitting they had something going. He should be rejoicing.

Except hiking back up that mountain was the last thing she should be doing.

"Stay here, Sunny, just until your dog's better, and then we can all three go together. I'll take leave before my deployment." Something he did not want to discuss right now and risk sending her running.

"I don't just want to go home, I need to go home."

He clasped her shoulders. "Tell me what's going on. Why all the secrecy? I think we moved beyond superficial when I tossed your panties into the fireplace."

She looked away quickly, staring out along the frozen bay and nibbling her bottom lip. "I'm freaking out over all my dead friends, okay?" She shook her head. "I can't accept that this was a random act. Why did some get away? Are they dead out there too? And what about those families that haven't been notified yet? The authorities aren't interested in me taking them up there until they finish their investigation here, and quite frankly I'm not sure I want them there. Just inviting you is a huge deal for me. I don't think you realize how big it is to bring a new person in, especially one who doesn't intend to stay."

Her arguments had meat to them. Almost too much. He covered her hand with his. "You know all of this only makes me want to tuck you away some place safe all the more. Let the authorities do their job."

Slipping one finger out from under, she stroked the top of his hand, a simple touch, strangely personal. "I don't mean to be insensitive. I'm just not used to…"

"Relationships?"

"Sharing, being open." She twitched, a small flinch, but telling. "I have a sister…"

Her words trailed off and he waited, letting her take the lead. "Our family lives remotely. A lot of people in Alaska live off-the-grid because it's just too far or too expensive to hook into a power plant. It's easier, cheaper even, to make use of what's here."

"And that's what your family has done." He'd already deduced as much, but she was talking and he didn't want to interrupt the flow.

"Hydropower from hot springs works year-round as long as you can keep the pipes from freezing. It's effective—"

"Why are you worried about your sister?"

She bit her lip and the words dried up. Frustration sharpened, its gnawing teeth slicing clean through the last of his patience.

"To hell with it all." He sagged back in his seat. "If you want to go, then fine. I promise to take good care of your dog. Have a nice life."

"Wait." She clasped his wrist.

Thank God. He swallowed back relief that she hadn't called his bluff, because yeah, it was a bluff. One thing was certain. There wasn't a chance in hell he could let this woman walk away alone. "I want to hear what you have to say, but I don't have the luxury of a lot of time. I'm in the air force. I have to report in, let my superiors know if I go too far from base."

Her hand turned cold under his. "You didn't have to go with me today. I appreciate your help this far, but I don't want to be the cause of your standing in front of a firing squad for going AWOL."

Firing squad? Where had that extreme statement come from? Pieces of this woman's life shuffled around in his brain with jagged edges that didn't come close to fitting together. He was missing something. "Where did you say your sister lives?"

"I didn't. We're private." She thrust her hands into her hair, her voice cracking. "Call us weird or freaks or whatever."

"Whoa, tone it down a notch there."

Her fists thumped the seats. "Okay, fine. My sister's deaf. She wants to get a cochlear implant. It's going to take some major maneuvering to make that happen for her, logistically and financially. But she wants it. I'm on board." Her words tumbled on top of each other, steamrolling through his brain, almost too much information to assimilate after so long of her parceling out every crumb. "Misty's planning to leave soon and I'm just worried about her alone out there if there's still some killer on the loose targeting people who leave my town."

"All the more reason we should just leave this to the authorities."

And still, Sunny evaded his eyes. "Everything I said about my sister is true. I'm scared for her, leaving on her own. I want to talk to her, to make sure she has solid plans in place. To tell her good-bye."

He studied her hazel eyes and for once he hated all the military training, because he could see she was still evading, still hiding a crucial piece of herself. "What aren't you telling me?"

"Believe me when I tell you, I'll do anything to protect my family." The honesty of her words was unmistakable this time.

He waited for more, for the rest.

Something shifted in her eyes, taking them from hazel to a dewy green. She cupped his face in her hands. "Our time together was amazing. Memorable. Special. I wish I had the luxury of staying longer, of basking in the afterglow. But I need to check on my sister."

The turmoil behind her eyes built, swelling with the sheen of tears, the last thing he would have expected from her. Then she sealed her mouth to his, her lips cool even in the warmth of the truck cab.

Her fingernails dug into his face, not enough to hurt but enough to hold. Not that he intended to back away from her, now that he finally had her in his arms again. Her tongue met his, fully demanding and taking. The salty taste lingered, mixing with coffee and the wild abandon of Alaska that seemed to permeate her. He took risks and lived on the edge as a rule, yet still she knocked him off balance.

The need to have her, to be inside her again, seared through him so hard and hot and fast he wanted to throw the truck in gear and take her home with him. Did that make him a caveman? Hell if he knew, and right now, hell if he cared. He just burned to keep her with him, to protect her from whatever it was out there that had her so damn frantic. And he could have sworn she wanted to stay with him too.

But then she tore herself away, panting, gasping for air and grappling for the door. "The plane leaves in twenty minutes. I hope I don't have to leave alone."

Without a word, she thrust the door open and almost fell out of the truck cab, uncharacteristically clumsy. She yanked her stuffed-full backpack with her and kicked the door closed.

She charged across the parking lot into the mist of blowing snow as if she truly didn't give a damn whether he joined her or not.

Sunny yanked her gloves on and scrubbed the tears from her eyes before they froze, clearing her view of the path to the tiny plane with a propeller on each low wing. A Cessna 303, her brother had told her in his email. As if that even mattered to her now, but she was desperately grasping at minute details to help fill up the gaping hole in her gut over walking away from Wade so abruptly. She'd really thought he would come with her.

Instead he'd only pushed for her to stick around on his terms.

She hefted her backpack into place, the weight some-how heavier than when she'd started out a few days ago. She couldn't turn her back on Phoenix, her sister, every-one in her mountain village. She had to make sure, in person, that he understood how important it was that he leave Alaska. Leave the U.S. with his family and start over in Canada, and if he'd chosen that option long ago, life would be so much simpler now. Why was he so damn set on staying in Alaska? She had to make every-one understand how important it was not to naïvely think they could block out the rest of the world through limited contact.

Now that she'd stepped out, she realized how fool-ishly they'd limited themselves in communicating dur-ing a crisis.

At least she'd gotten the email from her brother about the wire transfer of the money and how he'd arranged this flight. She didn't know how he'd worked that mira-cle and she didn't care. She just hoped her own warning to him and the community made it through.

She needed to get a move on fast and quit letting the good-bye with Wade tear her up. She would see him when she came back to get Chewie. She would tell him… something. She didn't know what yet, which of course only served to remind her of his words. Of how he knew she was holding back. He would know in the future too and she couldn't see how to get past that.

Time. She just needed time to figure out a way to straddle these two worlds.

The pilot stood beside the plane, waiting with a clip-board in his hands. Wearing Nomex coveralls that added bulk to what appeared to be a wiry frame, he jotted notes. With the earflaps down on his snow hat, he didn't hear her coming until she stopped almost in front of him. He looked up fast, aviator shades covering his eyes and a groomed beard shading his jaw.

"Are you Ms. Foster? Sunny Foster?"

"Yes, I'm here, just me though. My, uh, friend couldn't join me after all." Her throat closing with pain, with regret, she resisted the urge to look back at Wade. She juggled her backpack more firmly behind her so she could thrust out a hand. "Thank you for making this flight on such short notice."

"My pleasure, ma'am. This is how I make my living." He clasped her gloved hand in his. "My name's Brett."

———

His cell phone buzzed in his pocket.

Eyes locked on Sunny talking to the Cessna pilot, Wade ignored the call. He'd taken a week of leave to watch out for Sunny and he wasn't in the mood to talk to anyone. He would check the number and message as soon as the plane was airborne.

And he was inside it, planted right beside a certain infuriating woman.

Wade reached behind him for the backpack of survival and overnight gear he kept packed in the truck. Countless times he'd landed from one mission only to have the next waiting. And survival gear was a must in Alaska, where a broken-down car could be a matter of life and death.

The cell hummed again, any sound drowned out by the wind roaring down from the mountains to tear across the flat airport. Damn. It could be something about the

deputy or those other bodies. He couldn't afford to ignore it, especially when it could affect Sunny.

He tugged a glove off with his teeth and fished for his
phone. "Sergeant Rocha."

"Rocha, it's McCabe," the major said with clipped
efficiency. "OSI just passed along some more information on your friend Ms. Foster and I thought you would
be interested."

Wade's eye zipped back to the plane as Sunny passed
over her backpack. He exited the truck and thumbed the
automatic lock. "Your tone doesn't sound great."

Foreboding crept through him, but he needed every
ounce of information he could scavenge, especially with
Sunny still holding out on him.

"That's because the news isn't good," McCabe answered unceremoniously. "She and her family had a
reason for falling off-the-grid."

Possibilities raced through his head—criminal ties
topping the list. If she was on the run from the law, that
was it. His time with her was over. Except she said she'd
been in the community for fifteen years, just a teenager.
Still… "Details?"

"She has a sister and a half brother. That brother—
Phoenix Foster—joined the army straight out of high
school."

Brother in the army. Family slipping away, out of the
mainstream. Into hiding. Ah hell, he could already guess
at the deserter scenario about to unfold.

"He went AWOL the night before a deployment. He
and his entire family haven't been heard from since."

Shock, then the bitter taste of bile hit him.

Her brother was a deserter. Her brother had

abandoned his brothers in arms when they needed him in battle. Brothers and sisters in arms like his teammates… like his father…

Like his mother, who lived with nursing care round the clock because she couldn't even dress herself anymore.

What a helluva time to learn the person Sunny had been protecting was the same sort of person who'd turned his back on everything Wade believed in, worked for, was willing to die for just as the pararescue motto declared.

That others may live.

And that very same brother had a lot more reasons for making sure no one left the mountain than the deputy ever had. That didn't explain the deputy shooting at them, but then little about this had made sense from the beginning.

Charging across the lot, he shrugged his backpack more securely in place along with his resolve. "McCabe, can you do me a favor?"

"Sure. Anything. Ask and it's yours."

"Keep checking on Sunny's dog. Make sure he's okay. Sunny and I are going, uh, hiking. This could take longer than I expected—"

"No problem. That's all I need to know. Besides, it's not often that I get to hang out with a dog."

Their jobs made having a pet virtually impossible.

"Thanks. I owe you." He ended the call.

His resolve clicked into place faster than an icicle snapped under his boots as he charged toward the aircraft. He knew. Whether or not she was complicit in any of her brother's dealings, he couldn't just walk away. He was in for the long haul, following her to what many would label the ends of the earth, the place that God forgot. But he wasn't going unarmed. He had a beacon in his boot. And inside his gear, he'd packed a military-level GPS tracker. She might hate him for it later, but her home wasn't going to be a secret black hole any longer. He couldn't risk it.

He couldn't let *her* risk it.

Wade zipped his parka and tugged on his gloves, eyes homed in on the tiny airplane just visible through the haze.

With Sunny preparing to board.

Chapter 11

WHILE THE CESSNA'S ENGINES WARMED UP, SUNNY BUCKLED her seat belt in the back seat. Or at least she tried to, but her hands were shaking and she was totally about to lose her shit. All because a guy she'd known for a few days refused to follow her on what truly was a reckless trek.

To make matters worse, she was freaking out over not even having her dog beside her. Was the cosmos ganging up on her, telling her to turn back? She'd been taught for so long not to trust the outside, to trust only her judgment, lean only on her family.

Protect her family.

She pressed her hand to the window, staring at the mountains in the distance. The snowcapped peaks called to her. Would her sister delay leaving? God, she hoped so, but couldn't count on it. Not any more than she could brush aside what had happened between her and Wade.

How would he react when she came back? Because she would come back, damn it. Even if that meant she couldn't return home—oh God, her heart squeezed—she couldn't abandon Chewie. To be honest with herself, she also couldn't leave things the way they were with Wade.

She let her head sag back against the seat, staring at the back of the pilot's head for a few seconds before closing her eyes.

"What the—" The pilot's curse was cut short by the sound of the door opening.

Sunny bolted upright just as Wade filled the gaping portal.

"Got room for one more?" he asked simply.

Disbelief stunned her quiet, followed by a sunburst of joy. He was coming with her. She didn't have to face this journey, the fears, alone.

The pilot cranked around in his seat, pushing the mic on his headset away from his mouth. "Sir, ma'am, do we have a problem?"

Her heartbeat double-timing, Sunny held up her hand. "No problem at all. I mentioned there might be an extra passenger and he made it after all."

The pilot—Brett—just shrugged and turned back to the control panel. "Fair enough. Come on board."

Wade dropped into the seat beside her. His huge backpack thudded to the floor with what had to be an eighty-pound thump.

"What are you doing here?" Her voice came out breathier than she'd intended, but she was so damn glad to have a bright spot in this horrible day, to have someone to lean on.

"I'm taking you home." He snapped his seat belt over his lap and tightened the strap. "I thought since I'd compromised you and all, it's time to meet your family."

A laugh lodged in her throat. "Thank you."

"Good luck getting rid of me." He smiled, but it didn't reach his eyes.

Maybe it was her imagination. Her emotions were in such a tangle. So much had changed so fast. Finding her dead friends, being shot at, leaving the mountain for the first time in fifteen years.

Then there was Wade. Here with her. Here for her.

The propellers spun, engines powering up louder just before the small plane lurched forward. She gripped her armrests nervously as the Cessna surged down the narrow runway, faster and faster until the nose lifted along with her stomach. She couldn't help herself. She clutched Wade's arm.

Warm awareness seeped in and tingled through her body. They were connected by her touch, by this journey. By the attraction that crackled between them even with layers of clothes between them.

And they were airborne.

The roar of engines eased as they flew out over the bay. How strange to be this afraid of a simple flight when she thought nothing of kayaking down icy rapids or hiking through a mountain blizzard. But those were familiar. Air travel? Not so much. During the helicopter ride, she'd been too stunned, too distracted, for nerves.

Now, it was just her and Wade, winging away from the rest of the world. "Are you okay with work, coming with me?"

"No worries. I took care of it before getting on the plane." He shifted in his seat, the setting sun at his back so she could no longer read his face. "Did you email your family about your plans?"

"I tried. But email can be spotty around here, like cell phone service."

He straightened, brow furrowing. "You sent an email letting them know you're going to be out alone?"

"I had to let them know I was coming in order to get the money, and I had to be sure they had a heads-up to be careful. That's reasonable. And I'm not alone now. I have you with me."

"Thank God for that." He scratched a hand over his close-sheared hair. "No use getting worked up over what's already done. But could you try to keep a low profile from now on?"

Given the life she'd led for the past fifteen years, that should have been easy. Guilt tugged at her for bringing him into her problems. Life was moving so damn fast, with little time for second-guessing as she ran full out just to stay even a step ahead. "Were you able to get in touch with the people at work before you joined me? Major McCabe... Or was his name Major Walker?"

The plane cranked into a turn, streaming sunlight over Wade's face. His eyes said he wanted to press her for more information about contacting her family, much as he had pushed in the truck. But then his gaze shifted to the pilot for a second before settling on her again.

He leaned forward in his seat to shrug out of his parka, revealing his camo uniform. "My team leader's name is Major Liam McCabe, but his call sign is Walker."

"Call sign?" She settled into her seat, realizing this was the first time in nearly a week when she'd actually had the luxury—the security—of doing nothing. She could indulge herself in simply getting to know Wade.

"Nicknames," he said. "Like aviators have. Did you ever see the movie *Top Gun*?"

"Of course." Hadn't everyone? "I'm not that cut off from the world."

"Call signs are used by military members other than aviators, like say, in a special ops unit."

"And the PJs, pararescuemen like you, are special ops?"

"Yes, we are, about four hundred of us scattered around the globe at last count." He nodded simply. "And when we're in the field on a mission, call signs level the field. They keep ranks from getting in the way in a life-and-death decision moment."

She'd shut out her memories of her brother's time in the military so carefully in the need to make his new cover story a reality for her brain. But now, talking to Wade, a few old stories drifted up through that carefully constructed barrier. She hadn't remembered anything about call signs from Phoenix. He'd spoken more about the loss of control over his day-to-day life. "I thought what the officer said was always the bottom line."

"In essence that's correct. But different career fields have different dynamics. In those extreme situations that are a part of a special ops duty, I need to feel free to give my input without stumbling over a multitude of protocols and chains of command. There just isn't time when you're tiptoeing through a minefield."

"Tiptoeing through a minefield?" His words reminded her of the story he'd shared in the cave about his friend Franco parachuting in to save a downed airman as a part of his everyday job. A part of Wade's everyday job. "You're freaking me out a little."

He cocked an eyebrow. "Then I guess I'd better hold back on the story about my buddy Walker pulling a NASA astronaut out of a school of sharks after landing."

She hadn't thought about the rescue-swimmer aspect of the PJ profession. The frigid waters of the Bering Sea below them took on new dimensions as she envisioned Wade plunging into those depths to save someone he didn't even know. For the first time, she considered that she'd gotten a fairly skewed view of the military from Phoenix.

Angling closer to Wade, she soaked up details of his job with fascination, with admiration—and with a little envy. What would life had been like if she'd been the one to enlist rather than her brother? Maybe she would be traveling the globe by now, pulling downed astronauts out of the open sea. Plucking stranded climbers from mountains.

Even saving wounded soldiers in the middle of a battlefield.

Wade stretched his booted feet in front of him, linking his hands over his stomach. "There are also more practical reasons for the call signs. We speak over the radio to each other and to towers and command centers. Call signs help disguise our identity, our unit, even our mission."

She thought back over exchanges she'd heard between him and his friends as they transferred Chewie into McCabe's care. "And you're called Brick."

"As in brick or rock, for Rocha."

"And?" She leaned forward, sensing a bit more than he was sharing. "Isn't there usually a story to go with a call sign?"

"*Top Gun* has given you a wealth of knowledge about our world, I see." He tapped his temple. "I'm a rock head, thickheaded as a brick, immovable once I've set my mind to something."

"I would say that sums you up about right."

While some might find stubbornness a negative trait, she saw how he'd channeled that into a determination that saved lives. A loyalty to his team and his uniform. Admirable.

And a serious problem once he learned about her

brother, because she just couldn't see Wade understanding the choices her brother had made. Would he consider her whole family guilty as well because of their silence?

Her own sense of honor demanded she tell Wade the truth. The whole truth. She owed him the chance to turn back if he chose, because as much as she needed his help, she couldn't trick him.

She would have to trust her gut to know when the time was right to tell him everything. But she also knew that time would have to come soon. "What about your friends?"

"Hugh Franco, the big lug of a guy who sewed me up on the helicopter. We call him Slow Hand, because he plays the guitar and he's a bit of a player in other arenas as well."

"And why is Major McCabe called Walker?"

"He used to be an army ranger before he became a PJ. So we called him Walker, Texas Ranger, like the old television show, and it became shortened to Walker. He also does a great Chuck Norris impression. But please, don't ask him about his jokes or you'll get the whole stand-up routine."

"A guy with a sense of humor." Especially after a day spent working in a school of sharks. She reached for his hand. "I'll bet that comes in handy sometimes."

He linked fingers with her, but the walls stayed up in his eyes. "Insightful comment. Yes."

"What about the other guys?" She strengthened her grip. Such a simple pleasure to hold hands. Yet somehow this felt more intimate than anything they'd shared. Her stomach lurched again even though the plane continued to power smoothly through the darkening sky.

"You want to know about them all? We could be here a while."

"We have a while before we land, probably an hour." Not nearly long enough. "How about you tell me names for the other ones in the helicopter, the ones you're obviously close to."

He thumbed her wrist. "Jose 'Cuervo' James, self-explanatory. Ironic though, since he doesn't drink."

"Oh, and let me guess about the guy that scowls in the corner cleaning his gun all the time, never speaks."

"Gavin Novak."

When had she turned sideways in her seat until their feet almost touched? "His must be something dark like Dracula or Darth Vader."

"Not even close." A smile flickered, lightening his beard-stubbled face. "We call him Bubbles."

She laughed. How could she not? "Oh my God, that's great. Too funny. I never would have pegged you all for much of a sense of humor."

"We can read and cipher too, ma'am."

Preconceptions were rude, and unwise. She should remember that. For the first time she questioned how much of her perceptions of the military may have been skewed by her brother's experience. "What happens if Bubbles wants to change his call sign?"

"For the most part names don't change. Well, other than Fang, which stands for 'Fuck, another new guy,' who keeps that name until a new 'Fang' comes in. But back to your question, if someone like Bubbles insists on a new call sign, then we'll throw a keg party and give him a new name."

Didn't sound like much fun for Jose. Then she caught

a nuance in Wade's words. "*Give* Bubbles a new name? He doesn't get a say in it?" She held up a hand. "Forget I said that."

"There are three rules to the call sign system that are universal in the different services and units. Number one, if you don't have a call sign by the time you're assigned to your rescue squadron, you will be given one by your pals. Rule number two, you almost certainly will not like it. And rule number three, the most important of all, if you piss and moan about it, we will promptly give you a new call sign that you will hate even more."

"All righty then. I'm guessing Bubbles has learned to live with it."

"How would we ever know?" His big shoulders shrugged. "He doesn't talk."

She looked at him, really looked at him, sprawled in the airplane seat in his uniform, but cracking jokes to calm her in spite of his obvious reservations about being here. Wade the warrior merged with Wade, the man who cradled her injured dog so carefully.

Wade, the tender lover.

She clasped her other hand on top of his, needing to deepen their connection. "You're so different than I expected when I first saw you."

"You're not what I expected either from a tree-hugging granola girl."

"Wade…" She leaned across, closer, until a simple jostle of the aircraft would have had her mouth against his. "You're being so un-PC my teeth hurt."

His mouth curved at her whispered taunt.

"I could distract you from your pain," he offered confidently.

"I'll bet you could."

"And yet I can't get you to answer the simplest of questions. How damn ironic is that?"

The sensual thread between them snapped. She saw in his chilly eyes that he hadn't for a moment lost sight of his focus on finding out more about her life. She'd won her victory by getting on the plane.

Now she owed him the truth once they landed.

———

With the Cessna cruising on autopilot, Brett kept one eye on the darkening sky and the other on the strategically placed mirror that allowed him to monitor the two passengers behind him. He searched the horizon, clearing for other aircraft. With so many seaplanes zipping through the skies, it wasn't unusual to skip filing a flight plan.

That made his trip easier to hide, but did require extra vigilance piloting. The landscape filled with shadows, the water, the valleys and canyons going pitch-black well ahead of dusk because of the mountains hiding the setting sun.

His eyes dropped back to the instrument panel for a quick check of altitude, air speed, heading. He was organized. In control.

Intercepting Sunny Foster's email to her brother had been a piece of cake. And Sunny's email to her brother sure as hell hadn't gotten through. Setting up this flight was even easier since, like most Alaskans, he had his pilot's license.

If only he'd gotten it before, he could have rushed Andrea to medical help faster. That crucial hour could have given her full use of her arms, or even more.

He thumbed the pain building between his eyebrows. *In control. In control.*

Blinking away the red haze, he scanned his instrument panel. He did need to adjust his plans now that Rocha was on board along with Sunny Foster. Disposing of one female would have kept things cleaner and easier. But he wasn't the kind of person to let a setback derail him.

Already he'd put together pieces of a world-changing event—anonymously. He was smarter than either of those two sappy lovebirds behind him.

Definitely smarter than the pansy-ass deputy who'd choked when it mattered most.

How hard was it to walk up a couple of flights of stairs and pop two people in their sleep? It wasn't as if the guy hadn't killed before. Except now Rand Smith was dead, and that had brought a crap-ton of attention from law enforcement with military resources at their disposal.

Now he was stuck cleaning up the mess. Having to deal with Sunny's bulky military pal too made things a little trickier, but he could handle it. He tucked the lone parachute farther out of sight, tucking away the memory of jumps with Andrea before her accident. Change of plans, now that he had two passengers instead of one. Originally, he'd intended to parachute from the plane, leaving it programmed to fly into the side of a mountain. With so many aircraft in the skies, it wasn't unusual for one to crash.

End of Sunny.

Enough time bought to complete his week's work.

Mission accomplished.

But now he had to adjust that plan. He would go ahead

and land on the island as Sunny and her pal expected. They could head off for their trek up the mountain.

Wade glanced at them in the mirror, their heads tucked together so obliviously. He had plenty of connections now in the spies he'd helped place. He would simply have one of his people stage an accident for Sunny and Wade later, on their way up the mountain.

The power plant explosion would go off on schedule—and his most high value terrorist yet would slip into the U.S. with enough of a payoff for him to slip the other way, right out of the country and into a life of luxury, tucked away in Europe.

Again, he checked the altitude, air speed, heading. And ahead of him, miles and miles of nothing. No cities. No lights. So few people lived out here, he could get away with anything.

He was in control. The beauty of smuggling so many terrorists into the country? He had untraceable people to call on at the drop of a hat. He preferred to steer clear of the fanatics, but at least they could be counted on to plow through to the end.

Even Sunny's new special ops boyfriend wouldn't stand a chance against the unlimited resources at Brett's disposal.

—◆◆◆—

Misty stifled a yawn behind her hand, the fading sun and warmth of the truck's heater making her drowsy.

She couldn't believe she was sitting in the front seat with Flynn again. It had been so long. Everything felt familiar in some ways. And in others? The differences were painfully apparent.

He passed the thermos of coffee over. "Need some caffeine?"

"Thanks, I think I do." She took the metal cylinder, twisted off the cap, and poured herself half a cup. The rich java scent drifted up as she blew into the still-steaming drink. As she pursed her lips to blow again, she felt the weight of Flynn's stare.

She looked over quickly. "Keep your eyes on the road, Flynn."

"I want you to see what I'm saying."

"You assume I want to know," she snapped back.

"Then why aren't you looking away?"

Oh crap. She pulled her gaze off the potency of his pale blue attention. She gulped down her coffee and struggled not to wince as it scalded her tongue.

Holding a conversation in the truck had been difficult all afternoon. Signing was tough one-handed, and even when he tried to spell out words, he kept having to reach for the wheel. Maybe if they had practice communicating, time to be comfortable with each other. He couldn't turn fully toward her except when he stopped—not unless they wanted to risk sliding off the icy road and off a cliff drop. The dangerous curves in the roads and paths were all the more apparent in this nearly treeless landscape. Just ice and craggy angles.

Stark. Like her life.

Not for the first time, she wondered what her world would have been like if he hadn't cheated—or if she'd forgiven him—even if she'd still lost her hearing. They would have settled into their own routine, their own un-spoken ways of communicating. She likely would sim-ply have slid over to the middle of the seat. She would have leaned against him, soaking up her last view of the Aleutian volcanic mountain where she'd lived for the past fifteen years.

She would miss the summer thaw, the kayaking, even walking across glaciers. Sunny had always reminisced about California vacations and the openness of their Iowa home. Their home *before* this isolation.

But Misty? The silence here had a way of speaking, like a hum from the earth's core.

The movement of the snow across the road filled her with the haunting echoes of a howling wind.

Water trickling down a jagged rock whispered through her memory of the gushes beneath that would foam into a hot springs retreat.

The sun sank lower and she realized daylight was running out. Traveling this road in the dark and the snow would be dangerous. There weren't exactly Holiday Inns on every corner. God, it had been so long since that California family vacation she only dimly remembered. Once her parents had decided to leave Iowa and move to Alaska, they used a camper the whole way up the Alcan Highway.

Plane tickets would have left a paper trail to her brother.

She'd thought about how to handle all day in the truck, easy enough since they'd both opted not to converse. But she hadn't considered how they would spend the night.

"Flynn?" she said, pulling her eyes off the darkening landscape.

He slowed the truck to a stop, then slid it into park. He turned the power of his vibrant blue eyes her way. "Yes? Is there a problem? Do you want to turn back?"

Yes and no. She wanted everything.

"Where are we stopping for the night?" Why hadn't she thought to ask earlier? Maybe she'd been afraid to know, afraid she wouldn't be brave enough to face a night alone in a tent with Flynn.

"I had hoped to make it to an actual village, but it's been slow going with the snow earlier." He cranked open his thermos of coffee and took a swig. "I did prepare contingencies other than camping out. I went on the Internet before we left and found a bed-and-breakfast."

"A bed-and-breakfast? Out here?" Her mind filled with images of the old Victorian homes she'd seen in books. That didn't seem possible or probable out here.

"It didn't look like much in the pictures, which means it's probably worse in reality. But we'll have a place to sleep for the night before we head out in the morning."

He put the truck back in gear, tires crunching along the icy road. Tomorrow, she would tell him good-bye forever.

But first, she had to make it through the night with the only man she'd ever loved.

Chapter 12

THE SUN WAS SETTING FASTER THAN WADE'S FEET COULD carry him from the tiny landing strip to the lodge across the street. Salty wind tore in off the rural harbor. He hitched his backpack more securely over his shoulders, Sunny keeping pace beside him. But then she always did.

The woman was unstoppable. He admired the hell out of her, would give just about anything for a shot at a real relationship with her. But he didn't have a clue how that was going to happen while she protected a deserter brother.

There were a lot of things in life he could overlook or learn to live with. That was not one of them. He'd been too ingrained in military culture with his parents for too long to look the other way when it came to her brother.

So now he knew what Sunny had known all along. Their time together was limited, very limited.

In the morning, they would launch the final leg of their journey to her village. They'd reserved two snowmobile rentals to be picked up at sunrise tomorrow. For tonight, they were staying at the lodge perched on the shore. He waited for a moose to clear the road before continuing toward the one-story building of weather-worn wood.

Twice he'd flown rescue missions out here, once for stranded fishermen, and another time to save capsized kayakers. The water was so fucking cold he could have sworn his chestnuts retreated behind his lungs for warmth for at least a week.

He believed in the mission with every cell in his body, just as both his parents had been willing to give all for country. He squeezed his eyes closed against the headache throbbing at the thought of his mother, once every bit as take-charge as Sunny, whose battles now included struggling for words and learning to feed herself.

Beside him, Sunny gasped. He looked at her quickly, tracking her gaze to a couple of hunters walking across the street, their wolf-hybrid dog loping in step.

Sunny swiped her wrist under her eyes, and he followed her train of thought in a flash.

His hand fell to the back of her neck. "We can call McCabe and check on Chewie after we eat. So far I still have bars on my cell phone."

She smiled up at him as she stepped into the lodge lobby. "Thanks. I would really appreciate that."

"Before you go all mushy on me"—he closed the door behind her, sealing the wind away from the warmth of the wood-burning stove—"I'm also calling in to see how the investigation is going."

He ushered her through the lobby, which doubled as a dining area, tables packed with fisherman tugging off black stocking hats. Walls were crammed with mounted local catches. A stuffed brown bear loomed on its hind legs in a corner.

Five minutes later, he signed the check-in book. Wade collected the key. Neither of them had questioned staying together. The place only had a half dozen rooms, but after this morning's close call he wasn't letting her out of his sight.

Waiting beside him, she hooked her thumbs on her backpack straps. "A lot can change in a couple of hours." She chewed her bottom lip with uncharacteristic nervousness. "After you make your call, there are things I should tell you."

Yeah, he knew that too well.

This was it. When he had the conversation he knew needed to happen, things between them would change. Call him selfish, but he wanted this chance to be with her.

Once they crossed that line, saying certain things out loud, things would change irrevocably between them. "Sure, but first, I have something to say to you."

She stepped into the room, easing her backpack onto a split-log bench. "What?"

He carefully placed his own pack beside hers before pivoting back to face her.

"This." He closed the thick oak door and pressed her to the panel in one smooth move.

Hands bracketing her face, he kissed her. Hard and fast and with all the frustrated energy pent up from a day full of insane twists. They should have been lounging in bed for a lazy week off. He would have used the time wisely to learn every inch of her creamy flesh, to discover the precise location of every erogenous zone.

Instead she'd spent half her day identifying grisly crime scene photos and he was stuck finding out her secrets from OSI investigators. Whatever happened to exchanging phone numbers and astrological signs over drinks?

The day rolled over him. The insanity outside his apartment that morning. How close a crazed killer had been lurking, targeting Sunny. How close Sunny had come to walking away from him.

Tomorrow loomed with a big dark shadow of the unknown. But right here, right now, he had Sunny in his arms.

Her tongue searched his mouth every bit as boldly and thoroughly as he delved into hers. She tunneled her hand between them and unzipped his parka and shoved it from his shoulders and to the floor. A damn good idea. He set to work on her jacket until finally they could press chest to chest. The fullness of her breasts flattened against him, her curves familiar, enticing, and still entirely too covered up.

Wind howled beyond the curtains, bedside lamps flickering in response, bringing a momentary blink of reason.

He resisted the urge to tear every inch of clothes from her body. "We should slow down."

"Why?" she gasped, fumbling down the buttons on his uniform.

He covered her hands with his. "Because I don't want to be an insensitive jackass by taking you against this door."

"What if I like this door?" She nipped his bottom lip.

Fair enough. "That's all I needed to hear."

Finesse fell away faster than the rest of their clothes until they stood skin to skin, his hard-on pressing against the warmth of her stomach. He throbbed with restraint, aching to feel her all around him.

He dipped to snag his wallet from his pants and filched a condom. Sunny snatched it from his palm and sheathed him quickly, efficiently, her haste speaking loud and clear of her own impatience.

He thrust into her, the clamp of her body threatening to send him over the edge before he even really got started. His teeth clenched, hard. She kissed along his jaw, rocking her hips in encouragement as she whispered her need against his ear.

The pounding urge to come damn near deafened him, his pulse hammered so loudly in his ears. No doubt, this was going to be over quick, so he needed to work on making it happen fast for her too.

She writhed against him, scoring his shoulders with her close-cut fingernails, her motions jerky and a little frantic. "Quit thinking and start moving. I need... I want... Now..."

Didn't have to tell him twice.

Tucking an arm under the perfect curve of her bottom, he angled her closer, thrust deeper, faster, driving them both closer and closer until... her shout of completion mingled with his, echoing around the small room along with the crackle of the wood-burning stove, the slap of the tide against icy chunks just beyond their window.

His forehead thunked to rest against the door as he panted and prayed he wouldn't drop her. His legs weren't any steadier than his heart rate. When he could trust his arms to work properly again, he scooped her up and carried her to the split-log bed, caribou antlers over the headboard. She reached a limp hand down to sweep aside the patchwork quilt before he placed her in the middle of the mattress and slid in after her.

Now he just needed to wait for her to go to sleep so he could make his call.

—⁓—

Flynn swung open the door to the tiny attic room at the so-called bed-and-breakfast. More like a barn-and-breakfast. The small space had sloped ceilings, tucked away on the top floor of the A-frame house. The place was probably set up by the old hunter and his wife who lived here so they could close it off when it wasn't in use.

But it was warm and safe for Misty. Nothing else mattered.

He tossed his duffel bag and Misty's suitcase in a corner by the only chair and walked to the wood-burning stove to get some heat moving around. And to take his eyes off the iron bed. Not that he would be using that mattress. He would spend the night on the dinky futon that had been billed as a sofa bed on the website.

Kneeling in front of the stove, he opened the grate to find a preset kindling pile. Quietly, he eyed the room while Misty unpacked things from her bag. It was a house, but it wasn't. The cabinets weren't made of wood. They looked like wood but it was a veneer with particle board. The rug under his boots crunched. He reached down to test the texture. Nothing like the natural fibers he was accustomed to. The only things that appeared authentic were the hand-painted nesting dolls beside the bed. They looked like some of the crafts his brother's wife had her students make in school.

If things in this backwoods room seemed strange, how much more out of place would he be if he left the islands altogether? He didn't even remember another way of living. His parents had been one of the founding families, coming here from Washington State. His father headed up the village community council and talked about the day Flynn or Ryker would run for election.

Not that Ryker had much interest in anything other than smoking weed and sleeping with his wife.

Flynn had been the one to dream of having a simple life for himself like his parents'—a life with Misty.

Steeling himself for just how damn pretty she was, he turned to face her. Still, seeing her punched the air out of his lungs. Her silky hair brushed her shoulders as she pulled shampoo and a comb from her bag. Well-washed jeans hugged the curve of her hips. Her green flannel shirt had a little ruffle alongside the buttons that all but shouted to his fingers to slide them open.

He gripped his knee until it hurt. "Sorry there was only one room."

"I'm not worried." She added a bar of soap to her pile of toiletries, the scent of some kind of berries drifting across the room. "If you intended to hit on me, you would have done it long before now. It's been four years."

Since this was his big chance, might as well go for broke. "That doesn't mean I haven't been thinking about you."

"Tough not to, when we bump into each other all the time." She slammed closed the suitcase again. "You can take the futon."

"It's not exactly bedtime yet." Even to conserve energy, a person couldn't sleep all the time it was dark in Alaska. "We should eat something."

A tray rested on the end table, chair on one side, bed on the other. She eyed him for a second before plopping down on the edge of the bed, making it very clear he wasn't getting near the four-poster even for supper.

He took the chair as she pulled the napkin off a plate of salmon pie and blueberry cobbler. A pitcher of ice water and pot of hot chocolate rounded out the meal, the dinner making up somewhat for the ratty futon. He draped his napkin over one knee and divvied up the meal. At least he could feed one hunger. He tucked into his flaky crust, smoked salmon and cheese oozing out of the sides. With every bite he felt the heavy weight of Misty's gaze across the table as she pushed her food back and forth on her chipped pottery plate.

As he reached to refill his water glass, she dropped her spoon on the table with a jarring clatter.

"Flynn, I want you to know that I forgive you."

His hand froze with the fork halfway up, cobbler dripping off the sides. Stunned, he set the utensil down again. "What did you say?"

"I forgive you for what you did with... June. If you need it spelled out. I forgive you for having sex with her," she said curtly, her tight face not looking happy or at peace with jack squat. "I thought you should know that."

"Okay. Thank you," he answered, not knowing what the hell else to say. "I'm not so sure I could be as generous if the positions were reversed."

She cocked her head to the side. "If I had slept with someone you would still be angry?"

God yes, which is why he didn't understand why he'd done it in the first place. "If you cheated while we were dating, then yeah, I would still have a problem with it."

Picking up her fork, she looked away as if mulling his words over—and effectively making it impossible for him to speak, since she wouldn't see him.

She pushed her food around again, jabbing the cobbler until berries spurted purple juice into the crust the way she used to do with her mother's cobbler. "What about if I've slept with someone over these past four years?"

Her words stabbed him as effectively as her fork into that fruit even though he realized he had no right. He knew she'd dated a few times. He was painfully aware of each time, since his sister-in-law Lindsay made sure to pass along any gossip he might have missed.

But Lindsay had always done so assuring him none of them were serious.

Hell. As if he'd had any kind of relationship at all with June. "I guess I gave up my right to be upset about who you choose to be with, but yeah, it would bug me because I still regret how it ended with us. I wish things could have been different."

"Me too," she said simply.

With those two little words, Misty had reached out in a serious way here and he could, he would, do the same for her.

"I'll go the rest of the way to your appointment with you." Even if that meant he couldn't come back. He tamped down the panic, for her. He owed her. "I'll be right there by your side through the surgery, your recovery, all of it. Before you can argue, I'm not asking you to take me back. I'm only asking to be there for you now."

The way he should have been there when she got sick. His mom worked at the hospital and had given him reports. She'd told him how Misty seemed to have given up. They all thought she would die. He'd known he was the reason she didn't fight. It was a miracle she'd lived at all. He'd taken so much from her, from them both. He had to give something back.

She stared into his eyes and he started to hope that maybe, somehow, he could finally fix the mess he'd made. She opened her mouth, her hand sliding up to the side of her neck in that way he'd come to recognize she used to make sure her words came out right.

"You're misunderstanding where I was going with what I said." She covered his hand lightly. "I forgive you, but I don't need you, Flynn. Remember? I have someone else to hold my hand."

She'd said as much earlier, back at her house, but he'd assumed she was throwing words in his face. Certainly he would have heard about any serious relationship. But he could see the truth on her face now and it sliced clean through him.

The hell of it all? He couldn't make himself stop soaking up the feel of her hand on his again. "You said you have someone waiting to meet you. Someone who left before you?"

"It's not anybody you know." She slid her fingers away and back to her lap, twisting her napkin.

"Then I don't understand." He sagged back in the rickety chair.

"I met someone online."

He sat up straighter. "That's not safe."

"I'm not a child. I will be careful. Ted and Madison will help me as well."

Jealousy scoured his insides like lye on exposed skin. Adding heat to the already raging burn, he realized she'd never confirmed or denied anything that had happened over the past four years. He had no rights anymore.

But knowing it didn't stop the roar of jealousy inside him. Not that she could hear him even if he vocalized it. "I just want you to be careful. That's why I'm here with you."

"I'm grateful for your help. Truly." Her hand twitched as if she might reach out to touch him again. "I think we both need some closure."

He realized she was forgiving him so he could go home with a clear conscience. So he could get on with his life. So she could get on with hers.

She was telling him good-bye. Forever. Until that moment he hadn't realized how much he looked forward even to bumping into her on the street. The thought of never seeing her again slashed though him, incomprehensible.

Unacceptable.

He half stood and leaned across the table, cupping the back of her neck. The glide of her hair along his fingers almost made his knees fold. He angled his mouth over hers to stop the flow of words cutting him out of her life.

She felt familiar and still so much more than he could have remembered. He knew just how their mouths fit together, the scent of her, cinnamon. The taste of blueberries on her lips. Tracing the seam of her mouth until finally, finally, she opened for him with a sigh of encouragement he could never forget.

Her hands fell to his chest, her fingers twisting in his shirt as she deepened the contact, taking it to a new level. Not two teenagers, but meeting as adults, as a man and a woman. And his body was reacting 100 percent like a red-blooded man's.

He went so hard, so fast, his hands shook with restraint. After all day sitting in the truck with her, catching the scent of her with every gust of air his way, he hurt all the way to his teeth from having her so close and not being able to touch her.

Now, here she was, kissing him, and as much as he wanted more he was so damn scared that if he pushed her, he would lose this much.

She inched back, her green eyes wide with… horror. *Shit*.

He dropped into his chair, hope deflating as fast as his erection.

Misty scooped up her toiletries from the foot of the bed and scampered across the room and out the door as if she couldn't get away fast enough. The door clicked closed behind her, her footsteps growing fainter as she raced down the stairs to the shared bathroom on the second floor.

Then it hit him. She had kissed him back. And while that might have freaked her out, she hadn't slapped him. She hadn't told him to leave. She'd left, as if maybe she was every bit as off balance as he was.

He'd meant what he said about wanting to stay with her, to help her through everything ahead of her. No way in hell could he just walk away from her once they reached the mainland. He was making progress, but he'd almost wrecked that by pushing too hard, too fast, with the kiss. He needed to take a step back.

He had a chance with Misty, an honest-to-God second chance, and he refused to screw this one up. Even if it meant sleeping on the crappy futon.

—•∿•—

Sitting cross-legged in the middle of the bed, wrapped in the quilt, Sunny nibbled the edge of the oatmeal rhubarb bar. Today, she'd learned that amazing sex gave her the munchies. And since they'd had sex twice in the past hour—once against the door and again in bed—she was seriously craving snacks.

Even an oatmeal rhubarb bar. Not her favorite dessert by a long shot, but it would have to do. Right now she would give about anything for some of her mom's cobbler, but that probably had more to do with thinking about being home again than the actual food in front of her. Except it could never be home again for any of them.

As long as everyone was safe, she could deal with whatever else happened.

Wade knelt in front of the fireplace, their only source of heat right now since the local power plant seemed to be on be the fritz. Lights had flickered off and on for the past hour and she cringed to think what many in this area—so dependent on the power plant—would do if there was a long-term, major outage. The hotel had a backup generator, but Wade had said he figured he should stoke up the fire, just in case.

Light from the flickering logs played off the hard planes of his naked back. He had three tiny tattoos walking down his shoulder, green footprints, of all things. There had to be a story there, and she'd been meaning to ask him since she first saw them. Somehow life kept interfering in the craziest ways. She wondered if she would get the chance to ask before his learning about her family put a huge freaking wall between them.

He dusted his hands clean, a hefty sigh stretching his shoulders even broader. Pushing off on his knees, he stood, tugged on his pants, then faced her. Those stitches on his shoulder reminded her of all they'd been through together, how much they still faced. He'd insisted on changing the dressing himself—citing his medic training again. She'd tried not to feel rejected. It was such a silly thing to want to tend him, but he was clearly all hands-off.

His somber expression sent a skitter of apprehension down her bare spine.

She set aside the cookie bar with the others on the complimentary plate of snacks and tugged the quilt tighter around her. "What's wrong?"

"Time to talk about your brother."

Her stomach sank. She could see in his eyes that he already knew the truth.

So much for her big decision to come clean about Phoenix deserting.

As she looked at the cool anger in his face she realized what had been "off" about him in the plane. He must have just found out. He'd said he spoke with one of his teammates right before boarding the plane. Realization crept in.

He hadn't come on the flight to be with her. He'd joined her because he knew about her brother and there could only be one reason for him to follow her up the mountain. He wanted to see her brother jailed.

She sat motionless. Feeling so damn gullible. For once she didn't have a clue what to do. Stay put so he couldn't find her brother? Except then who would warn the community?

She had completely and surely boxed herself into a corner. "How did you find out?"

He dropped into a rocking chair beside the bed and it didn't escape her notice that he didn't choose the bed.

"The OSI lifted fingerprints from your backpack to

get an ID on you. Your brother's name popped up in connection to one of the prints in the database. He has a sister named Sunny and here you are. What're the odds on that?"

She stayed silent, her finger nervously tracing the appliquéd fish on the quilt.

"So much makes sense now." He clasped his hands between his knees, leaning toward her, his eyes pinning her as effectively as if he'd handcuffed her. "No wonder you freaked when I mentioned the need to report back in. You couldn't have been that old when he ran. Only a teenager."

"Sounds to me like you already know everything. Why didn't you say something sooner?"

"Waiting for the right time."

"Waiting until you could snag another quickie with the gullible woman?"

His head snapped back as if slapped.

She held up her hand. "Stop. Forget I said that. I'm the one who kept secrets. If anyone should feel taken advantage of, it's you."

His forehead puckered in confusion. "Damned if I can figure you out."

"It's probably best for both of us that you don't even try."

Her words, the wall they built, swelled between them. She inched off the bed and reached for a long T-shirt in her bag, one of Wade's T-shirts. Her wardrobe was seriously limited these days to what he'd given her and what she'd packed when leaving her apartment over the gym for what she thought would be a simple trip up and down the mountain.

Tugging the shirt over her head while keeping the blanket up would look silly. So she turned her back to him and yanked the cotton in place quickly. When she spun around, he was staring at the floor as if to give her privacy. God, how cold this felt, so different from what they could have had. Except if she had been up-front with him from the start they would have never even been here in the first place.

She sat on the edge of the bed. "What happens next?"

With her brother.

Between them.

"You need to face the possibility that someone in your community may be tangled up in this, that someone has a very compelling reason for wanting to keep the place anonymous."

His not-so-subtle hint sunk in.

"You think my brother killed all those people?" Horror almost made her vomit. "No! No, I would know. He's not capable of that."

He held up a pacifying hand. "Okay, I understand that isn't something you can consider. But you need to accept that it's possible—quite probable in fact—that someone inside your community is tied to this. Letting them know you've discovered the bodies, that you're on your way, could have alerted them."

His words made sense… blood chilling sense. "But I already sent that email."

"Telling them everything?"

"I explained about Ted and Madison. I warned that there could be others, and the investigation could sweep up there." She struggled to remember exactly how she'd worded her note. "I tried not to give too many details because I didn't want to freak out the families who had lost people, not to mention those who might think someone had died when they weren't on the list. And the OSI said not to give out all the names."

Her explanation sounded so damn lame now. She felt like a dog paddling in a frozen pond.

"You said the bodies found didn't account for everyone who'd left. Either we just haven't found them in the ice yet, or some did make it away." He thumbed between his eyes as if pushing back a headache. "Which makes me wonder, why kill those particular people? Was it simply a matter of impulse? Or targeting the weak? What do you know about the others?"

"I gave a list to the OSI of the other names and even though I didn't know them as well as the ones we…" She scooped the quilt off the floor, even knowing her chill went deeper than any blanket could help. "The ones we lost, I'm praying they're all still alive."

His hand fell away from his head, his brown eyes alert. "You didn't know them as well?"

"They were new to the community over the past couple of years."

"And the others?"

She thought through the names, those nightmarish dead faces, and realized… "They were long-term residents, people we were surprised opted to go. But they kept in touch by email for a little while. God, why didn't I think about the emails before? Someone is tampering with the email, pretending to be those murdered people."

"Could have been sent by someone who did leave, if that person was a part of some plan. But why?"

Hell if she knew. "Some nut job infiltrated our group to destroy the group?"

"You're quite the conspiracy theorist."

"Actually that would be Ryker Everett."

"Who's he?" Wade said a little too quickly.

And yeah, she enjoyed the hint of jealousy in his voice, especially after the sting of him staying in the rocking chair. "Twin brother of my sister's boyfriend. Or rather her ex-boyfriend." She thought about Ryker further and decided… "He's married to an art teacher in the community, Lindsay. They have a baby on the way." Lindsay even helped at the gym with aerobics.

Living in that small village had made her feel so connected to the people around her. What once felt close, comforting, now seemed tangled, choking… So damn scary.

She forced herself to keep talking, making public things about people who valued their privacy above all else. "Ryker's been a part of the group since he was a kid. His father's even one of the community's founding members."

He studied her solemnly. "You know I'm going to have to share the things you told me with the OSI."

He'd brought his cell phone in his survival gear. How could she keep forgetting that? Probably because she wasn't used to having one around all the time, as he was.

While she couldn't bring herself to give him a big thumbs-up to share details about people she'd trusted for years, she also knew she couldn't ask him to stay silent. Rights and wrongs were sometimes very clear-cut. And at the moment, the most important thing was keeping people alive.

Hugging her knees, she rested her forehead on her crossed arms. Sensing Wade standing, she heard the rocking chair thunk against the wall. The rustle of clothes told her he was dressing and then the door closed as he left to make his call.

And she wouldn't even get to hear his part of the conversation.

Misty scrubbed the travel grime off her and wished her pain was as easy to wash away. To hell with years of training to conserve water and power; she cranked the water hotter until her toes turned pink as she stood in the old-fashioned claw-footed tub. A blue plastic shower curtain hung from the ceiling, circling completely around and filling with steam.

She turned her face into the warm spray, a touch of sulfur smell seeping from the water and hinting it may have come in part from a volcanic spring. She bit back the urge to cry harder, louder. The thought that Flynn might hear her pain had her gasping for air.

She couldn't believe she'd actually let him kiss her. What's more, she'd enjoyed the hell out of that kiss. Only by running like a scared rabbit to the shower had she kept herself from hauling him into bed with her. But if she did—and God, did she ever want to—then he would know her secret. He would know she was still a virgin.

Either he would pity her, which she couldn't bear, or even worse, he would realize she'd never wanted anyone even close to as much as she wanted him.

And what about Brett?

Would he move her as much as Flynn? Could she

really bare her body, much less her heart, to a man she'd never even met face-to-face? Suddenly she felt so very foolish.

She needed someone to talk to and there was nobody to turn to other than Flynn. She wanted a computer, not just to reassure herself Brett was real, but to find her sister. For the past four years she'd been so focused on hating Flynn, convinced she'd numbed herself to what she once felt for him. With one kiss, he'd blown that out of the water.

A chilly burst of air cut through her steamy haven. Someone had opened the door. Squealing, she yanked the shower curtain to her naked body, peering around.

Flynn closed the door again, his hands behind his back. "You forgot a towel."

Chapter 13

SHOWER CURTAIN CLUTCHED TO HER CHILLY BODY, MISTY resisted the urge to smack the smirk off his face. If she ordered him to leave, she wouldn't get a towel. If she took one from the stack, she would have to step out of the claw-footed tub.

Anger spiked inside her, fueled, no doubt, by a hefty dose of sexual frustration. "If you think you can just waltz back into my life and pick up where you left off simply because of one silly"—*amazing*—"kiss, then you've been smoking some of that crap your brother grows in the attic."

"You know about that?" His eyebrows shot up into the hank of blond hair hanging over his forehead.

"Everybody knows." She snorted dismissively. "Stand underneath Ryker's open window and you can almost get high off the smoke."

Or maybe it was because her sense of smell was so much stronger these days. Regardless, she was so angry and confused, she couldn't even focus.

"Ryker will be crushed." Flynn leaned a hip against the sink, towels tucked against his chest. "He likes to think he's a badass."

"Flynn?"

"Yes, beautiful?" he answered, without taking his eyes off her for even a second.

"Put the towels down and leave."

"Right." He dropped them on the sink before reaching for the doorknob.

"And turning your head away may keep me from understanding what you say, but I know you can hear me. You shouldn't have come in here."

He glanced over his shoulder, his smile cranking back up to killer wattage. "So you want me to look at you?"

Squealing, she yanked the shower curtain in front of her again. "That's not fair. Now go."

"Yes, ma'am." He turned to leave, his hands behind him, twitching.

Signing.

"I have missed you."

━━━✧━━━

With the first rays of sunrise spoking in the distance, Wade strapped the backpacks into place on the snowmobiles—or as Sunny and other Alaska natives called the vehicles, snow machines.

His calls to McCabe and the OSI last night had netted nothing new that would be pertinent to them. McCabe had said the murders were actually being shuffled over to civilian police as the base went on high alert on another security matter altogether. He hadn't been able to go into detail over the phone, but Wade had gotten the gist. Spy satellites were picking up a new flurry of activity in Russia.

Meanwhile, it was up to Wade to keep Sunny safe. "All right, then, everything's locked down tight. We should make the most of the daylight."

From what she'd told him, they should be able to make good time with the snow machines. As long as the weather held. At least the skies looked clear, vast and brilliant blue like he'd never seen anywhere else in his travels around the world. No wonder Sunny loved her home state so much.

She gripped his wrist. "I know this is going to sound crazy after how hard I pushed for you to come with me. But you don't have to go the rest of the way. I'll tell you where I live. I realize that can't be a secret anymore. I know I'm going to have to fill in the blanks, but you don't have to do this for me."

"You're a little late with your willingness to pony up your life story, Sunshine." They were in a kind of limbo land here now, between her world and his, and once they finished? Likely it would signal an end to things between them.

"I believe it's never too late to make things right. You can go back now."

Not true. Some things in life were irrevocable. There was no going back for his mother. And there was no way he could walk away from Sunny, with her life in danger.

He was fast wondering how the hell he was going to walk away from her at all. "Are you trying to get rid of me?"

She exhaled a long puffy cloud into the chilly air. "I don't want to bring trouble down on your head at work because of my brother."

"Because of your brother, the deserter." He couldn't resist shooting straight to the heart of what they were talking about. It loomed between them like a purple elephant dropped right into the middle of the parking lot alongside the moose loping past.

She jammed her hands into her pockets. "The words

sound so stark when you say them out loud, but I understand you're right. That doesn't stop me from loving my brother."

"Then you'll do whatever it takes to make sure nothing bad happens to your sister or brother, and right now, I'm your best bet for a bodyguard. So let's go."

Cupping her waist, Wade dropped her onto her seat. He kissed her once, hard and fast and not daring to linger longer, or they could end up inside again.

He pulled down the faceplate on his helmet and tapped the mic. "Test, test."

"I'm here." Her voice caressed his ears, velvet smooth like her hands on his body.

Sleeping with Sunny complicated things. Seriously. He should be honorable and call a halt to all sex between them until this was settled. Except he couldn't see his way clear to a solution for two such mismatched lifestyles. The end of the road for them waited somewhere up that mountain, and Sunny seemed to realize that as well. Knowing that—even if he couldn't bring himself to accept it—fueled the need to make love to her, touch her, claim her every chance he got.

And those chances were fast running out unless somehow they could pick their way through a path to each other, a path far more treacherous than anything Mount Redoubt had to offer up.

He revved the engine and lurched forward full speed. He maxed the machine, peeling out of the parking lot.

———

Wind tore at Sunny's parka as she steered the snow machine open throttle over the ice and snow. The powerful engine roared beneath her, eating its way up the mountain. Carrying her closer to home.

She knew every crest and valley, every stretch of water rolling in the distance, broken up by the ice just starting its melting retreat. Short trees dotted the way ahead, kept from growing any taller by powerful wind surges snapping off the tops. The higher they drove, the less wildlife they saw. And the more she missed the comfort of her dog.

Life was so similar and so radically different all at once.

Wade kept pace alongside her, the path flattening out and widening for at least another five miles, if her memory served. And she knew it did. Even with the sheer drop off to her left, there should be enough width to ride the rest of the way in. She worked with the Everett brothers and their snowplow to keep the route clear for those departing and in case of extreme emergencies.

They'd even prepared for the possibility of the volcanic mountain erupting. But who could ever have foreseen something like this?

With each mile blurring past, Sunny found herself more and more needing the reassurance of Wade's voice in her ears. Even knowing she should focus on the treacherous landscape, conserve her strength, she couldn't stop pushing for him to talk. Pushing for a way to strengthen the connection between them. A connection that hadn't been given a fair chance or time to solidify.

She stole a quick glance at him keeping a steady pace beside her. "How do your stitches feel?"

"Not a problem."

The helmet mics delivered crisp sound, the nuances of Wade's clipped tone coming through loud and clear.

"Would you even tell me?"

"There's nothing to know."

Right. He would probably keep his mouth shut and her first sign would be blood seeping through his parka.

She surged ahead, guiding him into a turn, snow spitting behind them. "You're taking this military hero stuff pretty far. Do you spend all your free time helping damsels in distress?"

"What can I say?" his voice rumbled through. "The call to serve is in my genes."

And somehow she'd managed to bring them right to the purple-elephant subject between them. Family members and military service.

Well, she'd wanted him to talk, and now was as good a time as any to go there. They might not have another chance. "Your father and your mother both served, right? They've retired to Arizona with a pack of photos of the grandkids. Seems like a great choice for their golden years."

Sounded like a great way to celebrate a life together. She envied them that, especially right now, when she couldn't even envision what tomorrow might look like with her world ready to fall apart at any second.

He hesitated so long she wondered if he was going to ignore her question altogether.

"Wade?" she asked, sneaking a quick glance at him, big and bold against the expansive blue sky.

"Retirement wasn't a choice actually." His voice went huskier, downright gravelly with emotion. "My mom took a medical retirement and my father retired to take care of her."

The rockier ground jostled her in her seat, surprising

her almost as much as his words. "Were you all three on active duty at the same time?"

"It's not that unusual for two generations to serve at once. Guess you could say I joined the family business." Darkness tinged his voice, but his driving stayed steady. The man was a brick, steady on, nothing seemed to rattle him.

"Medically retired?" She sifted through his words that left so many unanswered questions. "But I thought you said she worked on medical flights."

"She did, on C-130s outfitted to be a hospital. She was a med tech. They flew into some hot spots overseas to pick up wounded. She was in a Humvee sent out to stabilize and transport wounded back to the plane. They hit a roadside bomb…" His voice trailed off, each breath heavier, like running a marathon. "She suffered a traumatic brain injury."

"Oh my God, Wade, I'm so sorry." She'd read an article about how even if a body stayed intact, the force of the explosion made the brain swell, causing permanent damage. Due to the roadside bombs, so many were coming home in one piece, but not at all whole.

And to think of that happening to Wade's mother…

She wished she could touch him, comfort him, but hopping over to his snow machine wasn't exactly an option. "And you feel like you should have been there."

"We all serve where we're called to be," he said starkly, almost like an automaton.

Snow swirled around them from the shifting winds, the powder they kicked up whirling right back toward them like an icy dust cloud.

"But no matter how many mothers, fathers, family

members, children you save for others, it's never enough." She felt the same responsibility to her brother right now all too well.

"She's alive, and I know to be grateful for that."

"And still?" She tightened her grip as the steering tugged left, working to gain traction along the snowy path. The rented machines didn't handle as smoothly as sleds she'd ridden in the past, but she seemed to have it under control again.

He exhaled so hard the vibration rubbed against her ears.

"My mother shouldn't have been working that day. She was pulling a shift for a guy with the call sign Seagull. You know why they called him that?" Wade bit out angrily. "Because he was like a Seagull. You damn near had to toss rocks at him to get him to fly. That day, supposedly he had the flu. Third time in a month."

His frustration, his pain, his anger were all understandable. She agreed, even understanding it must make looking at her, seeing her family, all the more difficult for him.

He eased back on the power to stay alongside of her as she fishtailed again. "Hell, I realize it would have still happened and the pain would have been hell for Seagull's family, but it was his shift to pull, the duty he signed on for. He cashed the paychecks, accepted the benefits, and then left my mother out there to take his place. My *mother* out there"—his voice cracked—"and I'm over here."

"You feel like you should have been the one to help her? Wade, you have to know you can't be everywhere in the world." What a heavy load to carry, the life of so many people on his shoulders.

"Saving people is what I do. Seems damn ironic I

couldn't help my own mom." His breathing came
through the headset heavier, emotional.

"Wade, I am so very sorry," she said again, knowing
it could never be enough.

Her grip tightened further, fighting against the whine
and drag as she all but willed her machine around a
boulder-size chunk of ice that narrowed the path to single file. She shot ahead and left, determined to conquer
at least one obstacle in her world where the insurmount-
able seemed to be piling up faster than she could kick
her way through.

Her snow machine lurched to the side. A scream
slipped past her lips before she could hold it back. Her
brain scrambled to assess what the hell was happening
as she spun out. From the corner of her eye, she saw
a blade from her vehicle skidding off and away. The
world became a blur of white as she skidded…

Toward the edge of the cliff, with icy waters below.

Chapter 14

HORROR SPIKED THROUGH WADE FOR A FLASH BEFORE instincts kicked into overdrive. Sunny didn't have more than an instant before her snowmobile would catapult over the ledge.

His arm snaked out. And right between spins, he snagged her around her waist. Muscles screamed as loudly as the shrieking engine beneath him.

He steered with his other hand, straining to keep his snowmobile level and on the path while he leaned. Eyes locked ahead, he was still too aware of the danger less than a foot away. A sheer drop-off into icy waters.

The back of Sunny's snow machine rammed into his, launching his ride sideways. He refused to let go of her. He clamped his legs tighter to the seat. Stayed put. For now.

Like with rescue missions in the past, he trusted his training and forged ahead. Yet, a flicker of doubt snapped at his brain, niggling him with the hellish possibility that he could fail Sunny.

But if he did, he would damn well die trying. He gritted his teeth and hauled harder, a shout punching through his body as he ripped her from her sliding vehicle.

She slammed against his chest. Her arms clamped around his neck and he cut the power. Fast. Praying he hadn't run over her legs in the mad flail of limbs. But thank God, thank God, she was alive. He eyed the trajectory of his snowmobile, gauging if he would need to bail before it… skidded… to a… stop.

The engine shuddered and choked, sputtering off sideways across the path.

"Sunny?" he shouted into the mic, into the air, not wanting to waste a second on finding out how best to reach her.

She stirred in his arms, twisting to turn around. "I'm okay… I think…"

His brain went numb with relief until everything else blurred except the feel of her alive and unharmed against him. He ripped his helmet off, flipped up her faceplate, and sealed his mouth to hers. Hard and insistent. She froze, but only a second, before locking her arms around his neck and giving back with every bit as much urgency. Her body pressed closer, firmer, against his. If it had been even remotely possible, he would have been inside her right here, right now, on the edge of a cliff in below-freezing temps. The magnitude of the moment, of what could have happened, scraped at his already raw insides and he tore himself from her.

He leaned over, holding his knees, sucking in gulps of air. Blinking back the fog, Wade looked down. An arm's reach away, the ground dropped off into nothing but air. Below, shattered parts of the snowmobile bobbed between chunks of ice floating like crystal barges in a small river.

Sunny had been that close to death.

Every other time threats had come their way, she'd been able to pull herself out of the fire. But it made him fucking ill to think what would have happened to her if he hadn't been here. He did this sort of thing for a living.

He'd plucked people from the jaws of death before. So what had him so off balance now?

She rested a hand on his back. "Maybe we could call for a tow," she joked halfheartedly.

"My phone was on your ride." He pulled away. Right now, he needed to get his head on straight and see to safety, to survival.

"But it was my backpack that went over."

"I tucked it into your backpack. If we got separated I wanted to be sure you had a way to call for help. I have a GPS tracker in my pack and a beacon in my boot, so we're not completely cut off from the world." He walked to his snowmobile, boots crunching over ice. "I need to make sure this ride wasn't tampered with too."

"Too?" She padded softly over to stand beside him. "What do you mean tampered with? And what about your GPS tracker and a beacon?"

"Did you really think I would climb this mountain without making sure I could be found?" His brain was shifting into professional mode again, leading him down the logical trail to what very well could have caused this seeming accident. "I don't have time to argue. We can't afford to think anything that happens right now is coincidental. As much as I want to get this trip over with as soon as possible, I'm not risking either of us using this vehicle until I'm sure it's in 100 percent working order."

He hunkered down for a closer angle at the skis along the bottom, not even certain what he was searching for but determined to find it. If they set off on foot, they would have to bunk down in a cave for the night. But if they could double up on the snowmobile, they had more options. It was worth giving the vehicle a look-see.

Besides, he could use the time to get his thoughts together so they stopped humming like a damn beehive in his head. But instead of dimming, the noise only increased, droning louder until he realized it wasn't in his head. He looked up sharply just as Sunny shaded her eyes.

"Wade?" Her hand slid to her waist, where she kept her knife strapped. "I think someone's driving down the path."

Brett flung his parka over the hook in the mudroom and unwound his scarf after his flight back from the islands that morning. He still had to go over to the plant, but since he would be working late, he wanted to stop by home first.

Seeing Andrea always brought his world back into focus again.

One foot at a time, he kicked off his boots in the mudroom, lining them up precisely. Andrea had always kept the house immaculately clean and organized before the accident and he tried to keep things as close to normal as possible. Otherwise, she fretted over things she wished she could do, the way life used to be. She had a live-in sitter, but as he knew well, caring for Andrea was a full-time job in itself.

He would hire a houseful of help in a heartbeat. He certainly had the money now. But he couldn't afford to draw undue attention to himself with conspicuous consumption. Especially not when he was so close to a bigger payoff. Large enough to finance a life of ease in Europe and access to every doctor, every experimental treatment possible.

Soon, baby. Soon.

Echoes of the helper clanking pots and singing in the kitchen drifted into the mudroom. He ducked his head inside with a finger over his mouth. "Shhh."

Mrs. Glotov waved from the dishwasher, loading lunch plates. Nodding his thanks to the widowed nurse's aide and all-around helper, he tucked his gift for Andrea on the counter. Treats from the fishing lodge, from her aunt who owned the place. Oatmeal rhubarb bars, her favorites.

When he and Andrea moved to Europe, she would no doubt miss her only remaining relatives—the aunt, uncle, cousins. It already frustrated her that she couldn't live on the island, but she needed to be on mainland Alaska with reliable medical care nearby.

Eventually, she'd conceded he was right, and she would see he was right about this move as well. Soon, he would give her the Swiss Alps for a view, along with a host of the best new doctors. He was doing everything he could to secure her future, to find the cure they'd hunted for so fiercely these past five years.

He pulled out his BlackBerry and checked the connection. Strong. Good. He logged onto the Web for a quick message check in his special account set up to deal with correspondence from the mountain village. A speedy look through showed nothing new from Sunny or Misty, but he hadn't expected any, as they were both away from computers. And Sunny should be dead by now from her rigged snowmobile. Wade would have to turn back.

With Sunny out of the picture, he could pull this off. He eyed the remaining thirteen messages, including ones from Ryker Everett, Phoenix Foster, and Astrid Foster… all of which he could take care of later.

For now, he needed to see his wife, to remind himself of the main reason he must succeed. Early tomorrow, the power plant explosion would rock Alaska. After that, he would be very, very busy.

Tiptoeing in his stocking feet, he started around the corner; a floorboard squeaked and he paused. But everything stayed quiet, other than the ticking grandfather clock and the wind whistling along the eaves. She usually napped this time of day, and he could think of nothing more perfect than sliding in bed beside her.

He opened the bedroom door slowly… and found it empty. He scanned the spotless room, decorated in her favorite vibrant reds, with a picture window and a huge, perfectly made bed.

Once she'd come home from the hospital, he'd brought in a special hospital bed, king size, with controls on her side as per her medical needs. But they could still sleep together. He scanned the room—her medications resting on a wooden tray, her favorite photos lined up along the dresser.

The two of them fishing together.

Snow-machine racing together.

Skiing together.

The last photo had been taken the day before her accident. Now she lived in a wheelchair. Which wasn't in the bedroom?

Frowning, he pivoted. Her helper would have called him if there had been an emergency. He walked deeper into their three-bedroom house, one of the spares used by the live-in, the other room used as a study.

He stopped outside the home office and sighed with relief. Sagging against the doorframe, he took a second to draw in the look of her, still alive. Even after all the years since her accident, he woke up at night in a cold sweat, reaching across the bed to make sure she was breathing.

Nightmares still tortured him. Seeing her crumpled and broken on the bottom of the icy slope, the snow around her tinged red with her blood, had been the most devastating moment of his life. He'd gotten another chance to be with her, to take care of her better this time around.

Andrea was his weakness. He knew that. But he'd channeled that into strength. He would do anything, anything, for her.

She sat at her computer, her link to the outside world, she often said. Her typing splint strapped to her wrist, she poked the stylus along the keyboard, using her other wrist to move the mouse. Andrea insisted on staying active, sharp, useful. Via the Internet. She called herself a "virtual volunteer," something he'd never heard of before, but hey, if it made her happy, he was all for it.

This year, she'd settled in as a grocery order taker for the elderly, doing store-to-door orders. She talked to the seniors on the phone, then entered their shopping lists into some online forms.

She damn near broke his heart every day.

Quietly, he made his way across the room, slid aside her thick red ponytail, and kissed her neck right where he knew she could still feel the press of his lips to her skin.

Her hand fell to the side and the stylus clattered against a pencil holder. Andrea turned her head, her green eyes sparking with tears…

And fury.

Raising her hand again, she rammed the keyboard with her stylus and demanded, "Who the hell is Misty?"

Shock nailed his feet to the floor. How the hell could she have stumbled on that name? That person? His thoughts raced about what else she could have discovered or what else she might have done to follow up on her fears. He was a man with too much to hide.

"Misty? I'm not sure what you mean." He chose his words carefully, unsure of how much she knew and not wanting to feed her a tidbit she hadn't uncovered.

Andrea nudged the controls on her electric wheelchair, turning to face him more fully. "I'm a lot more computer savvy than I used to be, so don't bother denying it. You've been cruising an Internet dating site, setting up a meeting with a girl named Misty."

"You seem to have everything figured out."

He was mad. Truly angry. How in the hell could she believe even for a second that he would cheat on her? There were a million different things his principled, honorable wife could have accused him of that would have been true. But this—not ever.

His nostrils flared and his pulse throbbed in his temple.

"I can't believe you aren't even going to try and deny it."

"And I can't believe we're even having this conversation."

"Do you think I want to believe this? This is killing me, you bastard."

He knelt in front of her, not to be in a position of pleading or supplication, but to bring himself eye-to-eye with her so she could see just how deeply her accusation cut. Andrea wouldn't appreciate groveling. She would mistake it for pity.

So Brett stared into green eyes spitting fire right back at him. Memories of their marriage before the accident scrolled through his mind. How she'd charged through life, even charged right over him when she was angry. And she hadn't lost an ounce of that fight even now.

"I'm going to tell you this once. I am not screwing around. You are everything I have ever wanted in a wife, and more woman than I can even handle. Believe me or don't. I will not beg you to trust me."

He shoved to his feet and turned to leave.

"Brett. Wait." Her words were tight. She wasn't over her anger, but then neither was he.

Stopping, he still didn't turn. He struggled to rein in his temper, reminding himself that sex was a sensitive subject for Andrea since the skiing accident.

Did he miss their old life? Hell yes. He wanted Andrea healthy again, and was willing to do anything to make that happen. But he thought they'd worked through the whole physical-intimacy issue. He'd told her it was an invitation to be more inventive and she'd taken up the challenge as firmly as he had. They had a full—although different—sex life.

And he wasn't willing to give that or her up because he'd been a dumb ass and used his home computer for some of his correspondence, which would ultimately make their dreams possible.

Thank God she hadn't stumbled on anything worse. His thumb drives with lists of names and contacts were safely locked away at work, with an emergency stash of getaway cash. Just in case.

"Yes?" he said, half glancing over his shoulder.

Her chin tipped. God, the woman had an expressive face, every nuance of her anger, confusion and pain shouting from the fine-boned features he'd loved for fifteen years. "Brett, don't play word games with me. There's a difference between screwing around and having an emotional affair. It's clear from the emails that you haven't met in person yet."

Her quick brain turned him on every bit as much as her beautiful body. He let himself smile for the first time since she'd hurled the inconceivable accusation at him. "I am not having an emotional affair with anyone. I am not trolling the Internet for babes. You are my one and only babe."

She searched his eyes for eight thumps of his pulse before nodding curtly. "Okay, I believe you."

Relief gut-punched him. She raised her arm, the one without the stylus, and stroked her wrist along his face. He closed his eyes and lost himself in the feel of her skin against his, the scent of her, like a Bali orchid. Just breathing in her perfume stirred him, making him ache to show her just how much he wanted only her.

"Andrea." He groaned her name into her curled palm.

Her arms slid farther upward to hook around his neck and draw him toward her. He leaned closer and claimed her mouth. His wife. His lover.

She eased back, eyeing him more seriously than he'd hoped.

"Brett, you know this means we're going to have to hire a new helper."

"I'm not following." He leaned back against the sleek steel desk.

"If you didn't send those messages, then somebody did, and she's the only other one who knows the password. She must have let her college-age son use our computer for his online courses." Andrea's fine, narrow jaw jutted. She was a tough woman who didn't tolerate betrayal. "That poor girl Misty is going to be so disappointed when she finds out her 'Brett' isn't at all what she thought."

And yet again, his brilliant wife was 100 percent on the mark.

His brilliant, *beautiful* wife.

Brett leaned to kiss her again, sliding his arms under her legs and lifting her against his chest. He would show her exactly how much he still wanted her.

And in the morning, he would launch the final stage at financing the life Andrea deserved.

————

Sunny felt Wade's hand fist on the back of her parka a second before he lifted her off her feet and thrust her behind him. The engine rumbled louder, roaring down the trail toward them.

From the direction of her village.

She thought about reassuring him it was probably nothing bad, but they both knew people had been murdered near here and they still had no confirmation that the deputy had acted alone. Until then, staying on alert made sense.

There wasn't anywhere to hide. No substantial trees, less than a half dozen short, stunted conifers, and plenty of craggy rock. What had once seemed majestic now felt painfully barren.

The growl of the engine, the crunch of the tires with chains eating up the ice neared, with another odd scraping sound. A three-foot wall of snow sluiced around the corner a second before—

A snowplow came into sight, a familiar snowplow on the front of a twenty-year-old blue Ford, carefully maintained for the Everett family business.

She gasped in recognition as she stared at the couple on the other side of the windshield. Even with the sun glinting off the glass, she could see the pair well enough.

Oh God, her sister had left the community after all. And since there was no way in hell Misty would ever speak to Flynn again, the Everett twin beside her must be Ryker.

Wade shifted in front of her, muscles rippling under his snow gear, his arm moving until he reached beneath the hem of his parka. He pulled out a heavy black gun—a 9 mm, she was pretty sure, the same one she'd seen him carrying before. He was careful to keep it out of sight of the truck, gripping the weapon behind his back.

"Wade…" She gripped his arms. "It's my sister. It's Misty."

"And the guy with her?" he barked over his shoulder. "Do you trust him?"

Did she trust Ryker Everett? She'd turned down date offers from the dope-smoking conspiracy theorist. But she'd always thought him harmless. She never thought twice if she was ever alone with him at the gym. Not that he even came by alone anymore, now that he was married with a kid on the way. So *did* she trust him?

"If you had asked me that last week, I would have said yes, unequivocally. But now?" She braced herself as the brakes squealed on the truck, Misty's eyes going wide inside. "I don't know who I trust anymore."

"Fair enough." Wade slipped the gun into the pocket of his parka. "I guess we're about to find out."

Chapter 15

WADE KEPT HIS HAND TUCKED AWAY IN HIS PARKA, holding the 9 mm as the snowplow slowed in front of him. Morning sun glinted off the windshield of the rusted-out blue truck with one helluva blade across the front channeling snow into a tidal wave that rolled over the cliff's edge.

Wind tore at his clothes, pummeling him so hard, Sunny gripped his coat to anchor herself behind him, her jagged-edged knife still in hand. He slid his other arm behind him to make sure she stayed on her feet.

She whispered from behind him. "My sister, Misty, is sitting in the passenger side."

He should have guessed that right away, since fear of Misty leaving had driven Sunny up this frozen hell on earth in the first place. Chances of running into a stranger up here were pretty slim.

Wade squinted against the sun, peering deeper at the woman with shoulder-length dark hair, the same color as Sunny's—without the sapphire streak. She also appeared to be a couple of years younger than Sunny, but he knew threats could come in any age range, any size package.

"And the driver?" Wade asked, tightening his hold on her against gale-force winds. "The guy with her?"

"Ryker Everett, twenty-two. I've told you about him before." She leaned into his back. "He's the one who runs a snowplow business with his father and twin brother, Flynn. Ryker's married with a kid on the way. A laid-back, free-spirit kind of guy. He's a big-time conspiracy theorist, but seems to be all talk, no action. But like I said…"

"You're questioning everyone now. Not a bad idea these days."

The brakes squealed, rocks and icy chunks spitting from behind the tires. The truck stopped a foot shy of the snowmobile.

The passenger-side door flung open. Misty leaped out, surprise stamped on her face.

"Sunny? Oh my God!" Her voice carried on the wind with a guttural sound that would have cued him in to her deafness if Sunny hadn't already told him.

Wade felt Sunny shift behind him, saw the blade of her knife reflect the sun's rays before she sheathed it again. She bolted around him and scrambled along the icy road toward the snowplow. Misty palmed her way along the truck's quarter panel, staying as far from the road's edge as possible. Meeting at the snowmobile, the sisters hugged each other, holding so tight their arms sunk into layers of winter clothing.

He kept his eyes on the other guy just past them. Ryker Everett, Sunny had called him. Everett slid from the truck, attention locked on the two women across the hood without intruding on the moment.

Wade studied the hulking Paul Bunyan wannabe in front of him and figured out one thing about the guy fast. Ryker Everett might be married with a kid on the way, but the man standing a few feet away had some hefty feelings for one of those two women. With the sisters still hugging tight, Wade couldn't tell which one the fella stared at with his heart planted firmly on his wind-worn sleeve.

But he intended to find out.

Sunny cupped her sister's face, tears streaking down her cheeks and glinting as they froze. "I'm so glad you're all right. I was worried about you." She turned to the guy still standing on the other side of the hood, shuffling from boot to boot. "Thank you for taking such good care of her, Ryker."

"Ryker?" Misty pulled back, then laughed. "You never could tell them apart. This is Flynn."

The other twin? Did that change Sunny's thoughts on whether or not to trust the man?

Misty cocked her head to look past Sunny. "Who's that with you? Where have you been? Are you 'kay? I was so worried 'bout you."

Sunny looked back over her shoulder at Wade, her hazel eyes relaying her uncertainty. He weighed the options and decided on the path that made the most sense.

Wade stepped forward, his fingers still wrapped around his 9 mm in his pocket. Just in case.

"I'm with a military rescue team. I helped Sunny when she got stranded up here. A lot has happened in the past few days." An understatement, for damn sure. "Why don't we all shuffle this conversation into the truck where it's warmer?"

They had a lot to discuss and a limited amount of daylight hours left to reach the community where hopefully they would find some answers. He just prayed those answers weren't going to plunge Sunny right back into harm's way.

———

Truck jostling in a pothole, Misty grabbed the cracked leather seat in front of her as she sat in the back of the extended cab with her sister. The world outside the windows was pitch-black, no city skyline. Nothing but the moon, stars, and twin beams of the headlights streaking ahead. The dim glow of the dashboard cast the men's faces in a spooky green glow as they talked to each other.

In the nine hours since they'd miraculously run into each other, she hadn't been able to peel herself from Sunny's side. The vehicle wasn't handling as well in the dark, but both Flynn and the military guy, Wade, had insisted on charging all the way back home, no stops other than refilling the tank with the extra fuel in the back. The last few miles were the clearest and easiest anyway, the ones traveled most around their village, which she'd once thought to be safe and remote.

She could still barely wrap her brain around the fact that so many of their dear friends had been murdered. What a devastating loss for their community. And why? It seemed so arbitrary, those who hadn't died. Unless their bodies simply hadn't been found. She shivered again in spite of the blasting heater. She could have been one of those corpses in the ice, if not for her sister.

While she'd wanted to leave and resented some of the restrictions that came with living there, she'd never expected to be afraid of her own home. She'd been so close to Deputy Rand Smith on more than one occasion when she'd helped Sunny, or when he'd come farther up the trail to get someone. And she couldn't help but wonder now if his trips all the way to the community had been for a different purpose, perhaps to touch base with an accomplice, someone who could be plotting new murders.

Tears stung her eyes every time she looked at Sunny. She hadn't fully grasped until now how horrible it would have been never to see her again. Close on that thought followed the sting of grasping how deeply she'd felt betrayed over Sunny not returning to say good-bye.

Somewhere in the back of her mind she'd wondered if her sister had delayed returning on purpose, to keep her from leaving. Yet now that she looked back she saw what she should have known all along. Sunny wasn't passive-aggressive. Sunny met life head-on. She'd been out there stranded in a snowstorm, with a mass murderer, and had come out alive.

With Flynn's handsome face reflected in the rearview mirror, she could see from his jaw that he was still talking—even if she couldn't hear him.

She nudged Sunny and signed for about the tenth time today. *"What's he saying?"*

Sunny's hands flew as she answered. *"We need to check in with Flynn's father, prepare him for the notifications about to come through."*

Misty kept her arms low, not wanting to draw attention to what they were discussing in case Flynn started watching in the rearview mirror. *"What about Phoenix?"*

Pain flashed across Sunny's face. *"We'll talk to him. Then we have to wait and see. I think he probably always knew this day was coming. It's up to him how to handle it."*

Nodding, Misty continued, *"Do you trust this guy Wade?"*

"Yes, I do, actually."

"Even though you've barely known him a week?"

"He's saved my life more than once, even today actually. He risked his own neck to pull me off my snow machine. I was so close to going over the edge of that cliff, no one in their right mind would have even tried. But he did. And after everything that's happened this week, I've learned knowing someone a long time—like the deputy—doesn't mean they're trustworthy."

Misty's eyes slid to Flynn as if against her will. She'd known him for fifteen years and still she didn't understand what happened four years ago. And yet the past couple of days, he had been the man she knew, remembered.

Sunny ducked into her line of sight. Her sister signed, *"Why are you with Flynn?"*

Misty sagged back against the seat. *"Because he offered."* And she finally admitted the truth to herself. *"Because I've missed him. And because today has made me realize how really rare second chances are."*

Her eyes slid back to the front seat even though that meant her world would go silent again without her sister signing the conversation. She wasn't even close to getting over Flynn, but she was still just as committed to moving into the real world and having the cochlear implant surgery. She was committed to leaving the mountain. And now she had Sunny and her military friend to escort her out once they'd cleared away matters here. Flynn didn't need to help her any longer.

He steered the truck round a jutting mound of boulders she recognized well, the final barrier shielding her village from anyone who may have wandered unwittingly into this remote corner of the world. The landscape opened up to her moonlit valley with a hundred buildings built alongside a small lake. So familiar. A place she could no longer call home. She'd said her good-byes, or so she'd thought.

Life had offered her a second chance here. A second chance for a last night to find closure with Flynn.

―⁓―

Wade paced in a circle around the open main floor of the log cabin that housed Sunny's business. Well past midnight, they had finally arrived at Sunny's home after meeting with Flynn Everett's father, head of the town council.

The bottom floor was sectioned off into four areas, mirrors all around and a skylight above making the small place look larger. One corner held fitness equipment. By the door, there was a check-in counter with fresh muffins, granola, coffee, and a water dispenser. Tucked behind it were two computers and some toys and kiddie tables set up with books, paper, and crayons. And the remaining space—not much—appeared to be used for aerobics or martial arts with mats. A narrow corridor at the end of the room led deeper inside the building. Given his view of the outside before they'd entered, there must be some sort of loft space upstairs— her apartment perhaps?

Sunny flipped on a single light over the workout equipment in a corner and stopped beside him, wearing her own clothes now for the first time since he'd seen her the day they'd met. Purple jeans hugged her legs, and a bold red sweater fit every curve. She was a splash of color in the middle of an oatmeal-colored world.

She toed an itch on the back of her calf. "That

hallway leads to a couple of bathrooms that double as locker rooms. Out the back door, there's a natural hot springs pool. My apartment is upstairs."

She didn't just manage this place. Apparently she also owned it with her brother.

He was impressed.

This whole little community wasn't at all what he'd envisioned for what appeared to be a town of no more than about a hundred and fifty people. It was much more organized and technological than he'd expected. When he met Flynn Everett's father, he'd been able to use the town leader's satellite phone to check in with McCabe. The conversation had been short and frustrating. Nothing new about the deputy, other than that he was from Oklahoma, deeply in debt, and moonlighting as a security guard at a power plant. There was nothing in his past to suggest he was a psychopath. Just flat broke.

McCabe had apologized for being abrupt, but he was heading into a brief about the security concern he'd mentioned earlier. Wade got the message. The defense issue with Russian intel leaks must have escalated. McCabe had quickly assured him the dog—Chewie— was recovering well. Wade had turned to tell Sunny.

But she'd disappeared and stayed gone for fifteen conspicuous minutes.

Wade walked along the dumbbell rack, shifting a twenty-pound weight that had been mistakenly placed in the twenty-five-pound slot. "What did your brother have to say?"

Sunny's legs folded and she dropped onto an exercise bike seat. "How did you know? Never mind. I didn't get to speak to him anyway."

"Are you covering for him?" He leaned back against the weight rack, wishing they didn't have all this crap between them and could just end the day the way he wanted. In bed with her, with him peeling the jeans off her legs.

"I realize you have plenty of reasons not to trust me, but all I know is that Astrid's parents were at the house baby-sitting my nephew. They said Astrid and Phoenix had gone camping together."

"Do you believe them?" Sounded too damn convenient to him that Phoenix would disappear right before the lid was about to blow off their private little village hideaway.

She shrugged. "They do that sometimes, go off together for time away from the stress of being new parents, enjoy back-to-nature kinds of meditation like they used to when they were dating. Yes, the timing seems coincidental, but the behavior is in keeping with something they would do."

"And your brother, do you think he got a warning we were coming?"

"I sent that email," she said carefully, resting a foot on a bike pedal, her red Converse high-tops as full of personality as she was. "He could have run, although I don't believe he would have left his son behind."

"And his wife went along too. I'm assuming she wouldn't leave her child either. All the more reason to assume he hasn't run. So why is he conveniently gone now? Something's off." He could sense it. "But still, I stick by my gut feeling that the wife—Astrid—isn't on the run with her husband. Plenty of wives I know aren't even willing to pack up and move to another state for even a job change. Your brother wouldn't be offering a helluva lot of security."

He knew he wasn't talking about just her brother anymore. He'd seen more than his fair share of military relationships hit the skids because of a transfer. The crackle of connection snapping from Sunny to him said loud and clear that she was having the same thoughts, the same concerns.

He waited for her to answer, to give him some kind of indication where they could go from here. If they could. Tough to figure out when he knew so little about her and her family. He'd slept with her, faced death with her, and he didn't even know the most fundamental things about her. And time was running out fast to learn.

Memories of the day and her brush with death came back to scare the hell out of him when he least expected it. He was pretty sure his insides were still a little numbed out about that.

"Where did you live before going off-the-grid?" Why hadn't he thought to ask that before? Had he been holding back too?

"On a farm in Iowa." She spun the bike pedal with her toe. "We grew corn and soybeans. The land was in the family for a couple hundred years. The farm barely paid for itself, but Dad had a store too, and Mom worked at a bank in town. They said moving here was the perfect way to get their priorities back in order."

"And your brother?"

"They wanted to help him. I was twelve at the time and I didn't ask a lot of questions." She looked around the small business she'd managed to build in the middle of nowhere as if seeing it with new eyes. "Maybe I should have."

They'd cut their two daughters off from the ability to

ask questions or reach out for any help, any other way of thinking. The place might not call itself a cult, but unquestionably there had been a closed society, cultish mentality at play.

Was Sunny even able to just break away from that? Sure she'd been scared of him finding out about her brother when he first found her, but she hadn't freaked out in the city when she was at his place. Looking back he knew now that she'd wanted to be at his apartment rather than base because of the intense proximity to the military. But she was comfortable enough there.

Seeing what she'd built here, with no help from the outside world, made him recognize how self-sufficient she was. What might she accomplish with the resources of the world he knew at hand?

He wasn't ready to say all their obstacles were out of the way. But for tonight, it seemed he'd cleared away a few.

Above all, Sunny was alive. Thank God, she was still alive.

Wade extended an arm to her. "Let's go up to your apartment."

A spark lit in her eyes. "I can think of nothing better than forgetting about all the things we can't change." She placed her hand in his, her smile almost chasing away the shadows in her hazel eyes. "But I have a better idea than going to my apartment."

Tugging him, she guided him toward the corridor, deeper down the hall, past the staircase leading to the second floor. Curious, he followed, his eyes gravitating to the sway of her hips, the swish of her ponytail, as she walked.

She unlocked and opened a door leading outside the log cabin. Turning, she clasped both his hands and pulled him out onto a huge deck overlooking... *Holy crap*.

The winding wood stairway with icicles led down to a bubbling pond of steaming waters. She'd told him the survival school sported a hot springs area, but he hadn't envisioned anything like this. A privacy fence wrapped around, stopping at the slope of a mountain wall with a waterfall trickling down over two tiers of rock slab.

Sunny peeled off her sweater and tossed it over her shoulder onto the deck. Her nipples went tight against her thin undershirt.

His jaw damn near fell there as well. "What are you doing?"

"Going skinny-dipping." She tugged off one red high-top, then the other.

He eyed the mounds of snow around the edges. "You're going to freeze to death before you make it into the water."

"Not a chance." She smiled at him with bold wickedness, the wind whipping her hair around her face. "Don't tell me you've lived in Alaska all this time and you've never hung out in a hot tub naked to watch the northern lights?"

His gaze slid from *nature's* hot tub to Sunny.

Best of all, the place was completely deserted. "Is that what we're going to do? Watch a cosmic laser show?"

"Afterward, perhaps."

"After what, exactly?" He stepped closer, closer still, until her hair brushed his chest. "I need to hear you spell it out."

"Take your clothes off and join me. I'll fill your ears

full of exactly what I want." She backed away, crooking
her finger and making it clear that she had more in mind
than lazing around. "It's the least I can do for the man
who saved my life today."

Just like that, his body remembered the intense
adrenaline surge that had accompanied that moment, the
fear and fierceness that had charged through him after
seeing her broken snowmobile in pieces at the bottom
of the cliff.

Hunger for her, for this moment to celebrate surviv-
ing the day, had him reaching for her.

She made fast work of the buttons down his camo
uniform and flung the top over the railing. "Take off
your T-shirt."

"You first." He tugged her undershirt over her head,
leaving her bared to the frigid air with only her purple
jeans and red bra. Her nipples beaded in the cold.

"You're such a guy." She yanked his T-shirt over
his head, careful of his shoulder. "Has anyone checked
your shoulder since you tangled with my dog and the
car earlier?"

"I'm a medic. I can look after of myself."

"You can't treat yourself or your family. I do have
some training in basic first aid—comes in handy on
survival treks." Staring down the icy steps, she flung
aside her bra, goose bumps raising on her flesh. "And
the sulfur in volcanic springs carries healing, *revitalizing* qualities."

Her eyes as steamy as the waters, she shimmied out
of her jeans and waded in, magnificently naked.

—◆—

Misty sat on her bed in her bathrobe, towel-drying her hair. She'd never expected to be back in this familiar shabby-chic room she'd decorated with her mother and sister, painting all the reclaimed furniture white. They'd worked together on patchwork curtains and a quilt made from outgrown clothes. Rag rugs lay on the floor to warm her feet in the morning.

Tonight should have ended so differently. She should have been back in civilization, meeting up with Ted and Madison, her heart breaking over saying good-bye to Flynn while trying to convince herself that Brett was really "the one."

But Ted and Madison were dead. Many more were gone as well. She'd dreamed of leaving here for so long, and now she could only mourn how the place would never be the same. She didn't even know what to think of her brother and Astrid disappearing. At least her little nephew was settled downstairs with his grandparents, who'd insisted on helping and staying here so he could sleep in his own bed.

She tossed aside the towel and reached for the comb beside her bed.

A cold rush of air blasted over her. She straightened, her stomach lurching with fear. The air smelled of outside, of an open window.

She started to scream just as the patchwork curtains flapped and Flynn's big head poked through. He pressed a finger to his lips. Just like all the times he'd climbed through her window during high school. She closed her mouth, her stomach flipping with a wholly different sensation that had nothing to do with fear and everything to do with anticipation.

Flynn swung his legs through and stood in her room, his head almost touching the sloped ceiling. "I'm not here to push you. I just needed to see you, to reassure myself that you're okay, and the stuffy old watchdogs downstairs insisted you need your sleep."

Her skin tingled with heated awareness under her robe. Her naked skin. She should tell him to leave.

But she didn't.

"Well, close the window before we both freeze to death." She swung her legs off the bed, waiting to take her cue from whatever he said next.

He shut the window and draped his parka over a bentwood rocking chair, then turned away abruptly to toss another log in the wood-burning stove, seeming hesitant. How strange to see him unsure, when his body and presence filled her room so vibrantly.

Abruptly, he dropped to his knees in front of her so they were eye to eye. He searched her face, his throat moving with a slow swallow.

His eyes glazing with unshed tears?

"Flynn?"

His chest pumped, his breathing ragged. "Everything's gone so crazy, all those people dead. And it could have been you. If that deputy hadn't died, if Sunny hadn't come back in time"—his eyes squeezed shut tight as if to hold the tears, the emotion, inside himself—"it could have been you."

True to his word to keep his hands to himself, his fists stayed plastered against his sides. The pain on his face was so real, so intense, it took her breath away. She thumbed a lone tear escaping from the corner of one eye. His weather-toughened skin felt so familiar, so dear.

She cupped his cheek. "Why did you sleep with June four years ago?"

"I honest to God don't know."

"That's bullshit." Her hand fell away.

He opened his eyes, finally meeting her gaze dead on. "I was scared."

"Bullshit."

A wry smile tucked dimples into his cheeks. "God, I've missed you."

"You have a funny way of showing it." Her pride still stung over his silence. Sure, he'd made an effort at first, but before that first year was out, he'd given up. People who loved each other never gave up, they never stopped fighting for the people they cared about, even going to the ends of the earth. Her parents had taught her that.

"I was an eighteen-year-old idiot. I heard you and your sister discussing what kind of wedding you would like to have, and I freaked out. I self-destructed. And I would do anything to change that day, anything. I knew it was a mistake the second after—"

She held up a hand. "I do not want to hear about your postcoital thoughts. Although it sounds to me like the sex sucked, and for that I am so, so glad."

His mouth went wide with laughter and her heart ached all over again that she would never hear the sound. She placed her hand on his chest to feel the vibrations. He stopped.

"Please, don't quit," she said quickly. "I miss the sound of laughter more than anything. I miss your laughter."

She signed, *"I miss you."* The same words he'd used back at the bed-and-breakfast.

He signed back, *"I am so very sorry. There is no one*

for me but you. If that means I live the rest of my life alone, then that's the way it will be."

This time, she believed him.

Her fingers crawled from his chest, up the strong column of his throat, and over his stubborn square jaw to his lips. She traced the chapped outline, remembered the feel of him nibbling along her bare skin. He'd been intent on learning what she liked, both of them so inexperienced.

So very hot for each other.

Carefully, hesitantly, he lowered his head and kissed her. He sealed his mouth to hers, fully. Her sigh slipped into him, his into her.

Without hesitation, she slid her arms around him, holding tight. His body was broader and harder than the teenage boy he'd been when they were together. The warmed flannel of his shirt was soft against her fingertips, the scent of him and the crisp air filling her senses. Muscles bulged beneath her touch in sleek definition from a combination of hours spent in the gym during the winter months and exertion outdoors.

Her need for him turned frantic until she could almost swear she heard it buzzing in her ears. She fumbled with the buttons, finally giving up on finesse and yanking his flannel shirt off his shoulders. Buttons popped and fell to the floor. She grasped for his jeans fly. He covered her hands and whispered something against her mouth.

She angled back, looking at him inquisitively.

"Are you sure?" he repeated.

"I have never been more certain of anything." She tossed aside the flannel and stared at his bared chest.

The washboard lines of his stomach contracted from

the caress of her eyes, his jeans open at the zipper and revealing a trail of hair. Her breath hitched in her throat, her limbs turning liquid with desire. She shrugged her robe from her shoulders, savoring the glide of the chenille along her skin, anticipating the feel of his touch.

His pupils widened with appreciation, never leaving her body as he tugged off his boots and shucked his jeans. Moonlight streaked across his body, casting shadows over every well-defined sinew. Her eyes dropped farther and her pulse quickened.

The length of him hard and standing upright against his stomach was so much more than she remembered. Before, she'd reveled in making him groan with the touch of her hand, her mouth. He'd returned the sensations to her tenfold. They'd fooled themselves into thinking they were holding back, but she'd shown him every inch of her body. Given him pleasure, taken pleasure, made herself vulnerable to him in sensual ways she'd never let any other man have.

Standing, she let the robe fall away from her body. His hands shook as he touched her, carefully, reverently, cupping her breasts. He stepped closer, the rasp of hair along his legs a sweet abrasion against her thighs.

And then he lowered her to the bed, his hands moving over her with a familiarity that spoke of how deeply ingrained their time together still was in his mind. He knew just where to touch to make her knees go weak, exactly where to kiss, lick, nip to make her thrash restlessly against the sheets, aching for release.

Her hands carried the memory of him just as firmly. Those recollections were burned in her mind, guiding her touch over him, around him, stroking until a slick creamy bead sliding over her fingers told her just how close he was to the edge as well.

His chest vibrated with what she knew must be a growl and he drew himself away from her. The brush of air across her overheated flesh made her whimper.

Until he nuzzled one breast, then the other, on his way lower, lower still. Her head pressed back into the pillow. She almost surrendered to the pleasure she knew was a simple flick of his tongue away.

Quickly, urgently, she grabbed his shoulders, pushing him off. He looked up at her, confusion staining his blue eyes.

"Everything," she said. "I want it all this time."

His face flooded with understanding a second before he crawled back up her body. She'd waited four years for the fulfillment she hadn't received all those nights he'd sneaked through her bedroom window. She wasn't waiting a second longer.

The weight of him was so dear and familiar she ached in corners of her heart she hadn't dared acknowledge for years. Inching her legs apart, she made room for him, her hands roving his arms and shoulders, soaking up the feel of him.

He kissed her jaw toward her ear, whispering sweet words that she felt in the movement of his lips and the warmth of his breath on her skin. The words didn't matter. He knew how he'd wanted this moment as much as she had.

Lifting his head, he pushed inside her, slowly, his eyes fixed on hers until he met the thin barrier of resistance. His eyes went wide with surprise that she didn't want to deal with right now. She arched up to kiss him

and wrapped her thighs around him, pushing, straining… A stinging burn throbbed through her as he broke
past, filling her, stretching her.

She buried her face in his shoulder while he waited,
holding her, stroking her with his hands and his mouth.
His chest vibrated against hers and she knew he spoke,
but his face was in her hair.

Dampness sealed her cheek to his and she knew the
tears weren't only hers. Her own had nothing to do with
pain and everything to do with the emotion welling inside her.

His hand in hers spelled over and over, *"I love you.
I love you."*

And he kept repeating the words in her palm as he
moved inside her, thrusting, determination stamped
on his face that he wasn't leaving her behind. And she
trusted him, with her heart and with her body. This was
the Flynn she'd known before, but stronger, more ma-
ture, the man she'd dreamed he would become.

Bliss swelled inside her, tingling and spreading until
even the roots of her hair shimmered with the impending…
Release.

Her arms flung wide, her fingers twisting in the
sheets as ripple after ripple crashed over her. Flynn covered her mouth with his and she realized she must have
been moaning with the power of the orgasm slamming
through her.

Or maybe he was covering his own shout of completion. His muscles bunched against her. His skin dark-
ened with the flush of desire culminating. Just seeing
him launched a fresh wave over her until her body lay
spent and his arms gave way. He collapsed on top of

her, his weight a welcome blanket grounding her to earth again.

His forehead rested on hers, his mouth so close she could read most of what he said, enough to understand the gist. "I love you."

"You told me." She cradled his face in her hands the way she still cradled his body inside hers.

"I want to be sure you believe me." He slid beside her, stroking her hair from her brow. "If I could go back in time."

"We can't go back. But we can start from here. A day at a time being honest with each other."

"Okay, then, I'll take that." Relief shuddered through him as he kissed her once, twice, again, punctuating his words. "God, I'll take that. Because it's more than I expected to ever have and more than I deserve. If you really can give this a day at a time, then I will work my ass off each and every one of those days, earning your trust back."

He tucked her closer to him, his chin resting on top of her head. His rapid breathing slowed, evened out until a slight snore ruffled her still-damp hair.

Holding him to her, holding on to the moment, she waited a little longer to be sure he slept deeply. Because she had one last loose end to tie up before she committed to him fully. She needed to send Brett an email to tell him she was sorry, but she had made a mistake. She couldn't meet him and she didn't love him.

Her heart still belonged fully and irrevocably to Flynn Everett.

Chapter 16

HOT SPRINGS BUBBLING AROUND HER, SUNNY STRADDLED Wade's lap as he sat on a submerged rock step. Only their shoulders and faces peeked above the lapping water. The springs refilled from the geyser in the middle, heated naturally from the mountain's volcanic core.

The ultimate place to make love.

Aftershocks from her release pulsed through her, steam wafting upward with a slight tinge of healing sulfur. She let the essence of it sink into her pores as she gave over control to pure, undiluted sensation. Sulfur was necessary for all living cells and she could swear she felt those revitalizing qualities now.

Her limbs went boneless and she almost melted against Wade, but remembered his injured shoulder at the last second. She flung her head back and let the tide tug her. She floated toward the geyser in the pool's center, her body barely submerged. Warm bubbles caressed her back while cool air sketched across her front. The swirling water played peekaboo, revealing patches of her skin.

Above her, northern lights painted the sky with green streaks and bursts of red. God, she never got tired of watching the aurora borealis, named after the Roman goddess of the dawn, Aurora, and Boreas, the Greek god of the north wind. This place was the closest thing to paradise that she could imagine.

The fact that she had a business here that also kept

her fed was just an added bonus. She eyed the outdoor haven with pride, the planked fence her brother had helped her build, the small dressing corner stocked with dry, warm towels and robes.

She chased thoughts of her brother from her mind. Not ready to go there yet in any way.

Being with Wade offered a temporary escape from the fast-encroaching reality. Here in her fenced Alaskan oasis, she had a stolen pocket of time before her town self-destructed when everyone woke up and news of the murders spread.

The water swirled faster around her, giving her a second's warning that Wade approached.

"This is not what I expected." He stopped beside her.

Underwater, his fingers stroked her spine, caressing with the bubbles until she almost couldn't separate his touch from the rippling rush. He moved down her back, over her bottom, and along the outsides of her legs.

She sighed with pleasure. "This is probably my favorite place in the whole world. Now I have all the more reason to love it."

A whisper of worry trickled through her brain like melting water down an icicle. What would happen to her little business, to her haven, to her way of life? It wasn't as if she could just put a survival school based in a log cabin on the market and folks would come streaming in with big-money offers.

Her feet started to sink and his hands closed around her toes, his thumbs massaging the arches. His artful touch chased away concerns and her eyes slid closed. The feel of his hands on her flesh sent a rush of aurora borealis behind her lids.

"Keep talking," he said, moving up her body again, between her legs.

Her throat closed up and she worked to push words past. "When I was a teenager, I dreamed of building a place around this spring."

"Why is that?" He massaged her thighs, higher inch by inch.

"I, uh, missed our gym back in Iowa, and it seemed like having at least a small workout space here would be the perfect way to stay in shape and burn off energy during those dark winter months." Right now, she was burning off more than energy. Her whole body was on fire from the subtle pleasure of his caress up her thighs.

"Talk," he commanded, "or I stop."

She flicked water on him, while clamping her legs around his waist. "You're not going anywhere."

Laughter rumbling, he moved closer, his thumbs at the juncture of her thighs, then…

He pressed against the oversensitive bundle of nerves that already ached for him all over again.

"Wade?"

"Let go, just float. I have you."

And he did. Her arms splayed out and she felt the waters tug her hair out into a fan around her. Her breasts peeked from the water, her nipples pulling painfully tight from the cold and desire. She tried to speak, but words wouldn't come.

Increasing the pressure ever so precisely, his fingers circled, plucked, teased. "All this heat with no electric bill." He stroked along her cleft, already moist from increasing arousal. "As long as the thing doesn't erupt underneath us."

She laughed softly, then gasped as his mouth closed over her, lapping, laving, until the aurora borealis wasn't just behind her eyes, it was exploding inside her. Wade braced her back and urged her farther, higher, milking every last sensation from her completion. Finally, seconds—minutes, hours, she lost track of time—later, her legs slid down him and she slowly righted again.

Looping her arms around his neck, she sagged against his chest and let him hold her, support her weight, as her legs probably wouldn't work yet anyway. "I think… I'm having… a heart attack."

"And living so deep on a mountain? That would make access to a major medical facility tough." He grazed her cheek with a kiss. "Lucky for you I'm proficient in CPR."

His words chilled her from the inside as she thought of her sister and wondered not for the first time if things could have been different for her if she'd gotten sick somewhere else. How could Wade help but think of his mother, cut off from help? No ambulance and ER right around the corner to care for her horrific injuries.

Sunny eased from him, her toes touching rocks along the bottom until she was grounded again, the fantasy dimming. She struggled to think of a way to get it back, her eyes lingering on her lover. Moonlight glinted off his short dark hair, slick with a mix of water and hints of ice, while his chest was flushed from the heated water and great sex. She knew his body so well in some ways, and in others not as much.

Desperate to chase away negative thoughts that threatened to steal this fantasy moment from her, she stroked his shoulder blade. "You have green footprints tattooed here." A strange color that seemed as out of place on his skin as the lights misting overhead. "What's the reason behind it? Because if it's a bar story, I'm betting it's a good one."

Laughing, he kissed the inside of her elbow, their legs brushing underwater. "It's a pararescue thing. Most of us have them somewhere on our body. It dates back to the Vietnam War, when the H-3 Sea King was the helicopter used most often to drop PJs in and pull us back out. The chopper was big and green—thus its nickname, the Jolly Green Giant. PJs started getting green footprint tattoos."

Her fingertips sketched along the rougher patches of inked flesh, her nerves still on heightened alert from the power of her orgasm... orgasms actually, as he'd brought her to completion three times since they'd entered the pool. "Any other tattoos I should know about ahead of time?"

"That's it. But you're welcome to look again." He kissed up her arm. "And again."

He pulled her closer until she pressed flush against him. The gush of water from the geyser echoed her speeding pulse in her ears. Her nipples skimmed his chest, his swirls of hair a gentle abrasion. She was definitely too spent to have sex again so soon, and even if she weren't she knew he was talking about the future. Which wasn't unreasonable, given the tenuous connection forming in spite of roadblock after roadblock.

He tucked her hair behind her ear, the longer ends floating out around her. "What am I going to do with you, Sunny Foster?"

"Could we just have sex twenty-four/seven?" she

whispered against his mouth. "Seems like we communicate best that way."

He nipped her bottom lip. "Believe me, I would if I could."

"You mean you're not a superhero?" She stared at him in mock surprise.

He scrubbed a hand over his face, not meeting her eyes.

Her hands grazed down his back until she cupped his tight, amazing butt. "No comeback, for once? That's a shocker."

He shrugged. "I don't really know how to joke about it. I've spent a lot of my life training for this."

"How long? Spell it out," she asked, hungry for everything she could learn about him. They had so little time left together, with his impending deployment, her own uncertainty about her future. "I can't know what you don't tell me."

"PJs spend nearly two years training overall. Indoctrination course at Lackland Air Force Base in Texas, then on to Airborne School at Fort Benning. Combat Divers School next." He paused. "Are you bored yet?"

"I'm impressed. Please continue. I wouldn't have asked if I didn't want to know."

"Okay, since you asked… Then Navy Underwater Egress Training at Pensacola Naval Air Station. Survival school up in Washington." He shivered melodramatically. "Freefall Parachutist School after that."

Now she was more than impressed, she was awed. "What else could be left to learn?"

"Special Ops Combat Medic Course, then our PJ

Recovery Specialist Course, finishing up at Kirtland Air Force Base in New Mexico."

"I knew PJs were a highly specialized group... but, wow, I didn't have a clue." She sifted through it all. So much training, so many places. "How do couples manage to stay together during all that time apart?"

He angled his head back, his cocoa-brown eyes meeting hers somberly. "If a couple can't handle the training, they aren't going to be able to handle the stress and separations of military life. Our divorce rates are high."

Her breath hitched in her chest at the shift in the conversation, the seriousness. The possibility behind the warning. "Are you proposing or warning me off?"

"I'm just telling you the facts so you have all the information."

A nonanswer if she'd ever heard one. She wasn't sure why she felt the need to push for more, but she couldn't stop herself from saying, "Your parents stayed together, in spite of everything life has thrown their way."

He stared up toward the northern lights, his eyes taking on a distant look. "Maybe I should bring my mother to one of the other, more accessible hot springs in Alaska, let her experience the hot springs, the healing waters." He glanced back down at her with a half-embarrassed grin. "I suffer no delusions that it'll fix everything for her, but at least I could give her something."

"That's a lovely thought." She cupped his neck, stroking along the shaved hairs at his nape, bristly crisp with freezing water. How ironic that she'd brought him out here for the soothing power of the healing waters without realizing how it might touch a deeper hurt than a couple of stitches in his shoulder.

His shoulder.

Just that fast, the levity evaporated faster than the steam dispersed by the cold Alaska air. How could she have forgotten even for a second that just earlier that week, Deputy Smith had shot wildly at them, trying to crush them with an avalanche?

Something tugged at the back of her brain, some detail, some sense that she was missing something. She searched though everything that had been said—tougher and tougher to do with Wade's hands making tantalizing forays over her breasts, his thigh working gentle, arousing pressure between her legs.

Her body warmed from the inside out, coming back to life as it always did with Wade, and she struggled to follow the elusive whisper of logic *tap, tap, tapping*. God, following it was as futile as kicking through an ice wall with bare feet. She needed serious firepower to let loose the avalanche.

She slid off Wade's leg and nearly slipped under the surface. Spluttering water, she resurfaced.

Wade braced her with his hands clamped to her waist. "What's wrong?"

"All this time we've been wondering if Deputy Smith was a serial killer who acted alone."

"Um, right, but what made you start thinking about that, right now?"

"Your injury reminded me of that day, when Deputy Smith was waiting for us, to shoot us."

"I remember it too damn well." His grip tightened around her.

"Serial killers have an MO, right? All the old cop shows stress that."

"Because it's true."

"So if Deputy Smith killed all those other people with a knife because he was a serial killer, doesn't it make sense that he would follow that same pattern in trying to take us down?"

Wade went still. Very still. The gush of water filled the silence between them as she could all but see the wheels turning in his mind.

Sunny continued. "Maybe he was just desperate, but it's worth considering alternatives to the serial killer scenario. According to every true-crime show I've watched, serial killers have their rules, their patterns— a particular method. They have to stick to the ritual to get the thrill. Rand Smith killed my friends by slashing their throats. If he's a serial killer, it stands to reason he would have used the knife on us instead of the gun. We have to seriously consider the possibility that he's an assassin, hired by someone higher up the chain."

Wade cursed low under his breath, his face hardening back into warrior mode. Her tender lover had faded away.

A noise cut the night, a door opening. He tensed, tucking her to his chest before she could say so much as "I can take care of myself." Although given that they were both naked, outside in Alaska, that made them both plenty vulnerable.

She looked to the entrance leading back inside. The brown door opened wide, the two figures backlit, faces indistinguishable.

They stepped forward as one, a man and a woman. The female eased forward and Misty's face came into focus. Sunny sagged with relief. Her sister stood with Flynn Everett, who apparently hadn't gone home for the night after all. Wade's uniform and Sunny's clothes littered the ground around their feet.

Now that the initial freaked-out fear had gone, awkwardness crept over her. She was in the middle of the hot springs, naked with a guy.

"Um, would you mind turning your backs for a second so we can get some towels and our clothes?"

"Of course," Misty said quickly, spinning around and pushing at Flynn's shoulders for him to follow. "Could you hurry? It's really important."

"Right…" She half swam, half walked across the small pondlike springs until she reached the steps, feeling Wade's bulk behind her.

She snagged a towel and robe, tossing one to Wade. Yanking the terrycloth over her body and half dancing to keep her toes from freezing on the deck, she allowed herself a quick glance at him. He pitched aside the robe in favor of yanking on his camo pants. So quickly his body had become familiar to her, from his taut butt to the green footprint tattoos walking up his shoulder. With the world unraveling around her, he was fast becoming her one constant.

As she rushed to follow her sister and Flynn inside, she saw Wade shrugging into the rest of his uniform, damp splotches mottling the camo pattern from where the fabric had rested on the icy deck. It was almost as if his body was immune to the cold.

The thick wood door eased closed, sealing the four of them in the dimly lit corridor. She started to suggest they go upstairs to her apartment, but Misty grabbed her by the arm.

"I got an email tonight from a woman named Andrea

Livingston. She forwarded documents and correspondence that suggest her husband plans to blow up a power plant. And he's doing so with the help of someone here."

Wade stepped forward, his face set. "Time to wake up Flynn's father and use his satellite phone again."

"Right," Flynn said. "He'll need to know the latest development anyway."

"Wait, Wade." Sunny clasped his arm, his muscles tensed under her grip. "Who are you calling? The police? Shouldn't we hear more about the emails to make sure we don't go off in the wrong direction?"

"I've done this your way since we started up the mountain. I've respected your boundaries, your way of doing things, your concerns for your family. Now it's become bigger than us. Bigger than your family. It's time to do this my way. It's time to set off my emergency beacon so my people can locate us. We need to call in the reinforcements."

<center>~~~</center>

The kitchen wall clock showed four in the morning.

Brett paced his way across the tile floor in the sleeping house. He couldn't risk going into the bedroom since Andrea might wake up and note what time he'd come in. The sitter slept like a log and didn't know yet that Andrea intended to fire her, so that wasn't a problem. The sitter only woke up for the alarm connected to an emergency button in Andrea's room and one on her chair.

He would stretch out on the sofa in the office. He would simply tell his wife he'd been at the plant late and didn't want to wake her once he got home, pretty much the truth. A dim glow lit the hall. Every room had night-lights rechargeable by the sun, so no matter what time of day, even in a blackout, Andrea would be able to find her way around the house.

Soon, he would be able to offer her so much more without worrying about the IRS questioning where all his extra capital had come from.

Pushing the office door open very slowly to avoid creaking hinges… he stopped short. Andrea sat at the computer. Awake. Her hair draped in a long red ponytail over one shoulder, a splash of color across her green silk pajamas. She was like a living, breathing aurora borealis for him.

But she was also a creature of habit in some things, like always turning in early. So why wait up for him tonight?

Was she still hung up on the suspicion that he was cheating? He didn't much care for having his itinerary checked, but he couldn't afford to cause any ripples now. She would understand more—if not all—soon enough. At least he'd erased all the old correspondence and anything to do with Misty. He would have just bought a whole new computer but he was afraid that would arouse more suspicions.

He tossed his coat on the sofa, one she'd re-covered in fabric bought on safari. "I had to work late. You shouldn't have waited up, although now that I see you, I'm glad you did."

"Oh, really," she said simply, keeping her back to him.

Her mood had been tough to gauge all day when he'd called, working at being an attentive husband.

Stopping beside her, he swiped aside her red hair to kiss his favorite spot on her neck. "Hello, beautiful."

She reached back, her wrist grazing his cheek, as she always did, even if she didn't answer. So close. They were so close to leaving this godforsaken patch of earth. So close to living a rich, full life together again.

His eyes opened... and he caught a glimpse of the computer screen. Of an email that began "Dear Misty..."

What the hell?

He straightened slowly as Andrea shifted aside, giving him a clear view. Damn it, he'd erased everything to and from Misty. He was certain. But as he scanned farther, he realized the note wasn't from him.

The post had been written by Andrea.

> You need to know that Brett isn't who he says he is.
> I hope to God he hasn't involved you in his dealings
> because if he has, there's nothing I can do for you.
> But you need to know someone in your community
> is helping him blow up a power plant...

He stopped reading abruptly. Stunned. Appalled. Scared.

He couldn't possibly be seeing what he thought. How had she found out? And he prayed to God she hadn't sent it yet.

"Andrea, what the hell have you done?"

"I should be asking you that, my love." Finally, she glanced back over her shoulder, steely fury glinting in her emerald green eyes. "But I'm afraid I already know."

His gut dropped harder than a ride in a g-force elevator.

"I thought we already cleared up this matter about the emails. Nothing is what you think." He was scrambling for possible explanations. And he had to think fast or she would sense the lie. "Okay, I'm not supposed to tell you this, but I've been working with local authorities to uncover a plot at the plant." His story was gaining speed in his mind. "The woman—Misty—is part of an ecoterrorist group that has been trying to blow up the place."

That sounded good, plausible. Maybe he could pull this off. He watched every nuance of her face as she searched his, waiting for her verdict, already prepping his next words.

She shoved his shoulder weakly, but oh so effectively. Her rejection of him and his story was clear in her upper lip, curled in disgust. "How could you so underestimate me? The accident took away the use of my legs but it didn't damage by mind. I know you so very well and I knew you were lying. And you should know I'm not the type of woman to let her man steamroll right over her."

A deeper fear took root. She really had figured out his plan, or part of it anyway. His perfect plan that could actually be coming apart. But then his mind hitched on something she'd said.

She'd called him her man. That was good.

He could salvage this. "I don't know what you think you've figured out, but there are layers to this you don't understand yet—"

"I don't 'think' I've figured out anything. I know," she hissed, speaking low enough that her aide wouldn't overhear. "I hacked your work computers. Once it became apparent every word out of your mouth has been a lie for the last year. Maybe longer. And now I know enough to put you in jail for the rest of your life."

Her voice cracked for the first time. Her pain stabbed clean through him. A fissure opened wide and kept cracking, his world coming apart of the seams. He dropped to his knees in front of her, desperate to make her understand.

"I love you, Andrea. Anything I've done I did for you, to get you the best doctors, the most cutting-edge new treatments. I want to take you to Europe." He rested his hands on her useless legs, which had once climbed mountains and tackled ski slopes with ease. "Even if you never walk again—and I'm praying you do—with the money I've made, we can go back to the way things used to be. We can still travel the world, still have adventures."

Her face creased with… pity? "You may have fooled yourself that you did this for me, Brett, but you did it for yourself. So you don't have to give up the 'adventures' now that I can no longer go with you."

After all he'd done, all he'd given up for her, this accusation cut the deepest.

"God, Andrea, don't say that. Do I want you out of that wheelchair? Of course. Do I wish that awful, awful accident had never happened? Every second of every day. But you have to know that I love you."

"And I love you for what we once shared," she answered without hesitation. "But I can't live with someone who would plan something like this, somebody who would risk so many lives. I can't spend the rest of my life knowing what you've done and living off the money you made from the pain, the suffering, the blood of others. And if you knew me at all, you would realize that."

She was serious. Dead serious.

However much she'd learned of his plans beyond the power plant, she'd figured out enough to put him in jail. She knew enough to connect him to murders. His pulse nearly pounded out through his eyes. Frustration roared through him, rage, years' worth. He'd been able to survive this frozen-in-time existence because he had a plan to get himself and Andrea out. He wouldn't be stuck forever working in a fucking cubicle, told to be grateful because he had a tiny-ass window and two real walls to tack up a picture and some antlers.

Trapped. He felt completely trapped like an animal. He was even panting like a dog. He was losing Andrea. He was losing Europe.

"Andrea"—his voice came out a hoarse croak— "after all I've done for you, for our future, you're going to spit on my devotion to you?"

"Oh God, Brett. You just don't get it. *Because* I love you, I've arranged it so you have a four-hour window to leave ahead of the police."

Four hours? It wasn't much, but maybe he could still pull this off. He sagged with relief. "Then it's not too late for us to—"

"Oh, no, it's too late to stop the notifications I've sent out to more than one person. I wanted to make damn sure the truth got out. I wasn't risking the possibility that you may have someone on your payroll that I haven't uncovered yet." She touched his hand, her face pulling tight with the first signs of real regret, even tears. "If you turn yourself in to the police, I will stay by your side, without fail. I will support you through the trial, through jail time, and if, Lord willing, you should ever see daylight again, I will be here waiting for you. If you make this right."

Nothing would ever be right again. He couldn't even bring himself to speak. He just stared at his wife, absorbing the beauty of her fine features, her ivory complexion, because he would never see her again.

"But if you walk out that door, Brett, if you run, you and I are finished. I will not follow you. And if you are captured, I will not so much as lay eyes on you again."

He knew without a doubt that she meant every word.

His heart was cleaved in half. She'd offered him two impossible options. Lose her or go to prison. Hell on earth either way. His grief turned to fury over her putting him in this position. Really no choice at all.

He would have to leave. Gamble everything on saving his ass and making it out of the country with what he'd saved. Gamble that maybe time would soothe Andrea's fury. Because no matter what she said, a strong woman like that would never want a man behind bars. How would she respect him?

Four hours? Once he picked up his stash of cash and thumb drives of data tucked away at the power plant, he would be on a private aircraft out of here in three.

The *whap, whap, whap* of helicopter blades in the distance cut the night.

Standing in the middle of Main Street with the rest of the community, Wade tipped his ear to the wind and listened to the approaching chopper. Yes, an MH-60, just as he expected. And making good time. Less than two hours had passed since Misty and Flynn had rushed out to the hot springs retreat.

Any thoughts of romance and winning Sunny over with tantric sex had been put on hold. Thanks to the senior Everett's satellite phone, Wade had been able to make contact with his base directly, speaking with both McCabe and their OSI contact who'd first questioned Sunny. Then Misty had forwarded all emails to a secure address via a secure cell phone link provided by the OSI.

The pieces had slid together quickly and neatly.

They were now racing against time to stop an attack on a major power plant on the Alaska Peninsula. Some group in this community was involved in making a statement in a very dangerous manner. Local police had been alerted and a military helicopter would transport them for on-site questioning.

A piercing light from above split through the dark. A searchlight from the approaching helicopter strobed over the crowd of people, some still wearing their pajamas under parkas. The helicopter banked toward the open patch of ground, a park beside the frozen river.

Sunny shivered in spite of the layers of clothes she wore now. She'd twisted her damp hair up in a knot and covered it with her hood, insisting she didn't want to waste even a second—or be left behind while they made the call.

He slid his arm around her shoulders. "Hang tough. Help is on the way."

"It's not that. I know we'll have the best of the best protection. I understand this is what needs to happen." She crossed her arms tightly over her chest as the chopper settled into a hover. "I just feel like I'm in the middle of that old movie about aliens, the one called something like *Close Encounters*. There's a big scene where the spaceship from another world comes in and everyone is staring up, gawking."

The roar and wind of the choppers beating blades cut

the air louder, louder still, until Wade had to duck his head to her ear in order to be heard.

"Aliens are not going to take over your town." He held her closer. "This is about keeping people alive and stopping an attack on a major facility."

"I know this is bigger than my worries about a changing way of life. I just can't believe I'm in the middle of such a horrible crime." She shielded her eyes against the searchlight. "I just want life to be good old boring and normal again."

The military chopper descended, the rotor wash of air stirring a ministorm. Snow swept outward, flakes and flecks of ice biting into his skin.

As Sunny grew paler beside him, he thought it was probably best not to tell her. For him, this *was* normal.

Chapter 17

SUNNY FELT AS IF SHE WERE IN THE MIDDLE OF AN OLD war film.

Strapped into the cavernous hold of the helicopter, she wore a helmet plugged into the central intercom system. At least three different conversations buzzed through. The pilots went back and forth about air speeds and headings. Something called "command post" added in weather and cautions. And then there were the people in back periodically piping in with everything else, yammering up the air waves. Roaring helicopter engines capped off the whole cacophony.

Like in the movies, all the big guns to save the day were geared up and ready for action. She felt… superfluous. She couldn't stand the sense of helplessness. She wasn't that kind of person. She needed to be able to do something. She had to contribute, to help put a stop to the horrible thing that had been planned right under her very nose for God only knew how long.

Her head was already spinning after how quickly things had happened—the helicopter landing, loading up her, Wade, Misty, and Flynn. Apparently people in her community, people she'd known and trusted, wanted to blow up a power plant and were hours away from making that happen.

She looked around at the packed webbed seats and recognized Wade's PJ team from the mountain rescue when

Deputy Smith had tried to mow them down. And the agent from the air force's OSI who'd questioned her was at work with some handheld device, scrolling and typing. She struggled for his name... *Special Agent Lasky*.

Bracing against the inevitable chill, she reminded herself he was one of the guys in white hats now. Could her brother possibly be involved in something this horrific? Would the OSI—would Wade—even believe her when she told them she truly had no idea where Phoenix and Astrid may have gone?

Wade leaned into her line of sight as if sensing her fears. His mouth moved as he spoke, but she couldn't make out what he said.

She felt like her sister right after she'd lost her hearing, first trying to read lips. "I can't understand you with all these voices in the headset."

"Here then. I'll swap to interphone, just us back here." A click cleared away the voices of the pilots and the tower until only Wade remained. "Is that better?"

"Much. Thanks." The silence felt exaggerated after the bombardment of so much noise. She looked around at the other passengers again and they all still seemed oblivious. Catnapping. Reading. Just hanging out, and in no way showing the magnitude of what waited for them once they landed.

"What do you need?" Wade asked.

"Isn't there something I can do? Talk to the agent over there? Tell him more about the possible players? There has to be something."

Wade rested his broad hand on her knee and squeezed lightly. "We've got it from here. I just want to see you and your sister safely settled."

Safely settled? "I thought you brought us along because we know the community."

"Flynn can help with that. Things could get really crazy down there if we can't stop the explosion in time. In order to focus, I need to know that you're locked down tight."

Surprise sparked through her. He really intended to shuttle her aside to some quiet little room at the station, or maybe he even planned to plop her in a hotel with a guard, for crying out loud. Anger flushed through her like splashes of red in the northern lights. "Wade, we've worked together for this whole week, helping each other stay a step ahead of whatever's going on."

He squeezed her knee a little tighter. "Sunny—"

She pushed his hand away. "Don't you dare think you can just distract me with a little sweet talk and stirring up my hormones again, Wade Rocha." She cut him short, on a roll and needing to be heard. "I may be from a small rural area and not some badass warrior, but that doesn't mean I'm less capable than you—"

A sneeze cut through the airwaves.

Wade stared back at her. And he hadn't sneezed.

She looked around quickly at a cargo hold of people working very hard not to make eye contact with her. Her gaze finally settled on the quiet, moody PJ, the one they called Bubbles. He had his hand over his mouth, his thumb and forefinger pinching his nose.

Bubbles glanced up slowly, brooding eyes at half-mast. "'Scuse me."

His two clipped words came through her headset loud and clear.

Jerking back toward Wade, she glared accusingly. "I thought this was a private line."

He scratched his jaw. "Private for all of us in the back. I tried to tell you."

"Oh."

The older guy—McCabe—stood abruptly. "Heads up. All ears cue in. Chopper's entering the approach pattern to land. We'll be rolling out right into the parking lot of the power plant. A SWAT team is already on-site. FBI is on their way."

Her gut knotted. All embarrassment evaporated. The helicopter banked left, swooping downward. In a blink of time they'd traveled what would have taken her days to accomplish on her own. Had her brother been gone long enough to make it here? If he was tangled up in such huge and horrible dealings, would he have access to faster modes of transportation now as well?

The chopper steadied into a hover, descent slowing until... *Poof*. The military aircraft settled with smooth precision. They had arrived at the Alaska Peninsula Power Plant.

And when she stepped from the military aircraft, she prayed she wouldn't find her brother waiting.

Binoculars in hand, Wade crouched on the rooftop of the outbuilding skirting the power plant. The sun just peeked along the horizon, sparking off the silver structure humming obliviously about fifty yards away.

The SWAT unit had already sealed the place off, bomb-sniffing dogs scouring every inch of the facility. The FBI had arrived minutes ago and the predictable territorial tussles for control had already started.

At least roof duty kept him out of the fray.

He and his team had spread out on top of various outbuildings to watch for suspicious activity and be on call for emergency medical treatment, if needed. They'd been this route hundreds of times, working training exercises and ops with SWAT and the FBI as standby combat medics.

Sunny, Misty, and Flynn were in a nearby trailer with Special Agent Lasky, studying security footage and suspect photos to see if any faces looked familiar. Hopefully by the time they hooked up again, this would all be over and Sunny's temper would have cooled. Given her brother's probable involvement, she had to be on edge.

It wasn't sitting all that well for him either, and he'd never even met the guy.

Major McCabe shifted from boot to boot as he crouched beside him, joints cracking.

Wind whistling fast and colder up high, Wade shot a quick glance sideways, ice pellets stinging his face. "Knees aching, old man?"

"Always." McCabe tweaked his binoculars, sweeping the side lot while Hugh Franco lay flat on his stomach with a rifle. "I know I'm too damn old to still be jumping out of airplanes, but, well, I'll keep on until the day they haul me off on a litter."

Franco kept his eye lined up on the scope. "If your knees hurt so bad from your ranger days, why didn't you choose something else after OCS, fly a plane or even a desk?"

"I said it hurts," McCabe answered fast. "I never said I could give it up."

Below them, SWAT team members darted around the

building, the front gates sealed closed. The power plant and grounds around it had been evacuated. Beyond the gate, however, the world carried on like normal, blessedly oblivious. At a harbor dock, a small fishing festival was under way. The FBI had decided the event was far enough away from the plant to continue safely, and too large to stop without creating a stampede.

Wade tweaked the focus on a news crew setting up cameras outside the main gate. "Then why aren't you still a ranger? Why bother with the swimming and mountain climbing?"

"I guess that's my story to tell."

"Fair enough." Wade scanned past the grid of scaffolding and wires surrounded by chain link fences. A K-9 cop jogged with his German shepherd toward a side entrance, but not with enough speed to cause alarm. The dog probably smelled the moose sausages and fish roasting at the bayside festival. How odd that just seeing the shaggy canine made him think of Sunny's big mutt. Seemed as if his every thought these days rounded back to her. "Aren't you going to ask me if I care about her?"

"Nope." McCabe just grinned.

"Everyone else did after our public argument over the interphone." He jerked a thumb at Franco. "Starting with this guy here."

Amazing how they'd found time to jab at him while in the middle of ramping up to catch a bomber. But then this was their life. Standard ops.

Wade glanced at McCabe. "At least you know it's none of your business."

"That's not what I meant," he said dryly, without missing a beat on his scan of the bay on the opposite side of the power plant. "I don't need to ask because I've known you a long time. I've seen how low-key you've kept other relationships in the past. Even that babe Kammi, the one you actually dated for three months, didn't get anywhere near this kind of reaction out of you. I can see straight up how far gone you are on Sunny Foster."

The words struck a little too close to the nerve for his peace of mind, especially considering how soon he would ship out. He needed his full concentration for his Afghanistan deployment. He didn't need attachments.

He didn't need to spend every waking minute of every day worrying about what kind of trouble a fearless woman like Sunny was getting into. He didn't need the mind-bending stress of worrying about her stepping on some kind of land mine—

Shit.

His mother was the one who'd stepped on a bomb. Not Sunny. And hello Dr. Freud, it was too creepy that he was mixing them up in his head.

Irritation grated his nerves much like how the ragged ice along the roof jabbed and poked, making him snap back. "What makes you such an expert on love? Last time I checked, you're as bad as Franco, never dating a woman more than a week—long enough for a one-night stand."

Silence settled on the rooftop thicker than a morning fog. McCabe was staring at him with a you're-a-dumb-ass look. Franco still stared through the scope of his rifle. But his knuckles were stark white.

Damn.

Franco had been a serial dater since he'd lost his

wife and kid. Razzing the guy about his relationship history was pretty much taboo, and if he weren't so damn wrapped up in himself he would have remembered that. His pal had been wrecked then and was still half-cracked now.

And Wade was wondering if maybe he understood where Franco was coming from a little better today than he ever had before. With torturous images of his mother being caught in a bomb's blast hammering through his brain, all he could think of was keeping Sunny safe. She needed to take off those Pollyanna rose-colored glasses from her isolated upbringing and stay put, stay safe. Let people like him, like his team, like Agent Lasky, handle bomb-building fanatics.

"Heads up," McCabe called, tapping a finger to his earpiece. "One of the explosives-sniffing dogs have found something."

How did bomb squads manage to do this for a living, day in and day out?

Sunny hooked arms with her sister and watched the power plant in the distance, the metal structure nearly swallowed by morning mist. And watched. And watched with Flynn and Agent Lasky and his team once the bomb had been located. The rest of the plant workers were still behind the fence, about fifty yards farther than where they'd been since the initial evacuation. At least she hadn't been hustled out of there, that much farther away from Wade.

As much as she tried to help, he kept shuttling her behind guards and into a secured room to look at pictures. She wanted to protect herself as much as anyone, but she knew her community. She had valuable profiling insights to offer on every person in that town. They'd all come through her business at one time or another, working out, grabbing a quick muffin, or using the Internet service.

God, she felt so helpless and angry. She hated not being able to help and was so enraged that she hadn't somehow known a person in her community, a person close to her, could be capable of something this horrendous. To think that all of their emails, their primary form of communication with the outside world, had been so horribly manipulated made her ill. How many town members had used her Internet?

A hand clamped around her arm and she damn near jumped out of her skin. Looking up sharply, she bumped her head against... Wade's chin.

She sagged with relief. "Thank God, it's you. You scared the crap out of me, sneaking up like that."

"You need to go," he said abruptly.

The roots of her hair burned with apprehension. She lowered her voice to keep from risking a panic in the crowd. "Have they found a bomb? Is it about to go off? Is that why we were all evacuated so quickly?"

His face tight and closed off, he ducked his head to her ear. "Yes, they've found an explosive device. The bomb squad feels confident they can defuse it, but I don't want you anywhere near here."

"Wade, if this wasn't a safe distance, I believe the authorities would have moved us farther out. I want to be on hand in case they catch whoever's responsible..." Dread closed her throat for a gasp. "Or do they already have someone? Is my brother here? Are you trying to get me away from here so I won't freak out about my brother? Be honest with me."

Her voice rose with panic, but it was all she could do not to grab Wade by the parka and shake some answers from him. She could handle anything, except being kept in the dark.

He clasped her shoulders and guided her away from the eavesdropping crowd. His steady, determined step crunched along the ice until he stopped beside a boat dock tucked by the bay. "You need to calm down and do what I say."

And didn't that just rub her every last independent nerve the wrong way?

She jerked out of his grip. "Excuse me? Are you ordering me back to the kitchen to rustle up some supper while you go save the world? Do you not grasp that I've guided tour groups from our town out of blizzards? Pulled survivors out of avalanches?"

"Is it so damn wrong of me to want you to be safe while I do my job? I can't be in the middle of a mission in Afghanistan wondering if you're back here tangling with ecoterrorists or falling off the side of some mountain."

She resisted the temptation to check for water in her ears because she couldn't possibly be hearing him correctly. Since when were they talking about his deployment? Wasn't this an argument about the here and now?

"Is this a backdoor way of asking me to wait for you while you're overseas?"

"And if it was?"

"I don't think this is the time to talk about that."

"Fine, then I'll make sure one of Lasky's agents

escorts you on the boat over to the lodge where we'll be staying—"

"I am not leaving. Get that through your head. I have a stake in this today."

"You're here to protect your friends."

"I'm here to protect the ones who aren't involved. The home I love is about to have the foundation crumble under it. I can't just drink cocoa by the fire at some lodge and pretend it has no effect on me."

He clammed up with the stone face and stubborn thrust of his jaw that had earned him his Brick call sign.

"I get that you're a superhero, macho guy, but that doesn't mean you can steamroll over me or that you need to protect me." She rested a hand on his chest, hoping he would reach back and meet her halfway. "It may have escaped your notice, but I've done a fine job of taking care of myself this past week."

"Tell that to the snow machine floating around somewhere in pieces," he said starkly.

Her anger lost some steam, her heart softening a little as she remembered how freaked-out he'd been then.

"You saved my butt that time, and I'm grateful. But I've also carried my own weight. I'm not a wilting flower, and I thought that was something you liked about me."

"There's a power plant about to be blown up by some wacko ecoterrorists who lived right under your nose for the whole planning of their crime. Excuse me if I'm not so certain of your objectivity in sifting through the evidence."

His accusation slapped at her as coldly and harshly as the wind rolling in off the bay.

"I can't believe you would say that about me. How can you think I would ever let anyone get away with something like this, even subconsciously?"

"You've been protecting him for fifteen years. Some habits are hard to break."

She wanted to throw up. How could he think that of her after all they'd shared, how close they'd been? Or maybe she'd only imagined the connection on his side. Because it was very clear right now that he wasn't budging.

Still, she had to say her piece. "That's totally different from this. I can love my brother without loving the choices he's made... But I can see that you don't believe me."

"I can't risk it."

Did he believe she might try to alert her brother? Sneak him away from a military op involving enough firepower to blow them all sky-high? She shook her head in disbelief.

Her heart shattered into a thousand pieces at his words, like the final tap on a pristine sheet of ice that fractured it apart, nothing left but deathly cold water beneath.

"That's it for us then. You go do your job, and I'll do my best to stay out of your way. But you do not have the authority to make me leave. As long as Lasky believes I'm a valuable asset, then I'm staying right here."

She backed a step from him, her eyes memorizing the bold, strong lines of his face. Snow flurries fell between them, melting on his hair and sleeves. Her fingers ached to test the stubble along his jaw one last time, to brush the beads of water from his head.

"Good-bye, Wade." She forced herself to turn away fast, before she weakened and changed her mind.

Or before he saw the tears clouding her eyes.

Through the sheen, she saw Flynn in the distance, standing just past the boathouse. At least they could work together to try and make some sense of what had happened in their village. Together with Misty they could try to find the people responsible.

Before she'd made it two steps, Wade clasped her arm. "Stop. We can talk later. But for now you just can't wander off."

What good would talking do? She didn't, couldn't, face him. "I'll stay with Flynn and my sister. We'll stick by Lasky. Now please. Let. Me. Go."

He held her arm so long she thought he might argue. Part of her wanted him to stay and hash this out, reassure her she'd misunderstood somehow. His fingers slid away, releasing her with his own unspoken good-bye.

Her feet moved ahead of her heart, making fast tracks across the deserted frozen lot, needing to put distance between herself and Wade. She searched, anger clouding her mind. Finally, she caught a glimpse of a familiar figure outside the power plant gates. Flynn. He must have taken Misty away to find something to eat at the fishing festival.

She doubled her speed, sidling out a gate, past a guard, racing toward the dock. She glanced back over her shoulder quickly, only to find Wade stalking off into the swirling snow. Collecting his thoughts, maybe? She couldn't blame him.

Approaching Flynn softly so as not to startle him, she called out quietly, "Flynn? Are you okay? Where's Misty? Did you find something good to eat, because I just realized I haven't eaten yet."

He pivoted on his boot heel toward her slowly. The morning sun streamed down over his windburned face, creased in confusion. "Did you need something?"

"I just wondered if you're ready to go back with me to talk to Agent Lasky. They're ready for us to look at some more photos, help figure out who may have been responsible for the bomb."

A creaking dock plank sounded behind her, giving her only a second's warning before something solid jabbed against her back. "Don't make a sound," a female voice ordered, "or I'll be forced to shoot you. The gun has a silencer, so no one will know."

Her eyes shot to Flynn quickly. Why wasn't he helping her? And then she couldn't think of anything other than the familiar voice behind her.

Astrid.

The awful, awful recognition gelled inside of Sunny that her brother's wife had a gun wedged between her ribs and might truly shoot.

Sunny looked back over her shoulder at the woman she'd called family for nearly two years. "What are you doing here? I thought you were camping with Phoenix."

Some camping trip. Oh God, was her brother here too, somehow tangled up in this nightmare?

Her sister-in-law tugged her hood more firmly over her blonde hair. "Your brother is off doing what he always does, communing with nature as if somehow that's going to heal the earth. I'm taking action. Since he won't help me, I've just found others who will." She jabbed harder. "Now, since you interrupted our getaway, you're going to come along with us in the boat."

With us? Her eyes went to Flynn. To the line of

fishing vessels tied to the moorings down at the dock. To the SWAT team and Wade, all too far away to be of any help.

Oh God, why hadn't she listened to him about the danger here? All the information they'd gathered and put together with intel pointed to the power plant, but maybe someone on the inside knew there had been a leak, because this group sure as hell appeared to carry off their plan with adjustments to work around the police and military forces in place. Now she truly was alone to fight this battle that could create such far-reaching horror for so many if Astrid got away.

And Flynn. She couldn't even bear to think of what this would do to Misty. Sunny could have sworn his feelings for her sister were genuine. Maybe there was some hope in getting through to him. "But Flynn? I don't understand."

"Flynn? That's Ryker." Astrid laughed. Her voice, which had once seemed so lyrical when singing to her infant son, now sounded harsh and discordant. Her eyes lit with fanaticism. She swept a hand toward the nearest fishing boat, with a lean man, his back to them, already at the helm. "And that's Brett—our partner in the biggest, splashiest front-page news this area has ever seen and just what we need to make people sit up and take notice."

Chapter 18

MISTY SLIPPED AWAY FROM AGENT LASKY, ACTUALLY fairly easy to do since it had turned into a ghost town, with everyone evacuated. Authorities were confident about their security in place and busy as hell searching for more bombs. Sidling past two local cops on their radios, she scanned the huge parking lot, the outbuildings, the perimeter trees by the bay, for Flynn and Sunny. Sometime over the past twenty minutes she'd lost track of them and as much as she hated to admit it, she needed them.

Winding her way through the festival, she was scared and feeling her deafness more acutely than ever in the four years since she'd lost her hearing. Out of her comfort zone, away from everything familiar, she found this overcrowded, fast-paced world overwhelming. There was so little time to react and so many surprises—people, carts, cars, you name it—zipping past and startling her.

Of course it didn't help that she was positively nauseous over how she may have unknowingly aided the people responsible for this through her emails with Brett. How easily she'd been lured in. Somehow, he'd known all the right buttons to push to get close to her.

To learn more about the people around her.

A body jostled her from behind as she stuck close to the sidewalk near the water. She jolted, spun around, and sagged with relief at a father kneeling to help his kid with a fishing rod. "Sorry, ma'am."

She just smiled her apology, painfully aware of how her voice would label her now, make her more vulnerable.

Had she even eased Brett's path in staging this bombing attempt? Or had he merely worked his way into her affections so he could keep tabs on when she planned to leave? Agent Lasky seemed to think the murders may have been an attempt to keep the community contained. Either the rest of the unaccounted-for people were dead as well, or they were somehow involved in this plot.

Or worse yet, other plots.

So where was Brett now? According to his *wife*— Misty swallowed back bile—he was on the run and she had no idea where. Andrea Livingston was being questioned further and her home was staked out, only twenty miles away. How much more betrayed must that woman be feeling?

The wind carried the scent of the sea as she circled past a line of three boats on trailers with the power plant logo stamped along the side. Beyond the gate, a small fishing festival was well under way. Looking down the length of the dock, Misty's eyes locked on Flynn with Sunny. His broad shoulders and back were so wide and dependable. She was lucky to have this second chance with him. She wouldn't throw it away.

Sunny turned to step from one level of the dock to the next, her face tipped toward Misty for the first time. Misty waved and started to call out across the fifty yards or so that separated them.

Sunny's eyes went wide. And not in happiness or surprise, but with unmistakable terror. Misty had spent too much of the past four years reading people's nonverbal cues to doubt herself, even from a distance. She froze in her tracks, half-hidden behind the row of boats and meandering people.

"No," Sunny signed fast, one hand low behind her back. *"Gun. Hostage. Help."*

Horror iced through Misty as her sister was loaded into a security boat tied to a mooring.

Frantically, she studied Sunny closer. The early morning sun caught a glint of metal pressed into her sister's side. Most definitely a gun held in the mystery woman's hand. And oh God, Flynn was actually helping by hauling Sunny along? She couldn't wrap her brain around the possibility that he could do something so horrific, that he could be involved in this criminal nightmare…

Because it couldn't be him. Somehow, even if it seemed impossible, that had to be Ryker. Her brain began to register the differences. Now she just had to figure out what to do next.

Misty's chest went tight with panic, her knees wobbly, and she grabbed the nearest mooring post for support. Only a split instant to make a decision whether to press ahead and scream or slip away and search for help. And if she chose wrong, her sister would die. Others could die from the stray gunfire.

Her grip numbing as she held on to the boat for balance, she looked behind her for help, but Agent Lasky was out of sight. Everyone else at least a hundred yards away on the other side of the fence. God, why had she wandered so far away?—but if she hadn't she wouldn't have found her sister. And why weren't there more police on the dock?

She made her decision. She couldn't even waste a

second for a final look, or good-bye, or I love you. But then her sister had to already know.

Misty spun on her heel and ran full out toward Agent Lasky. She didn't have to be able to hear to know the boat carrying her sister was already roaring away.

Wade had once held immeasurably still for five hours in a Central American jungle after stabilizing an injured pilot who'd punched out of his F-16 doing drug interdiction patrols. Their ride out had been diverted due to antiaircraft fire, and with drug lords crawling around behind every banana tree, he hadn't dared move.

He'd only been on this frozen rooftop a half hour, scanning the perimeter for suspicious activity, but it already seemed twice as long as that jungle stint. He would feel a helluva lot better when he had a chance to talk to Sunny, to figure out a way to sort through the anger in her eyes. Still, even knowing that the SWAT team and the local police were crawling all over the place, even sending out a boat to patrol the bay, didn't ease the knot in his gut at the thought of her here helping.

His earpiece buzzed with chatter from the bomb squad as they discussed ways to either disable the device or contain the blast. Fire trucks and EMTs waited outside the fence. And the MH-60 was still parked right where they'd landed a couple of hours ago.

"Hurry up and wait" had never felt so damn excruciating before.

McCabe's knees popped again as he shifted positions. "Wanna swap places? I just got a clear view of your girlfriend."

"Where? What's she doing?" Damn it, she should be far, far away from this place. "Hang on and I'll be over in a second. There's something funky going on outside the gate."

He didn't like the look of four people confabbing a little too tightly. He didn't want to take his eyes off them just yet.

"She was over by the docks with her buddy Flynn. I think her sister was beside her, but then a chick in a parka is pretty much a chick in a parka, you know. Sunny with her hood down though? Can't miss that blue stripe through her hair."

Franco laughed low. "Better get your eyes off his woman's stripe or you're liable to get your ass kicked, old man."

"Hmmm..." McCabe said. "That's interesting. Your girl and her pals are taking a ride in one of the fishing boats by the festival. She must be going back to the lodge like you told her."

He couldn't imagine her doing that, not after the fire she'd just spit his way. The hair on the back of his neck stood up. "Where's Lasky? Have they checked this place out? Or are they all still too busy arguing about who's in control?"

The chatter in his earpiece grew louder, the intensity indicating something was heating up down there. Wade pressed his finger to the device, his buddies beside him going silent too just as Agent Lasky barked through the airwaves.

"Red alert, all eyes and ears up. We've got a hostage situation. I repeat, a hostage situation."

Wade's instincts blared and his gut clenched with the

undeniable surety that Sunny was somehow in danger. As he shot to his feet, charging toward the metal stairs wrapped around the outside, he swept his binoculars around the power plant, praying he would find her...

He swept past Lasky. Then back again sharply, bringing the view in tighter. Flynn and Misty stood with the agents, their hoods down, so there was no mistaking them.

The same two people McCabe had just said he saw with Sunny in a boat.

Sea spray stung Sunny's face like a thousand frozen needles. She suffered no delusions that these three people wanted to keep her alive. She'd stumbled into their getaway and now she was disposable. It was a race against time for Misty to find help soon enough to save her life.

How had Astrid and Ryker gotten tangled up with this man Brett? She recognized him from their plane trip earlier and shuddered to think she and Wade had been that close to death.

The hull chopped through the waves, farther from the power plant until it was just a speck. Farther and farther the craft raced from Wade and help.

She'd been so naïve to think she could save her sister, but God, how could she have foreseen something this huge? This evil?

And Wade had stood by her through it all. Even when he charged ahead full speed, he was doing it for her. And she'd pushed him away, rather than considering his reasons. He'd been right to be cautious, albeit he could be heavy-handed at times, but given what had happened to his mother, that was understandable.

Morning rays shimmered off the icy bay. Fishing charters in the distance were all oblivious and too far away to signal. Even if Astrid didn't still have the gun wedged into her side.

Brett eased back on the throttle, the boat slowed, and her heart sped.

Not yet, not yet.

She needed more time. Misty, Wade, the authorities needed more time. Damn it all, she wanted more time with Wade, another chance. She tucked her hand inside her parka to touch the survival knife, strapped to her waist.

One-on-one odds in a fight, she could handle. But three against one was beyond hopeless. The best she could do was stay alive long enough. If they threw her overboard, she would be unconscious in thirty seconds, dead in ninety. Without some kind of protective clothing, she couldn't survive in the freezing waters.

The boat drifted past a small iceberg, swirling turquoise streaks through the black Alaska waters.

Brett turned from the helm to the others behind him, his face paler where his beard had once been. He was frighteningly normal looking. "This hasn't gone quite as we planned."

His hand slid from his pocket, holding a gun.

Her hand clenched tighter around the knife handle as her mind raced for ideas, for anything, but she couldn't see a way. Her mind filled with images of Wade.

Before she could finish registering that the Beretta had a silencer lengthening the barrel...

Hiss. A bullet ripped through the air. Bracing, Sunny stifled the urge to scream.

Ryker crumpled against the railing, his eyes wide with shock—and lifelessness. His body toppled over and into the water as Astrid's scream filled the air.

Screw inaction. She wanted that gun. She whipped around—

Brett's Beretta hissed again.

Astrid jerked, stumbled, then slumped over a seat, the back of her skull covered in blood. Her sister-in-law went limp, so horribly dead, as the weapon tumbled from her limp grip.

Sunny lunged for the gun. A revolver beat a knife, hands down, and this was a fight-to-the-death moment. But Brett scooped it a second ahead of her. Frustration, fear, rage all howled through her in a typhoon of emotions. How could the world just continue to spin so normally in the distance, unaware? Houses on the far shore with families. A news helicopter overhead in search of a story for the 6:00 p.m. news, but flying obliviously past the horror happening here.

"Why are you doing this?" she screamed at him, the boat rocking beneath her feet as she stared down the murderer. "Why did you have to kill them?"

The bastard stood still as an ice sculpture, emotionless after having snuffed out two lives with no explanation. So much for Astrid's faith in her "partner."

"Count yourself lucky that I chose you for my hostage, my insurance." He tapped under her chin with the lengthy barrel before backing up a step and pocketing Astrid's weapon. "I'm big on having insurance. Accomplices don't hold much weight with the authorities when it comes to hostage negotiation. Now, get yourself under control and maybe you'll be able to walk away from this alive."

At least he was talking instead of driving, killing time instead of people. "How could you just murder them?"

She struggled against distracting thoughts of the two people who'd just been murdered, the mother of her nephew, the young man who'd made them grin with his outlandish conspiracy theories.

Wind whipped past her ears, bringing tears to her eyes.

"Who are you to judge me?" he sneered, grabbing the back of Astrid's jacket, hauling her up, then flinging her overboard as if she were nothing more than a piece of trash rather than a human being. "You helped your brother hide out for years even though he turned his back on his country."

"What do you know about my brother?" Please, no more betrayals today. Still, she had to know.

"I know your brother wasn't man enough to see what was going on right under his nose with his wife. He thought he could sit up there on that mountain and avoid the rest of the world forever. He still does, poor idiot."

And with those few words he'd put to rest her fears that her brother might be involved, in spite of what Astrid had said. Sunny wouldn't have covered for him, not on something like this. Maybe not at all, anymore.

"Do you think it's better to mow down innocent people, disposing of their bodies on a mountain and in the sea?"

He cocked an eyebrow. "Keep that up and damn straight you won't be arguing with me because you'll be dead. If that damn deputy had done his job right you would be taken care of already, just like he took care of your friends on the mountain. I have that kind of power you know—to decide who lives and dies. Which makes me wonder why you would risk pissing me off." His eyes narrowed, his Beretta raising back to point dead center at her head.

The feel of cold steel pressed against her skin was an effective reminder of her need to stay calm in the face of hearing how coldly he'd ordered Deputy Smith to execute so many of her friends. To execute her. She needed to think, to stall.

"Wait!" she rushed, wind tearing through her hair much as the fear ripped through her body. Help—Wade—had to be close. "You're right. You do need a hostage in case they come looking for you. So where are we going? You can't expect to get away in this boat. The gas will run out."

Heartbeat tumbling over itself, she was running on adrenaline. Icy waves lashed at the sides of the craft. The backs of her legs pressed against the leather seats behind the captain's chair.

He lowered the gun from her head. "Have you forgotten already that I'm a pilot as well? Now that I've picked up some important data from the plant"—he toe-tapped a slim briefcase under his seat—"I can fly out of here. The people I work for? Well, let's just say I have some names and records that are very valuable to them. This is my ticket to a lot of money once I land at my final destination on the other side of the Bering Sea."

Names? Of people involved in the bombing plot? Did he intend to blackmail them? And why would that be valuable to him in Russia? But he made it sound like there was someone higher up the chain.

"How do you intend to get rich off bombing power plants?" She inched her hand back into her parka as if warming herself, all the while listening for the sound of another boat or any sign of help from the shore. Her fingers brushed the handle of the knife. Ready.

"Oh you rustic little bumpkin, just like your two friends there. They were all too willing to help me out, imagining I was every bit as dedicated to their cause as they were. This is so much bigger than that. Now sit back down, right here where I can keep my eye on you. Be a good girl or you'll be swimming with your friends."

She dropped into the seat beside him, for now her will to live strong, but her legs still not all that steady. The murderous bastard eased the boat out of idle, and they surged ahead. Sea spray needling the air again, he steered around small icebergs littering their path.

The magnitude of what she faced threatened to overwhelm her. This man was certifiably evil. Her fingers slid around the knife handle again and this time she wouldn't let go, even for an instant. She had lost any hope that he would let her live, and the farther away they went, the less chance Wade had of saving her. The Bering Sea, the islands, the mountains, all provided vast wastelands in which to dump her body.

No damn way. She wasn't giving up on life. She wasn't giving up on a future, a future with Wade, her rock-headed, stubborn, honorable lover. The only man ever to move her all the way to the core of her being. She wanted his body. She admired his integrity.

And just flat out loved Wade, the man.

The nose of the hull smacked a wave, hard, yanking her from her thoughts and jerking Brett's gun hand for an instant. All the opportunity she needed.

Sunny whipped her hand free, blade reflecting the

sun's rays. She jabbed upward into the bastard's gut. He stumbled from the steering wheel, the boat screaming forward through the waves. The heated gust of Brett's shocked "Oomph" washed over her face. His mouth moved soundlessly, a trickle of blood sliding from the corner of his mouth. The gun fell from his slack hand...

Just as the boat rammed into an iceberg.

Chapter 19

IN THE BACK OF THE MH-60 PAVE HAWK, WADE YANKED on his antiexposure suit. Watertight rubber, it resembled the type skin divers used, but cinched in around the neck and feet. He pulled his focus in as tight as the seals on his suit, trying his damnedest to lose himself in training and routine.

Because if he let himself think about Sunny out there with terrorist bombers, with murderers, he would lose his mind.

To his right, Franco tugged on his gear. Out the open side hatch, his other four team members stood on the concrete landing pad by the power plant. It was agreed they would stay behind in case they were needed for triage in the event of an explosion. The bomb had been defused but the bomb squad still hadn't finished inspecting the entire building. Lasky and the FBI wanted the kidnappers alive for information.

Wade just wanted Sunny.

Thank God for the MH-60 in the lot and years of training at their fingertips. They were in the chopper and ready to lift off in under five minutes. The door closed, sealing him into a dimly lit cocoon of wires and gear, mustiness of old equipment drenched in the fumes from hydraulic fluid. He welcomed the familiar in a day turned upside down.

He shot a quick glance at Franco, suited up now as

were the two pilots. Those suits were crucial gear when flying over the life-sapping cold waters of the Bering Sea. Without the suits, someone in the water would be dead within just a couple of minutes.

Sunny would be dead.

Never had the speed of his mission been more important.

"Ready in front. How're we doing in back?" crackled over Wade's helmet.

Franco nodded, eyes a little crazier today than normal, but Wade welcomed that edginess now more than ever.

He shot a thumbs-up to the pilots and replied, "Ready in back."

The pilots turned their attention to starting engines, running a checklist in a professional call-and-response manner that always seemed to bring Wade into the zone. The singsong of the pilots focused him in on the mission ahead. Finally the rotors began to turn, the grinding whine growing louder, faster.

The copilot called for clearance to take off and track down the fleeing fishing boat. The chopper rotors *whomp, whomp, whomped* overhead in a deafening drumbeat as they flew out over the icy bay. Wind roared beyond the open side hatch, snow flurries picking up speed, a storm brewing.

The chopper banked hard and fast, flying balls-out toward the open bay. With the boat hauling ass, they could be out in the Bering Sea all too soon. The Coast Guard had been alerted, but would be at least five minutes behind them in responding. Minutes were everything in this climate.

He and Franco were Sunny's best chance of coming out alive.

The copilot began tweaking the radar to spot boats. "I would say that we look for a boat going mach-snot and perform a close flyby to see if we can identify it. But extra eyes are welcome."

Wade didn't need to be told that one twice. He sensed Franco sliding into place as well. They'd worked as a team for so long, he didn't even need to check.

"Moving over twenty-five knots." The copilot's voice piped low and calm over the air waves. His New England accent growing thicker betrayed the only sign of any nerves. "Let's give him a look-see first. Come thirty degrees right, target is about three minutes out."

Less time than a damn commercial break, but in waters like these, that was more than enough time to freeze to death.

Wade craned his neck to search out the starboard-door window. He kept his eyes trained on a speck speeding away in the distance, weaving a reckless hell-bent path around floating segments of ice, some bigger than the boat itself. Hand locked around a handle bolted by the door, he got the okay to open the hatch and swung out farther into the whipping wind for a better look. God, why had he been such a jackass to waste time with her, fighting? It wasn't as if he'd accomplished a damn thing. He wasn't going to change her. In fact, he'd only succeeded in pushing her away from him when, if anything, they should have been sticking closer together.

But then the last thing she'd wanted was his protection. Well, after this, he couldn't imagine letting her out of his sight. Which would be damn tricky once he was in Afghanistan.

Shit.

Clear the brain of distracting thoughts. Focus on the mission.

His headset hummed to life. "Target in the camera," the copilot barked. "Target in the camera. I have our boat in sight. And—what the hell? It's not moving."

The implications of "not moving" were like a sledge-hammer on Wade's back.

Swinging back into the chopper, Wade launched himself through the hold and behind the pilots. Eyes narrowing, he scoured the radar display, scrambling for every detail he could find, anything that would help him haul Sunny out of this alive.

He braced his hands hard against the pilots' seats to keep from shaking. He watched the radar, desperate for any sign of life on that boat. The airwaves went silent, the helicopter flying closer, the image growing clearer, larger, as they neared.

Movement. "There!"

Wade pointed, refusing to believe he could be mis-taken. Again, he caught the hint of motion as a person rolled to their knees on the deck, slowly uncurling and standing. Alive.

He looked up through the windscreen as they neared, his view of her clearer. Long dark hair streaked behind the woman. Sunny. It had to be her. Relief nearly took out his knees until he straightened with the infusion of a new sense of purpose because he *would* save her.

Hang tough. He willed her to hear his thoughts as he charged back into the belly of the chopper, to the open hatch. He would winch down into the boat in another two minutes, tops. If she could just hold on, he and Franco would be there.

As he looked down, she staggered toward the rail of the boat and his gut lurched. *No, no, no*. If she went in the water she would be dead before the helicopter could get close enough for him to go in after her.

The boat listed left. Sharply. She stumbled again, her feet splashing in pooling water inside the craft.

"Holy shit," he shouted into his headset. "It's sinking. We need to get there now."

Planting his feet on deck, he gripped the handle, leaning farther from the chopper, snow stinging his face. He willed the aircraft to fly faster.

The fishing vessel was taking on water fast, sunlight glinting off the ripples gushing into the craft. Sunny grappled along the rail, her arms flailing toward something he couldn't make out.

She jumped up and he held his breath, certain she would go tumbling overboard. Her hand connected and she yanked.

A burst of yellow shot away from the boat, a life raft inflating and settling onto the choppy sea. Good God, she was saving herself. She was getting away from the boat and whoever else was on board.

Sunny leaped from the edge, airborne for what felt like an eternity as he watched the life raft tossed about on the churning waves. She landed in the raft, tumbling against the side and almost pitching over. She held fast.

Relief raced through him again along with a ridiculous hint of pride in her fast thinking. God, she was an amazing, strong woman. She wasn't in the sea. And most importantly, she wasn't in the sinking boat.

Now, rather than winching down into the sinking boat, he would drop into the water with survival gear, keep her safe from exposure or tipping until they could haul her up.

Wade sank down onto the cabin floor and started to put on his swim fins. "Get the basket on the line. I'll go out and get her. Franco can lower into the boat with the winch to check for any other survivors."

"Roger that," the pilot answered.

Franco keyed up the radio. "Got your back, Brick. Will clear the boat."

The helicopter began a slow turnaround, nearing the drop site. Sunny waved, clutching with her other hand as the raft kicked up on waves, each swell threatening to pitch her out. Rotor wash pushed the sea into higher swirls as the MH-60 hovered as close as it dared.

Wade pulled his goggles and snorkel on, and stepped back into the open hatch. He sat with his legs dangling out the door, put one hand over his mask, and slipped out of the helicopter. He floated through air for what always felt like the longest glide of his life until abruptly…

Freezing water swallowed him. Actually, *freezing* didn't even come close to describing the walls of ice encasing his body. Through his mask, he kept his eyes fixed on the raft above him, the tiny inflatable holding his entire world. That woman had come to mean more to him in a few days than anyone in his life. So much so, he couldn't imagine his life without her.

Pumping his feet, he surged upward, bubbles streaming past in the murky underwater until… He burst free from the icy clamp of the underworld. He bobbed to the surface and gave a thumbs-up to the helicopter overhead.

Slicing through the sea with stroke after stroke, his body rode waves as he swam. Needing to see her. Hear her. Hold her vibrant, alive body so he could stop the shaking inside him that had started the second he'd learned she was taken.

His palm slapped the edge of the rubber lifeboat and he grabbed hold with his other hand as well. He peered up and found Sunny looking down at him, shivering and drenched, with her lips turning blue, but *alive*.

"Wade, I can't believe it's you." She grabbed his arms and tugged. "You're here."

The raft lurched, nearly pitching her out, rolling water splashing her in the face. Her grip loosened, her legs sliding around on the rubber raft until she nearly tumbled into the churning ice below.

"Let go," he ordered, "and back to the other side of the raft so I can bring myself in."

If she got dumped into the water without an anti-exposure suit it would be bad, beyond bad. Carefully, as if his life depended on it—and it did, since Sunny's life was in the balance—he hefted himself into the raft. Her teeth chattering, she wrapped her arms tight around him.

"You're okay, you're okay," he said, more to reassure himself than her, wanting to hang on, rooted in the knowledge that she was alive and whole.

But with regret, he pried her off him. He needed to get her covered.

He unstrapped the survival gear from his back and whipped free the Thinsulate blanket. He held it open just as she fell into his arms. He wrapped her and he gathered her to his chest, against his pounding heart.

Out of the corner of his eye, he saw a cable from the chopper lowering Franco into the boat. Franco would search while they raised Sunny back up into the helicopter in a metal basket. He would have to let Sunny go, and that was going to damn near rip his heart out when he'd only just got her back, but Franco might need his help.

"Sunny?" He squeezed her gently. "How many people are still in the boat?"

"One man alive, stabbed and t-t-tied up," she chattered. "T-two dead, he shot them. He shot Astrid and Ryker." Her hazel eyes turned murky and haunted. "Their bodies are both in the water."

He ticked through his memories of the people in her community. Ryker was Flynn's brother. Astrid was her brother's wife. Innocent victims, or had they been caught up in the bomber's plan? They must have been, given how unlikely it was for anyone in that community to be here. Now.

What the hell had she been though? "Are you hurt? Do you need medical attention?"

He picked up her hand where he saw blood on it. No wound. Just a long streak up her arm. Under her nails. Dear God, she'd been the one to do the stabbing. He placed his fingers on her wrist to measure her heart rate.

"N-not hurt," she murmured through her chattering teeth. "J-just possibly going into shock."

She blinked up at him, eyes wide. And wasn't that just like her to assess her situation with a cool head even as her pulse slowed, her skin frighteningly pale? But she would be okay. He kissed the top of her head, where icicles formed in her hair.

Sunny burrowed closer, tighter, and he braced his back for a swell to keep the water off her while he waited for the helicopter to return with the basket. Until then, Sunny would be safe with him.

"J-just don't let go." She shivered against him. "Please God, don't ever let me go."

That was a request he intended to honor with every fiber of his being.

———~w~———

With Flynn standing tall beside her, Misty stared up at the landing helicopter, almost afraid to hope what Lasky had told her could be true. That Sunny was safe, inside that descending military chopper.

Wind from the rotors stirred up a swirling snowstorm as the MH-60 landed in the parking lot. With her sister inside. The pilot had called in the successful rescue to Agent Lasky, but Misty wouldn't be able to breathe freely until she saw Sunny with her own eyes.

What a difference an hour could make. Her sister had been saved. The bomb had been defused. And the power plant had been declared clear.

Now the authorities would be turning their attention to questioning Brett Livingston, once he got his gut stitched up from the stab wound Sunny inflicted. And they would work to locate and retrieve Astrid and Ryker's bodies. She slid her hand into Flynn's. His face was stoic. But she knew him well enough to sense he was shell-shocked and hurting underneath. Her heart ached for him.

The helicopter finally touched down and ground crews rushed forward just as the hatch opened. Wade Rocha leaped to the ground, sure-footed, then held out a hand. Sunny stepped into view in the open portal. Alive. Her sister was really alive and appeared unharmed, as best she could tell from the blanket that swaddled her.

With Wade's help, Sunny stepped out onto the pavement, her steps slow and shaky as she searched the crowd. The second her eyes landed on Misty, she smiled, trying to move faster, but her ordeal had obviously taken a toll. Misty sprinted to her, wrapping her sister in a hug so tight it was almost painful, but she couldn't bring herself to let go. She'd been so terrified, so scared she wouldn't find help in time, second-guessing herself the whole way.

Sunny eased back, tears streaking into her smile. Her hands raised. *"Thank you. Thank you."*

"I'm sure someone else could have done something more."

"You were the completely perfect person I needed at the right time."

And Misty realized it was true. Her signing, her heightened sense of nuances in facial expressions had served her—had served Sunny—well. For the first time in four years, she felt strong.

Wade slid an arm around Sunny's shoulders. "We really need to get you checked out by the doctor."

Misty nodded too. "Go, really. We'll have plenty of time later. A lifetime."

"Okay," Sunny agreed. "Just one more thing." She hugged Flynn, squeezing hard.

Sunny's mouth was moving but Misty couldn't catch what she was saying. Likely it had to do with Ryker's last moments. And then Wade was hooking his arm around Sunny, pointing to one of the EMT trucks. Even her indomitable sister needed to be reminded she was mortal. It appeared Sunny had found a person strong enough to stand with her—and up to her—in Wade Rocha.

Misty turned to her own man, one she'd loved for years and had finally found a path back to. "I'm so sorry about your brother."

He stared out over the bay, snowflakes catching on his blond hair he stood still so long. "I'm sorry I didn't see what he was into. I'm sorry he wasted his life. And I'm sorry about how this is going to break our father's heart."

"Your dad will get comfort from having you near." She dusted the snow away and wished it could be as easy to ease the burdens on his heart.

Flynn looked down at her, the full power of his pain showing through. "Or will looking at me remind him of my brother? God knows, I'm not sure I'm ready to look in the mirror yet. Even Sunny thought he was me out there."

"But I know who you are." She stroked the side of his face. "I knew then."

Turning into her hand, he kissed her palm, lingering long enough for her to know he took comfort from her touch. Anything more overt out here in public wasn't possible, but there was an unmistakable connection in the moment. An unmistakable connection between them.

A sigh shuddered through him and he tore his eyes away from the harbor. He looped an arm around her shoulders and steered her back toward the heated RVs set up for questioning and waiting. Not fancy, but definitely warmer. And there was just something scary about going into the power plant, even if it had just been given the all clear.

Sighing, she tucked against Flynn's side, his arm solid and familiar. "What should we do now?"

With ease, he positioned his face so she would see

his mouth even as they stayed side by side. "I need to tell my parents about Ryker, and I would like for you to come with me." He guided her past a fire truck that had blessedly been unneeded after all. "But after that, I want us to go to Anchorage so you can have the surgery. I want to be there with you."

His plan seemed so perfect it broke her heart that they couldn't have figured it all out sooner. "That's not possible now. So much of the logistics depended on staying with Ted and Madison." So many deaths, so much grief to be spread out in such a tiny community. "How can I complain about a missed appointment with the specialist when they lost their lives?"

He gripped both her shoulders and turned her to him just outside the nearest RV, their last chance for privacy for what could be many hours of intense questioning. "And they would want you to go after life and grab it with both hands, whatever it is that you want."

For the first time today, she let herself voice the fears that had been hammering around inside her brain. "What if the doctor who agreed to take my case pro bono won't do that anymore once all the scandal of our village hits the paper? What if he wasn't even real, just another lie pumped through our compromised Internet?"

"Then we'll find a real doctor, one willing to do the procedure." The determination and honesty on his face all but vibrated the air between them. "I can drive a snowplow anywhere with snow, and while I won't ever be a rich man, I will do work until my last breath to give you what you need. I will stand by you every step of the way until we figure out how to make that surgery happen."

"You would do that for me? Leave the only home

you've ever known?" She'd seen the claustrophobia close in on him when they'd been stuck in the room with Agent Lasky. She could see the homesickness in his eyes when he'd stared out over the bay. And yet she saw none of that now.

"I've thought every day for four years that I would do anything in my power to be with you again. Being with you *is* home for me. In case you haven't noticed, Misty, I love you."

"I do know. And I hope you know I love you too."

The reality, the honesty of that emotion between them was so strong, she could hear it *singing* through her veins.

Twenty-four hours later, Sunny stretched out on the bear rug in front of Wade's fireplace in Anchorage. The fur tickled the backs of her legs peeking out of the oversized T-shirt she'd borrowed from him. "I'm really going to have to invest in some clothing of my own."

"But you look so smoking-hot in mine."

"And you look so damn adorable hugging my dog."

Wade stoked the fire with one hand, his other arm hooked around Chewie. Bare chested and wearing only low-slung sweatpants, he sent her pulse racing again even though they'd already made love twice since reaching his apartment.

The past twenty-four hours had passed at a frenetic pace. Brett Livingston was in police custody at the hospital. He'd survived surgery and faced a lifetime in prison for the murders and the bombing attempt.

If not more.

She'd told the police about Brett's "insurance" plan

in his briefcase, and they were sending electronic divers down in an attempt to retrieve it from the boat. She couldn't even begin to fathom what it might contain, what could possibly be worse than had already happened. But at least she could know the authorities weren't in the dark any longer.

Still no word from Phoenix, and she was beginning to wonder if maybe he had run after all. The thought that he would actually abandon his wife and child was more than she could wrap her brain around, but she still had to hope he was alive out there somewhere. Thankfully, her nephew was safe with Astrid's parents.

At least she knew her sister was happy, already making plans with Flynn. The two of them had accepted the helicopter ride back up the mountain to be with Flynn's parents right now. And Misty wanted to stay near their nephew until the police officially cleared everyone in the village—or made any necessary arrests. What kind of legacy was that to leave a child? A criminal for a mother and a father who ran? Her chest grew tight with regrets.

Wade replaced the poker and stroked back her hair, still damp from the shower they'd shared. "I can arrange for a flight home for you, if you've changed your mind."

She shook her head, certain in her decision to stay right where she was. Working things out with Wade. "I want to be here with you, for as long as we can be together before you have to leave. Correct me if I'm wrong, but I thought that's what you wanted too."

Especially after the way he'd held her so fiercely in the life raft and how tenderly he'd made love to her.

"Can you tell me you aren't having regrets about not going back home with your sister?"

"I have regrets about what happened, about not picking up on the signs. It's become clear to me in a hundred different ways how cutting ourselves off has left us open and vulnerable. The place I knew as home isn't going to exist anymore after this."

"I'm so damn sorry for that." He tugged her to his chest and she leaned into him, the steady thump of his heart under her such a welcome sound she'd feared never hearing again.

Chewie nosed her knee insistently, shuffling into the circle with determined garbled noises until she couldn't help but laugh. God, it felt good after the horror of the past days. "I haven't forgotten about you, Chewie. Not for a second."

Her dog was recovering well from his pulled tendon, thank goodness, and should be back up to speed in another couple of weeks. Burying her fingers into his thick fur, she collided with Wade's hands right there alongside hers.

Wade grinned. "What can I say? I'm getting attached to your dog."

"Oh really?" she teased back, inwardly breathing a sigh of relief because she and Chewie were pretty much a package deal. "I haven't had time to think through all the details about where I want to live yet, but I do need to be with my sister to help see her through her surgery. I should have known that at the start."

"So you are willing to move." His fingers linked with hers in the husky mutt's thick pelt. "For Misty."

"For Misty, yes, but for me too." And for Wade, if this relationship was going where she thought, where she *hoped* it was going. "My skills as a guide and workout trainer can be used just about wherever I go, so while I may not own the place, at least I would have a marketable job history. A small town would probably suit me best, some kind of rural community."

One with mom-and-pop diners, rustic B and Bs, and wood-burning fireplaces crackling a hand's reach away. Most of all, one with wildernesses to explore.

"Alaska has plenty of those," he agreed. "And what if once I return, I wanted you to come where I'll be? What if I could find a nice rural town nearby?"

"That sounds… huge. But workable. You understand though that it would take an independent, strong person to make such a radical change. A damsel in distress just isn't going to cut it, especially for a guy who's got a scary dangerous career that takes him all around the world for extended periods of time."

He raised his hands in surrender, angles of his beard-stubbled face starker with the morning light streaking through the windows. "Okay, I get the message and completely agree. You are not the clinging-vine sort, and believe me, I respect that. You can take care of yourself, and quite well, I might add—"

"Thank you." She stopped him with a nip to his bottom lip. "I needed to hear you say that and know that you mean it. I think we make a formidable team, you, me, and Chewie."

"I concur." He nipped her right back, then again, until his hands were in her hair and his body covering hers on the rug.

Gliding her hands over his shoulders, along his back, she stared up into his beautiful cocoa-brown eyes and realized she could lose herself in those no matter where she lived. "Where will you be transferring to once you return from your four months in the Middle East?"

"Ever heard of Patrick Air Force Base?"

"No. Is there snow?"

He winced, rolling onto his side, worry furrowing his forehead. "Actually, it's in Florida, near Cape Canaveral."

"No snow then."

"Afraid not. As a matter of fact, you'll need lots of sunscreen."

Florida? Somewhere like Washington State or North Dakota might have been a little easier to grasp, but then she'd never been one to embrace ease. "I've always dreamed of visiting the beach again. And in the meantime, it's not like you're going to the moon. We'll be able to talk, right?"

"Periodically, yes. Some of the guys set up Skype accounts."

"I definitely prefer face-to-face Internet now." She shivered to think how easily her seemingly innocent Internet café had been a portal for such evil. Brett Livingston had set up shop in her backyard, closing down their communication to the outside world so that everything was filtered through him.

Funny that she'd grown up in a community that shunned most technology, while she'd embraced it, setting up a business that helped residents connect to the world. Yet she'd probably walk away from this nightmare more wary of technology than most people.

"You'll always know who you're talking to," Wade promised as he knuckled her chin upward and kissed her frown away. "And I'll be able to tell you to your face how very much you mean to me."

Her heart did a little flip over the touch of his mouth, the promise in his words. "How much would that be?"

"More than you can imagine. More than I could have imagined feeling for someone." His chocolate-brown eyes deepened to molten sincerity. "I'm falling in love with you, Sunny Foster. And I say falling, because what I'm feeling increases every time I see you. And my gut is telling me I'll keep right on falling in love with you more and more every day."

He kissed her before she could answer back, and she so very much wanted to share the words bubbling up inside her. Love for him had rolled over her fast and fierce, but then she wasn't a woman to shy away from a challenge. And one thing was certain: Wade Rocha was a brick-headed, sexy, loyal-to-the-end kind of man who'd taken her whole heart.

Cupping his beard-stubbled face in her palms, she vowed, "I love you too, so much I can't even come close to telling you in just one night. I'm going to need lots of nights and days, months, years, to express it all."

His forehead fell to rest against hers. "I'm sorry we don't have longer before I leave."

She grazed her heel up the back of his leg, already planning a homecoming to remember. "Then we'd better start making every minute count."

Epilogue

HE'D NEVER LOOKED FORWARD TO A HOMECOMING MORE.

Inside the cavernous C-17 cargo plane, Wade lined up with his PJ team and other airmen returning from their rotation in the Middle East. Beyond the open load ramp, the sun beat down on the crowd of waiting families and friends with flags and banners. A military brass band played, but it was tough to tell which was louder, the music or the cheers.

He'd gone from Alaska to his deployment in Afghanistan and was returning to his new duty station at Patrick Air Force Base in Florida. All his household goods—not much to speak of—were in storage. But he had somewhere to bunk in the meantime. At Sunny's place.

The fact that she'd actually moved here still stunned him, humbled him. In fact, she'd embraced the adventure of it all, as he should have known she would. After seeing Misty through her surgery and recovery, Sunny had landed a job at the Patrick AFB gym and even found a tiny bungalow to rent, tucked away in a marshy cove. Nothing here would be as isolated or open as Alaska, but she assured him an ocean view provided some of the vastness her pioneer soul craved.

One shuffle at a time along the cargo deck, he moved

forward as they gathered gear and made their way toward
the back ramp. Anticipation hummed inside him as tangi-
bly as the idling jet engines. He ached to hold her, catch
the scent of her hair, the taste of her. They'd spent every
day together before he deployed, but still had spent eight
times as many days apart as with each other.

They'd done their best to stay connected, talking and
cyberdating via Skype, and true to his word, he'd stuck
to webcam, face-to-face discussions where they'd actually learned a lot about each other—beyond where to
touch to drive her over the edge fastest. Although he
was looking forward to resurrecting that knowledge the
second they got to her bungalow.

As much as he'd missed sleeping with her, he most
regretted not being with her during all the massive
changes in her life. Not everything that had come into
the community via email had been a lie. The surgeon
Misty had communicated with was real and the offer to
perform her surgery at his teaching hospital had been
valid. It hadn't been completely free by a long shot, but
she had her hearing back. She and Flynn had decided to
move back home, raise her nephew, and lead the community in rebuilding with a more open environment.

Not that a mountainside on the Aleutian Islands was
ever going to be a vacation playground. But there would
most definitely be watchful eyes on that little off-the-
grid village from now on.

The records recovered from the boat wreckage had
rocked the intelligence community. He was privy to
just the tip of the iceberg, and only that much because
Lasky needed help connecting some dots. Asking
Wade sat better with the agent than letting Sunny in on

such explosive, top-secret information. Wade was still rocked to his boots over learning Brett Livingston had been aiding Russian mob groups smuggling terrorist spies into the U.S. through Alaska. Deputy Rand Smith had been his hired assassin. Sunny had been that close to death so many times. That bastard Livingston had cut a deal to avoid the death penalty. Already over a dozen arrests had been quietly made, all prior members of Sunny's community. She and the rest of the village would never know the full extent of how horribly they'd been manipulated.

For the best, in his opinion. Sunny already had enough pain to carry around, with her brother still missing.

Wade's boots thudded down the metal ramp and finally the bottlenecked human traffic jam eased. He stepped out onto the tarmac, searching the masses behind the roped off area until finally he saw *her*.

Sunny.

Her hair loose and lifting in the wind, she wore a floaty green dress and a smile brighter than the Florida rays. A pink stripe gleamed in her hair these days and he loved her unpredictability. Hell, he just loved her.

Dropping his gear, Wade double-timed toward her. The ropes gave way and things got more than a little chaotic. He sidestepped a family of five huddle-hugging and a young couple crying buckets.

He found Sunny just as she found him, meeting him halfway. Before he could speak she was in his arms and he wasn't sure who was holding tighter. His eyes closed and for the most awesome second he could remember, he just breathed in the scent of her hair that somehow still carried the crisp perfume of wide-open

Alaska spaces. The sound of the band and other reunited couples faded away.

Cradling her face in his palms, he kissed her, then kissed her again because he could, and that was something he did *not* take for granted. Words became jumbled in between, but no doubt they were on the same page. *I love you. I missed you. God, I've waited so long to hold you again.*

A jolt against his leg finally hauled his attention back to the crowded runway. He looked down to find Chewie head-butting his leg, demanding equal time.

"Well hello, big guy. Sorry I didn't see you there at first." Wade dropped to his knees, scratching the dog behind his ears. "Thanks for taking such good care of her while I was away, pal."

The malamute mutt garbled a half-howling response.

A *second* dog peeked its head around Sunny's leg. Now that, he hadn't expected.

Laughing, Wade patted the wirehaired scrap on a leash and looked up at Sunny. "Who's this fella?"

Sunny scooped up the little terrier mix of some sort. "This is Princess Leia. Or Princess, for short." She straightened the dog's patriotic bandanna. "Your mother responded so well to Chewie when I flew out to meet her, your father and I thought a small lapdog might be a good idea. He asked me to pick out a good candidate and suggested we bring it to her."

That she would reach out to his family on her own, that she would find a way to give his mother comfort… So much emotion welled up inside him he cleared his throat, twice, before he could push words free. "You're too amazing, do you know that?"

"You're not a slouch yourself there, superhero." She pressed a hand to his chest, then his neck, his cheek, as if she couldn't get enough of touching him in the flesh.

He folded his hand over hers and pressed it to his heart, which damn near thumped through his chest just because he stood next to her. "I don't take for granted how difficult this move must have been for you."

"Thank you. I appreciate you saying that." She sidled closer, a glint of promise in her hazel eyes. "And you can show me just how grateful you are once we get back to my place."

"Roger that, pretty lady. I've got you covered."

Acknowledgments

While reading an article in National Geographic about kayaking in the Aleutian Islands, I was completely fascinated by this region that Russian missionaries labeled "the place that God forgot." Upon further research, I realized the Aleutian Islands have a long and fascinating history, in spite of their sparse population. I knew I had found the perfect setting for a book bubbling to life in my brain. While the story may have been inspired by an article and its amazing photographs, the people and the towns I have written about are completely fictional. In telling their tale, I hope to have captured the vast Alaska spirit and the breathtaking bravery of elite pararescuemen. In my hope of doing so, I have had the generous help of many. However, any mistakes, inaccuracies, poetic license, overall stretching the realm of possibility, rests completely on my shoulders!

Thank you, Deb Werksman, a gifted editor with endless energy and wit. I'll be forever grateful for the day you said, "I have this idea…" It's a delight to work with you and the entire Sourcebooks team. Barbara Collins Rosenberg, my longtime agent and trusted champion, I appreciate all you do to keep me focused, steady—and under contract. Sending a huge shout-out of gratitude to my author peeps, Joanne Rock and Stephanie Newton. I don't know what I would do without your brilliant critiques, genius brainstorming, and amazing taste in junk food.

Technical advisors rock! And I have been truly blessed to hear the daring PJ tales shared by former air force pararescueman Dr. Ronald Marshall, DC. And as always, I would be lost without my own air force aviator husband, Robert, who is always ever ready with brainstorming help and fact-checking reads. Thank you both for your brave and selfless service to our country! Much gratitude goes to Karen Tucker, RN, who so generously offered her medical knowledge and eagle eye for detail. Thanks also to my go-to pals for insider tips on Alaska living, Leah Marie Brown and Patricia Marshall Brow.

Most of all, thank you to my precious children, Brice, Haley, Robbie, and Maggie, for your love and patient restocking of my Diet Cokes during deadlines. And as always, all my love to my hero husband, Rob.

About the Author

USA Today bestseller Catherine Mann has won both the prestigious RITA Award and Booksellers' Best Award. With over two million books in print, her work has been released in more than twenty countries. Catherine resides on the Florida coast with her aviator husband, their four children, and an ever-growing menagerie of pets. For more information: http://www.catherinemann.com

HOT ZONE

Book 2 in the
Elite Force series

CATHERINE MANN

Coming December 2011
From Sourcebooks Casablanca

Chapter 1

THE WORLD HAD CAVED IN ON AMELIA BAILEY. LITERALLY.

Aftershocks from the earthquake still rumbled the gritty earth under her cheek, jarring her out of her hazy micronap. Dust and rocks showered around her. Her skin, her eyes, everything itched and ached after hours— she'd lost track of how many—beneath the rubble.

The quake had to have hit at least seven on the Richter Scale. Although when you ended up with a building on top of you, somehow a Richter scale didn't seem all that pertinent.

She squeezed her lids closed. Inhaling. Exhaling. Inhaling, she drew in slow, even breaths of the dank air filled with dirt. Was this what it was like to be buried alive? She pushed back the panic as forcefully as she'd clawed out a tiny cavern for herself.

This wasn't how she'd envisioned her trip to the Bahamas when she'd offered to help her brother and sister-in-law with the legalities of international adoption.

Muffled sounds penetrated of jackhammers and tractors. Life scurried above her, none of whom seemed to have heard her shouts. She'd screamed her throat raw until she could only manage a hoarse croak now.

Time fused in her pitch black cubby, the air thick with sand. Or disintegrated concrete. She didn't want to think what else. She remembered the first tremor, the dawning realization that her third floor hotel room in the seaside Bahamas resort was slowly giving way beneath her feet. But after that?

Her mind blanked.

How long had she been trapped? Forever, it seemed, but probably more along the lines of half a day while she drifted in and out of consciousness. She wriggled her fingers and toes to keep the circulation moving after being immobile so long. Every inch of her body screamed in agony from scrapes and bruises and heaven only knew what else since she couldn't move enough to check. Still, she welcomed the pain that reassured her she was alive.

Her body was intact.

Forget trying to sit up. Her head still throbbed from trying that. The ceiling was now maybe six inches above where she lay flat on her belly. Again, she willed back hysteria. The fog of claustrophobia hovered, waiting to swallow her whole.

More dust sifted around her. The sound of the jackhammers rattled her teeth. They seemed closer, louder with even a hint of a voice. Was that a dog barking?

Hope hurt after so many disappointments. Even if her ears heard right, there had to be so many people in need of rescuing after the earthquake. All those efforts could easily be for someone else a few feet away. They might not find her for hours. Days.

Ever.

Still, she couldn't give up. She had to fight to the end. If not for herself, then for the little life beside her, her precious new nephew. She threaded her arm through the tiny hole between them to rub his back, even though he'd long ago given up crying, sinking into a frighteningly long nap. His back rose and fell evenly, thank God, but for how much longer?

Her fingers wrapped tighter around a rock and she banged steadily against the oppressive wall overhead. Again and again. If only she knew Morse code. Her arm numbed. Needle-like pain prickled down her skin. She gritted her teeth and continued. Didn't the people up there have special listening gear?

Dim shouts echoed, like a celebration. Someone had been found. Someone else. Desperation clawed up her throat.

Time ticked away. Precious seconds. She clutched her left hand around the rock, her right hand around the tiny wrist of the child beside her. Joshua's pulse fluttered weakly against her thumb.

Desperation thundered in her ears. She pounded the rock harder overhead. God, she didn't want to die. There'd been times after her divorce when the betrayal hurt so much she'd thought her chance at finally having a family was over, but she'd never thrown in the towel. Damn him. She wasn't a quitter.

Except why wasn't her hand cooperating anymore? The opaque air grew thicker with despair. Her arm grew leaden. Her shoulder shrieked in agony, pushing a gasping moan from between her cracked lips. Pounding became taps... She frowned. Realizing...

Her hand wasn't moving anymore. It slid uselessly back onto the rubble strewn floor. Even if her will to live was kicking ass, her body waved the white flag of surrender.

—⁓—

Master Sergeant Hugh Franco had given up caring if he died five years ago. These days, the Air Force pararescueman motto was the only thing that kept his soul planted on this side of mortality.

That others may live.

Since he didn't have anything to live for here on earth, he volunteered for the assignments no sane person would touch. And even if they would, his buds had people who would miss them. Why cause them pain?

Which was what brought him to his current snowball's-chance-in-hell mission.

Hugh commando-crawled through the narrow tunnel in the earthquake rubble. The light strapped to his helmet sliced a thin blade through the dusty dark. His headset echoed with chatter from above. Familiar voices looking after him and unfamiliar personnel working other missions scattered throughout the chaos. One of the search and rescue dogs aboveground had barked his head off the second he'd sniffed this fissure in the jumbled jigsaw of broken concrete.

And now, he burrowed deeper on the say so of a German shepherd named Zorro.

He half listened to the chatter in one ear, with the other tuned in for signs of life in the devastation. Years of training honed an internal filter that blocked out communication not meant for him.

"You still okay down there, Franco?"

He tapped the talk button on his safety harness and replied, "Still moving. Seems stable enough."

"Says the guy who parachuted into a minefield on an Afghani mountainside."

"Yeah, yeah, whatever." Somebody had to rescue that

Green Beret who'd gotten his legs blown off. "I'm good for now and I'm sure I heard some tapping ahead of me. Tough to tell, but maybe another twenty feet or so."

He felt a slight tug, then loosening to the line attached to his safety harness as his team leader played out more cord.

"Roger that, Franco. Slow and steady man, slow and steady."

Just then he heard the tapping again. "Wait one, Major."

Hugh stopped and cocked his free ear. Tapping for sure. He swept his light forward, pushing around a corner and saw a widening cavern that held promise. He inched ahead, aiming the light on his helmet into the void.

The slim beam swept a trapped individual. Belly to the ground, the person sprawled with only a few inches free above. The lower half of the body was blocked. But the torso was visible, covered in so much dust and grime he couldn't tell at first if he saw a male or female. Wide eyes stared back at him with disbelief, followed by wary hope. Then the person dropped a rock and pointed toward him.

Definitely a woman's hand.

Trembling, she reached, her French manicure chipped, nails torn back and bloody. A gold band on her thumb had bent into an oval. He clasped her hand quickly to check the thumb for warmth and a pulse.

And found it. Circulation still intact.

Then he checked her wrist, heart rate elevated but strong.

She gripped his hand with surprising strength. "If I'm hallucinating," she said, her raspy voice barely above a whisper, "please don't tell me."

"Ma'am, you're not imagining anything. I'm here to help you."

He let her keep holding on as it seemed to bring her comfort—and calm—while he swept the light over what he could see of her to assess medically. Tangled hair. A streak of blood across her head. But no gaping wounds.

He thumbed his mic. "Have found live female. Trapped, but lucid. More data after I evaluate."

"Roger that," McCabe's voice crackled through.

Hugh inched closer, wedging the light into the crevice in hopes of seeing more of his patient. "Ma'am, crews are working hard to get you out of here, but they need to stabilize the structure before removing more debris. Do you understand me?"

"I hear you." She nodded, then winced as her cheek slid along the gritty ground. "My name is Amelia Bailey. I'm not alone."

More souls in danger. "How many?"

"One more. A baby."

His gut gripped. He forced words past his throat clogging from more than particulates in the air. "McCabe, add a second soul to that. A baby with the female, Amelia Bailey. Am switching to hot mic so you can listen in."

He flipped the mic to constant feed, which would use more battery but time was of the essence now. He didn't want to waste valuable seconds repeating info. "Ma'am, how old is the baby?"

"Thirteen months. A boy," she spoke faster and faster, her voice coming out in raspy croaks. "I can't see him because it's so dark, but I can feel his pulse. He's still alive, but oh God, please get us out of here."

"Yes, ma'am. Now, I'm going to slip my hand over your back to see if I can reach him."

He had his doubts. There wasn't a sound from the child, no whimpering, none of those huffing little breaths children made when they slept or had cried themselves out. Still, he had to go through the motions. Inching closer until he stretched alongside her, he tunneled his arm over her shoulders. Her back rose and fell shallowly, as if she tried to give him more space when millimeters counted. His fingers snagged on her torn shirt, something silky and too insubstantial a barrier between her and tons of concrete.

Pushing further, he met resistance, stopped short. Damn it. He grappled past the jutting stone, lower down her back until he brushed the top of her—

She gasped.

He looked up fast, nearly nose to nose now. His hand stilled on her buttock. She stared back, the light from his helmet splashing over her sooty face. Her eyes stared back, a splash of color in the middle of murky desperation.

Blue. Her eyes were incredibly blue, and what a strange thought to have in the middle of hell. But he couldn't help but notice they were the same color as cornflowers he'd seen in a field once during a mission in the U.K.

Hell, cornflowers were just weeds. He stretched deeper, along the curve of her butt, bringing his face nearer to hers. She bit her lip.

"Sorry," he clipped out.

Wincing, she shrugged. "It was a reflex. Modesty's pretty silly right now. Keep going."

Wriggling, he shifted for a better path beyond the maze of jagged edges, protruding glass, spikes…

"Damn it." He rolled away, stifling the urge to say a helluva lot worse. "I can't reach past you."

"Thanks for trying." Her fingers crawled to grip his sleeve. "I'm just so glad you're here, that everyone knows we are here. Joshua's heart is still beating. He's with us. There's hope, right?"

Nearly forty-eight hours had passed since the earthquake occurred, and while he'd participated in against all odds rescues before, he had a sick sense that the child was already dead. "Sure. There's always hope."

Or so the platitude went.

But if he told the woman as much, she would freak out and above all she needed to preserve her strength by staying calm.

"I'm going to hang out here with you while they do their work upstairs." He unstrapped the pack around his waist and pointed his headlight toward the supplies. "Now I'm gonna pull out some tricks to make you more comfortable while we wait."

"Happen to have an ice cold Diet Coke? Although I'll settle for water, no lemon necessary."

He laughed softly. Not many would be able to joke right now, much less stay calm. "I'm sorry, but until I know more about your physical status, I can't risk letting you eat or drink." He tugged out a bag of saline, the needle, antiseptic swabs, grunting as a rock bit into his side. "But I am going to start an IV, some saline to hydrate you."

"You said you're here to help me," she said, wincing at a fresh burst of noise from the jackhammers, "but who are you?"

"I'm with the U.S. Air Force." Dust and pebbles showered down. "I'm a pararescueman, which also includes medic training. I need to ask you questions so I know what to put in your IV. Where exactly did the debris land on you?"

She puffed dust from her mouth, blinking fast. "There's a frickin' building on top of me."

"Let me be more specific. Are your legs pinned?" He tore the corner of a sealed alcohol pad with his teeth, spitting the foil edge free. "I couldn't reach that far."

Her eyes narrowed. "I thought you were checking on Joshua."

"I'm a good multitasker."

"My foot is wedged, but I can still wriggle my toes."

He looked up sharply. If she was hemorrhaging internally, fluids could make her bleed out faster, but without hydration…

The balancing act often came down to going with his gut. "Just your foot?"

"Yes. Why? Do you think I'm delusional?" Her breath hitched with early signs of hysteria. "I'm not having phantom sensations. I can feel grit against my ankle. There's some blood in my shoe, not a lot. It's sticky, but not fresh. I'm feeling things."

"I hear you. I believe you." Without question, her mind would do whatever was needed to survive. But he'd felt enough of her body to know she was blocked, rather than pressed into the space. "I'm going to put an IV in now."

"Why was it so important about my foot?"

He scrubbed the top of her hand with alcohol pads, sanitizing as best he could. "When parts of the body are crushed, we need to be… careful in freeing you."

"Crush syndrome." Her throat moved with a long slow swallow. "I've heard of that. People die from it after they get free. I saw it on a rerun of that TV show about a crabby drug addict doctor."

"We just need to be careful." In a crush situation, tissue died, breaking down and when the pressure was released, toxins flooded the body, overloading the kidneys. And for just that remote possibility, he hadn't included potassium in her IV.

Panic flooded her glittering blue eyes. "Are you planning to cut off my foot?" Her arm twitched, harder, faster until she flailed. "Are you going to put something else in that IV? Something to knock me out?"

He covered her hand with his before she dislodged the catheter in her hand. "There's nothing in there but fluid. I'm being honest with you now, but if you panic, I'm going to have to start feeding you a line of bullshit to calm you down. Now you said you wanted the unvarnished truth…"

"I do. Okay. I'm breathing. Calming down. Give me the IV."

He patted her wrist a final time. "I already did."

Blinking fast, she looked at the tape along her hand. A smile pushed through the grime on her face. "You're good. I was so busy trying not to freak out I didn't even notice."

"Not bad for my first time."

"Your first time?"

"I'm joking." And working to distract her again from the rattle overhead, the fear that at any second the whole damn place could collapse onto them.

She laughed weakly, then stronger. "Thank you."

"It's just an IV."

"For the laugh. I was afraid I would never get to do that again." Her fingers relaxed slowly, tension seeping from them as surely as fluid dripped out of the bag. "The second they uncover us, you'll make Joshua top priority. Forget about me until he's taken care of."

"We're going to get you both out of here. I swear it."

"Easy for you to claim that. If I die, it's not like I can call you a liar."

A dead woman and child. He resisted the urge to tear through the rocks with his bare hands and to hell with waiting on the crews above. He stowed his gear, twisting to avoid that damn stone stabbing his side.

"Hey," Amelia whispered, "That was supposed to be a joke."

"Right, got it." Admiration for her grit kicked through his own personal fog threatening to swallow him whole. "You're a tough one. I think you're going to be fine."

"I'm a county prosecutor. I chew up criminals for a living."

"Atta girl." He settled onto his back, watching the hypnotic drip, drip. His fingers rested on her wrist to monitor her pulse.

She sniffed. "I prefer to be called a woman or a lady, thank you very much."

"Where I come from, it's wise not to be nitpicky with the person who's saving your ass."

"Score one for you." She scraped a torn fingernail through the dust on the ground. Her sigh stirred the dust around that shaky line. "I'm good now. So you should go before this building collapses on top of you and keeps you from doing your job for other people."

"I don't have anywhere else to be." He ignored a call from McCabe through his headset that pretty much echoed the woman's words. "The second they give the go ahead, I'm hauling you out of here, Amelia Bailey."

"And Joshua. I want you to promise you'll take care of him first."

"I will do what I can for him," he answered evasively.

Her wide eyes studied him for seven drips of the IV before she cleared her throat. "You don't think he's alive, do you? I can feel his pulse."

"Yes, ma'am."

"I'm not imagining it, damn it." Her hand flipped and she grabbed his arm, her ragged nails digging deep with urgency. "I can feel his pulse in his wrist. He's a little chilly, but he's not cold. Just because he's not screaming his head off doesn't mean he's dead. And sometimes, he moves. Only a little, but I feel it." Her words tumbled over each other faster and faster until she dissolved into a coughing fit.

Ah, to hell with it. He unhooked his canteen. "Wet your mouth. Just don't gulp, okay? Or they'll kick my butt up there."

He brought the jug to her lips and she sipped, her restraint Herculean when she must want to gulp. Sighing, she sagged again, her eyes closing as she hmmmmed, her breathing evening out. He freaked. She needed to stay awake, alert.

Alive.

"Tell me about your son Joshua." He recapped the canteen without wasting a swallow on himself.

Her lashes fluttered open again. "Joshua's my nephew. I came with my brother and his wife to help them with the paperwork for their adoption. They don't want any legal loopholes. What happens to Joshua if they're…?"

She bit her lip.

His brain raced as he swept the light along the rubble, searching for some signs of others. Although if they'd been outside, chances were next to nil. All the same, he made sure they heard upstairs, by speaking straight into his mic as he asked her, "Where were your brother and sister-in-law when the earthquake hit?"

"They were in the street, right outside the hotel. They went outside to buy lunch. They waited until Joshua was asleep so he wouldn't miss them." Her voice hitched. "I promised I would take care of him."

"And you have." He pinned her with his eyes, his determination, the swath of light steady on her face. "If your family is outside, they stood a much better chance of being okay. They're probably over in one of the camps right now going nuts trying to find you."

"I've read stories about how babies do better because they have more fat stores and they don't tense up or get claustrophobic." Her eyes pleaded with him. "He's just napping, you know."

The force of her need pummeled him harder than the spray of rocks from the jackhammered ceiling. The world closed in to just this woman and a kid he couldn't see. Too clearly he could envision his wife and his daughter, trapped in the wreckage of a crashed plane. Marissa would have held out hope for Tilly right to the end too, fighting for her until her nails and spirit were ragged.

Shit.

The vise on his brain clamped harder, the roar in his

ears louder, threatening his focus. "I'm changing your IV bag now, so don't wig out if you feel a little tug."

She clenched her fist. "You must get pretty jaded in this line of work."

"I've got a good success rate." He didn't walk away from tough odds. Every mission was do or die for him.

"About my foot," she started hesitantly, "am I imagining it's okay? Be honest. I won't panic. I need to be prepared."

"The mind does what it needs to in order to survive. And that's what you need to focus on."

Not that it had mattered in the end for Marissa or Tilly. They'd died in that plane crash, their broken bodies returned to him to bury along with his will to live. A trembling started deep inside him. His teeth chattered. He dug his fingers into the ground to anchor himself into the present. Amelia Bailey would not die on his watch, damn it.

But the trembling increased inside him. Harder. Deeper. Until he realized… the shaking wasn't inside, but outside.

The ground shuddered with another earthquake.

SEALed
with a Kiss

BY MARY MARGRET DAUGHTRIDGE

> **THERE'S ONLY ONE THING HE CAN'T HANDLE, AND ONE WOMAN WHO CAN HELP HIM...**
>
> Jax Graham is a rough, tough Navy SEAL, but when it comes to taking care of his four-year-old son after his ex-wife dies, he's completely clueless. Family therapist Pickett Sessoms can help, but only if he'll let her.
>
> When Jax and his little boy get trapped by a hurricane, Pickett takes them in against her better judgment. When the situation turns deadly, Pickett discovers what it means to be a SEAL, and Jax discovers that even a hero needs help sometimes.

"A heart-touching story that will keep you smiling and cheering for the characters clear through to the happy ending." —Romantic Times

"A well-written romance... simultaneously tender and sensuous." —Booklist

978-1-4022-1118-8 • $7.99 U.S. / $9.99 CAN

SEALed
with a
Promise
BY MARY MARGRET DAUGHTRIDGE

**NAVY SEAL CALEB DELAUDE IS AS DEADLY AS
HE IS CHARMING.**

Professor Emmie Caddington's quiet intelligence and
quirky personality intrigue him. When he discovers
that her personal connections can get him close to the
man he's vowed to kill, will their budding relationship
be nothing more than a means to revenge...or is she
the key to his salvation?

Praise for *SEALed with a Kiss*:

"This story delivers in a huge way." —Romantic Times

*"A wonderful story that will have readers experiencing
a whirlwind of emotions and culminating with an
awesome scene that will have your pulse pounding."*
—Romance Junkies

*"What an incredibly powerful book! I laughed and
sniffled, was turned on and turned inside out."* —Queue
My Review

978-1-4022-1763-0 • $6.99 U.S. / $7.99 CAN